WHITE HOUSE STORM

Dale Napier

ISBN: 0692253262
ISBN 13: 9780692253267
Library of Congress Control Number: 2014910446
Mastersoft Media, LLC
Las Vegas * Houston

PART I

OPTIONS

I don't know when I started noticing changes ... little things, creeping up on me. So much change ... three years of campaigning, every day a new challenge. Now President for how long – two years, three? – so many changes in every way. No privacy. No personal space. Sometimes I miss the old days, the daily, predictable grind at Charley's Gym. But even that changed ... one day, I was pumping iron; the next day I was pumping investors to buy my franchises. Then movies. Then ... Governor of California. How did that happen? Such a blur, and now I'm president. Time to show the generals what a truly strong man looks like.

The Chairman and his Joint Chiefs of Staff stood in a straight line in front of their designated seats, saluting their Commander in Chief with robotic precision. Surveying them, President Charley Davidson wondered whether they were really all the same height, or whether it was a visual trick of some kind. He saluted right back at them, snapping a knife-edged right hand against the side of his forehead. In his youth, America's latest chief executive had led a self-absorbed life with no room for military service. Davidson's feelings on the subject were complex: Although he felt no regret about his life choices, he had this idea that he *should* support and respect the military, so he behaved as if he did, without giving much thought to whether that respect came from anywhere other than an idealized model. Today he knew that guilt or no guilt, respect or no respect, he would have to rein them in.

The President and the Chiefs sat down. The Chairman, Army General Gus Caesare, remained standing. Caesare was a man with big bones but a gaunt frame. Originally from Brooklyn, he came from a sheltered prep school environment that he had fled for the Army after college.

"Mister President, we have a lot of ground to cover today, so I've taken the liberty of having my media guy work with yours for the presentation." As he spoke those words, he waved a soft, manicured hand at a non-comm near the door. The sergeant—a short, thin, young man with a pale complexion—passed a remote-control unit through the door to one of the chiefs, who passed it to Caesare.

Caesare clicked the remote unit with a melodramatic flair. A four-screen display came to life on the wall adjacent to the President's desk.

"Mister President, we've seen enormous change in Iran since you took office. Their desire to revert to the appellation *Persia*, the Democratic Republic of Persia, at that, is the least of those changes. Even by itself, many of our experts see that as an ominous sign."

Davidson nodded. He had asked for this presentation because he knew there was a split among the service chiefs over the best strategy. Though not interested in their political views, he knew that political decisions often had military consequences.

"In the space of six months, we've seen a new secular revolution. The new President of Persia is lobbying to enter the U.N. Security Council. Now we have confirmation, from more than a dozen sources, that they have successfully detonated a test nuclear device."

Davidson nodded again. All this was old news. He spoke strongly with the trace Germanic accent for which he was famous.

"Generals, thank you all for coming. What we discuss today must be completely confidential. Note that not even my own chief of staff is present. Not even the Vice President. I have the utmost respect for her, but we must set limits. Only you, me, and the Secretary of Defense, since he is in the military chain of command.

"Gentlemen, we have before us nothing less than the task of shaping a new Iranian – excuse me, *Persian* – policy. The stakes are enormous, but I want to make it clear that I believe the options are many. I seek your counsel in examining the military considerations before I decide how we must proceed. General?" He looked back at Caesare to continue.

"Mister President, let's start with the nuclear detonation itself. Tehran was quite cooperative in providing us footage of the actual event, along with markers that give a clear indication of the scope of the event." Caesare selected a couple of menu items on the screen. A seemingly empty screen with a small tower appeared. After a moment, it was followed by a sudden burst of white light that briefly burned out the ability of the camera to handle it. As the brightness of light lessened, the shape of a tall, thin mushroom cloud appeared high above the desert where the tower used to be. The men watching all flinched slightly with the burst.

"Interesting, General, but we've all seen videos of nuclear detonations before. What can you tell me about this test?"

At this point, the Army Chief of Staff, General Strom Thornton, took over. Thornton's sharp chin and angled jaw gave him a harsh countenance that he had learned to use to his advantage, especially when trying to get his way.

"Mister President, our scientists rate this as a smallish fission device, approximately thirty kilotons. That's twice the size of Hiroshima, but it's an A-bomb, not a full-blown nuke."

Davidson furrowed his brow. Only recently had serious wrinkles appeared on his seventy-five-year-old face, a fact remarked upon by those who worked closely with him. His movie-star good looks were finally falling to the depredations of time.

"A nuke's a nuke. I know the difference between uranium fission and hydrogen fusion with plutonium. For our purposes here today, the only difference is size. It does not require a thermonuclear device to destroy Tel Aviv or Jerusalem or Baghdad. Or one of our aircraft carriers.

"One question is, how many arrows do they have in their quiver? We know they have intermediate-range missiles that can hit all over Europe and the Middle East, but how many?"

"Still working on it, Mister President. Best guess, five to ten, with five to ten new ones each year."

"If we're wrong by even one device, hundreds of thousands of souls could be lost," Davidson snapped. "When I want guesses, I'll call the CIA. This is essentially a political problem, gentlemen, as it always has been, but I can't deal with the Persians unless I know our full range of options. That's the main reason I called you here today. So let's get on with it."

"Mister President," Caesare said, "we have a full spectrum of options for you. Five options that pretty well exhaust the possibilities. Maybe a little room to mix and match. I'm going to present these to you in order of strength, with the strongest option first." With a click of a button, a new PowerPoint slide appeared, with five bullet points on it. They all read it quickly but waited for Caesare to elaborate.

"Obviously, the strongest possible action is a preemptive nuclear strike. As you know, this is well within our means. It is consistent with doctrine that has been discussed internationally. However, it has disadvantages too numerous to go into at this moment. Suffice it to say that launching a preemptive nuclear strike might give some of our enemies cause to strike at us as well."

Davidson nodded.

"Not to mention poisoning the Middle East, Europe, and eastern Asia for years or even decades to come," he said. "That's a lose-lose option. Next?"

"Next is a comprehensive but conventional strike, largely from the air, at all of its nuclear-production facilities. This might seem the most advantageous, but our intelligence people will not promise we can get it all. There is no guarantee we can shut it down for good. For that matter, we do not know where their current devices are stored. The best we could hope for would be a temporary postponement. Meanwhile, we would have a regional war on our hands, maybe worse."

"Next?"

"Next is a conventional attack to further cripple their capacity to produce oil. Air attacks and perhaps naval bombardment would do in some cases. Like the economic embargo, it would do damage."

"But not enough to guarantee acquiescence," Davidson completed the thought for him. "And just like option number four, it could destabilize the new regime. And while we do not know their true intentions at this time, for the moment, that seems unwise."

"Just so, Mister President."

"And next? Number four."

"Number four is even less ambitious but has some things going for it. Embargo all refined petroleum products going *in* to Persia. Keep in mind, they produce the oil, but they don't have refining capacity. They actually have to import their gasoline, and it's costing them an arm and a leg. We could make this problem much worse for them."

"But do we really want to jeopardize the new regime?" the President asked. "Gasoline was one of the triggers that set off the Persian revolution to begin with. They may have The Bomb, but otherwise, this whole thing looks like a blessing in disguise."

"That's a political decision for you, Mister President," Caesare said. "All we can deliver are military solutions."

"Nothing military about that last one," Davidson said. "What else?"

"The polar extreme," Caesare said. "We stand down."

● ● ●

Outside in the nearby hallway, Army Sergeant Sam Conway stood at parade rest while two young White House aides eyed him with curiosity. Neither had served in the military nor knew anyone who had, so they considered it an unusual calling, like the priesthood.

Conway, noticing their stares, gave the smallest of smiles and nodded slightly to them. The older of the two was a tall, twenty-year-old Yale graduate who once had thought of himself, mistakenly, as CIA material. After nodding back, he spoke up.

"Say, Sarge, don't take this the wrong way, but is it true what they say about your boss in there?" He said it in a friendly Southern way that was intended to lure the unsuspecting. The sergeant, five years his junior, seemed like a ripe candidate.

Conway relaxed slightly and turned toward him.

"Depends on what they say," he said.

"They say he's a faggot," the Southern Yalie said. "Is it true?"

Conway's face turned bright red.

"If I knew the answer to that, what would that make me?" he asked. "Tell me, is it true what they say about *your* boss?"

Now it was the Yalie's turn to look unsettled.

"What do they say?"

"They say he's pulling a Reagan."

"What's that supposed to mean?"

"Do I hafta spell it out? He's losing his mind. At least, that's what they say."

The thin, young sergeant returned to parade rest, staring at the wall, while the two aides stared at him in disbelief.

● ● ●

"Do nothing?" Davidson said. "I know some of my people love that idea, but it's the last thing I expected to hear you recommend."

"Not recommend, Mister President. That was just a list of options. My men here have a lot to say about what we *ought* to do."

Until then, the generals and admiral had said nothing. Sitting impassively during presentations was a skill at which they all excelled. Caesare's words animated them enough to confirm Davidson's belief that nothing about this situation would resolve with ease. His plans began coming together.

"Let's get the big one off the table. Is there any conceivable reason why a nuclear strike on Persia would be to our advantage?"

"Obviously it would end that threat once and for all, Mister President," said the Air Force Chief, General Don Martin. Martin had a pinched face with a nose like a long, crooked thumb. "But I'm afraid it would create a new threat even worse than the old one."

"Elaborate," the President said.

"It makes *us* the target, doesn't it? Think about it. America invented the nuclear bomb. We are the only nation to use it in war. Forget about how justified we were. The whole world knows us as history's only nuclear aggressor.

"Right now that seems like a distant memory of history. What happens if we bring it back to the present with another nuclear strike? Every country in the world suddenly has to reassess the threat from us. The nuclear powers, they have to wonder whether they're next. Let's not forget that we have established preemptive attacks as morally and militarily justified. Couldn't they turn that against us if they felt the need?"

"When you say 'nuclear powers,' General, realistically, you can only mean China and Russia. No one else has the delivery systems to threaten us," Davidson said.

"Short of a backpack nuke, that's true," Martin said. "And they are exactly who I mean. Both countries have exhibited friendship toward Persia. Not just symbolically, either. We want to keep them out of it, so this option is off the table."

"Agreed," Davidson said in a decisive tone. "My doctrine, which is not for public consumption, is to go nuclear only as a response to a nuclear attack on U.S. soil, or that of its closest allies. Never as a first strike unless an attack on us is clearly, unquestionably imminent."

"Mister President, we must act *decisively*," Thornton said. Clenching his distinctive jaw, he stood and waved his right hand with a clenched fist, smashing it into his open left palm. "We cannot let this situation go unsaid."

"Thank you for your advice, General," Davidson said. The cool, dismissive tone to his voice came naturally. After walking around his desk toward the generals, he stopped and looked at all of them.

"Generals, so far, I do not see this as a military problem. I see it as a political problem, Clausewitz notwithstanding. I will consider this matter further. You will know my plans soon."

With a curt nod, he saluted them in dismissal. One by one, each stood stiffly, saluted in return, and filed out in silence.

Secretary of Defense Fleming D'Enfant stood. D'Enfant's background was originally in intelligence, not the military, which accounted for his portly stature. As the generals departed, the President took his elbow and drew him away, toward his desk. Davidson noticed that the younger, out-of-shape man was sweating and obviously uncomfortable in clothes that fit poorly.

"You're out of shape, Mister Secretary," he said. Davidson looked up and down as if sizing up a new recruit. D'Enfant knew he would have to redirect the conversation quickly, because the President was infamous for his impromptu exercise sessions.

"Are we going to stand down, Mister President?" D'Enfant asked. Davidson looked at him again, tilted his head, and laughed, recognizing the ploy.

"I'm still considering the options," Davidson said. "The Israelis are sure screaming for a military solution, but I'm not convinced this is a military problem. Tomorrow I want a complete update on our preparedness status, on all fronts. Focus on the carriers and subs."

"Yes, sir," D'Enfant said.

"What are you waiting for? It's time for my workout," Davidson said. He stalked out irritably without waiting for his subordinate.

2

NEW JOB

Lieutenant Colonel Samuel Chin strode into the E-ring office with a proud military bearing, his broad shoulders square and back. He felt conflicted by the impending opportunity but saw no choice except to meet it head-on. A good military officer could do no less, and he had always tried to be a good military officer.

As he checked in with the "secretary," a young male captain with the countenance of an old maid, he tried not to look too much like a tourist. Having reluctantly grown accustomed to khaki green furniture and walls, he felt almost giddy in the E-ring office, like a kid in Disneyland. Caesare's furnishings, while elegant and tasteful, were surprisingly understated. Assuming the general made his own choices, which the colonel assumed, he preferred exotic wood inlay work over ornate stone or glittery metal.

At his approach, the captain jumped to his feet and saluted. He stared into the distance to avoid eye contact.

"Sir!" he said. He stood stiffly.

"At ease, Captain," Chin said, saluting in reply. "I have an appointment to see General Caesare." He pronounced the name carefully and correctly, *cheh-zuh-ray*. He knew some generals' aides who contemptuously called the Chairman *Cheezy* behind his back. Chin spoke carefully to avoid committing an unpardonable *faux pas*.

The captain sat down but did not seem any more relaxed. Chin looked more closely at the young officer and realized his hair was actually permed. And did he smell a whiff of cologne? He had a sinking feeling but saw no way out. Caesare's aide looked down at some papers as he spoke.

"Sir, the general has not returned from lunch. I apologize for the delay."

A nice touch, since we both know the general won't apologize. Having stars means never having to say you're sorry. And how far am I from a star? Forty-two and stuck at light colonel for five years now. A tour of duty at the top like this should get things going. Then maybe another combat posting, knock on wood. The last thing this country needs is more war.

An average-sized soldier but with a powerful build, Chin the warrior loved the fight of war, but not the large-scale death and destruction. As he waited, Chin stood and examined Caesare's power wall. Like any general's power wall, it was covered with photos of him paired with other men of power – generals, presidents, American and foreign leaders of all types. Unlike most generals' displays, however, Caesare's included a heavy smattering of Hollywood celebrities, all male A-list actors under thirty-five. Chin winced as he considered the general's reputation, which carried a serious downside for this posting.

They warned me not to work for Gay Gus, but how could it be a mistake to work for the top general in the country? That has to be a plus no matter what he does on the side. Ike got started working for MacArthur, didn't he? Patton got started with that old Indian hunter, Black Jack Pershing himself. Pershing was a pariah because he commanded black soldiers. But he ended up as lead general in World War I. The first five-star. Maybe an unorthodox assignment is what I need to spice up my career.

"Ten-shun!" he heard the captain shout. Chin wheeled around with a sharp turn and snapped to attention as General Gus Caesare walked through the door. Caesare's golden, wavy hair appeared to glisten with an oily sheen. After saluting each man individually, he walked over to shake the colonel's hand.

"Follow me, Colonel," he said. Before Chin could react, Caesare turned around and headed for his office. As they entered, he waved to a row of wing chairs lined up along one wall.

"Help yourself. Grab a chair and come on over here." He walked behind his desk and stood there as Chin pushed a chair to the designated spot.

"They were in here working on my carpet, so everything got moved around," he said by way of explanation. Never before had Chin come even this close to hearing a general apologize for anything, even halfway. It made an impression. Chin had never met Caesare before, so he silently appraised him but did a terrible job of hiding it.

"Go ahead, *look*," Caesare said with a smirk. "If you look at women the way you're looking at me, I bet you get slapped a lot."

Chin looked so startled that the general laughed, a nonthreatening laugh that compelled him to join in with a grin.

"Sorry," Chin said.

"Don't be sorry, son. A good officer always takes a hard look at all the pieces on the board."

Hearing the general call him *son*, he realized for the first time their age difference. Caesare's dress was impeccable. That was typical for top generals, but there was something extra ... the manicure, perhaps, or the peroxide (it was rumored)-blond hair, styled and longish by military standards. It made him seem younger, more like a big brother.

Chin sat down, but Caesare remained standing. He paced around behind his desk, holding his hands behind his back as he walked. The general was off in his own little world. He looked at Chin infrequently as he began "lecturing," as other colonels called it.

"America has the finest, most professional military the world has ever known," he said. "But life at the top is different from boots on the ground. I spend my time fighting the politicians and my own generals, instead of some enemy abroad. It requires a special kind of man. Boldness is still called for, but finesse rules over force. A strong man can be beaten by a ninety-eight-pound weakling if the weakling is popular and the bully is not."

"Yes, sir," Chin said. He nodded his head with the words. This was starting to sound like a lecture about the importance of discretion and diplomacy.

"If you're thinking that this sounds more like a challenge to your discretion and diplomacy than your fighting ability, you wouldn't be far off," the general said. He had a well-earned reputation as a mind reader, because he was good at anticipating next thoughts. "Make no mistake, we need fighters. And your Medal of Honor brings instant respect like nothing else." Caesare had stopped pacing. Now he faced him, this time with his hands on his hips. The pose made Chin uncomfortable.

Great, Chin thought. *He needs a poster boy.*

"But that's not the real reason you're here. I think your work at Oxford could make you perfect for this position. Keep in mind that as my top aide, you will attend all meetings and events with me, everything except those closed to you by the President. A man of the proper disposition will thrive here. Are you of the proper disposition, Colonel?"

"I hope so, General," Chin said. His discomfort was obvious, which Caesare liked.

"You *hope* so?"

"I mean, yes, General, certainly. But I hope I can turn to you for guidance, sir. If needed."

"Of course, Colonel, of course. We'll try this out. I think you'll work out. By the way, that's *full* Colonel now. I can't have a half-bird working for me."

"Yes, sir. *Thank you*, sir. When do we begin?" Chin generally kept a poker face, but he was smiling now.

"You've already begun, Colonel, you just didn't know it. As we speak, your effects at that B-ring office are being carted over here." Chin's temporary assignment had been a minor make-work job, so minor he had been concerned for his career. He knew there had been gossip among his comrades in arms back in the Endless War, as they called Afghanistan.

"Now, let's talk about Persia."

• • •

The President strode into the press room. He stopped along the front row of reporters to shake a few hands like on a campaign stop. Those he knew best, he would trade personal small talk with. His charisma, coupled with fanboy syndrome, made it easy to leave a positive impression that guaranteed favorable coverage.

Walking behind the podium, he looked down, as if consulting some papers. After a moment, he glanced up and signaled he was ready to begin. His decades of work with TelePrompTers on Hollywood sets gave him the ability to appear as if he was speaking directly to each and every viewer.

"My fellow Americans, thank you for taking a moment of your valuable lives to share with me," he said. The press was rarely disappointed by his unorthodox openings.

"Let me get straight to the point. As most of you know, there has been much turmoil this year in the country we used to call Iran. Now we call it Persia, again. Persia, of course, is an ancient civilization with much to be proud of.

"Before the Persian Revolution, we had many problems with the Iranian government. Their uprising in 1979 was a revolt against the United States just as much as against the old shah.

"During the Shah's time, Iran was America's greatest ally in the Middle East, even greater than Israel. The new President, Fahrook Arkhami, is not the Shah, but I think he does want to be our friend. I am not foolish. I will not simply take him at his word. But I am hopeful enough to give him a chance. I believe the entire community of nations wants peace in the Middle East. God willing, a Persian-American friendship could help make that possible.

"We will stand aside and let events take their course. We are not stupid or naïve. We know there are many ways this could go wrong. But we are an optimistic, forward-looking people. Americans want to hold out their hands in friendship. Perhaps it is a little too soon for that, but to begin with, we can at least give peace a chance.

"President Arkhami, I call on you to exercise the leadership you promise. Show us the nuclear restraint that proves you are civilized and capable of sitting at the table with the leaders of civilizations. We await you, with strength and hopeful resolve."

With a nod to the camera and the reporters, he strode out of the room, leaving the reporters shouting their questions behind him.

• • •

Chin made a face.

"What?"

"I just feel funny calling it that. *Persia*. I always thought the name sounded cool, but I guess in a soft, ancient kind of way, you know? Persian rugs. Persian cats. But *Iran*. Now *that's* a hard-core name."

"A funny comment, Colonel. I'm as concerned with the name as the fact of the change. What does it imply?"

"Conventional wisdom around B says they want a new, modern Persian empire."

"Conventional wisdom around the B-ring is about useful as conventional wisdom from *People Magazine*," Caesare said. He took a slightly harder tone and looked at Chin as if seeing him, the real him, for the first time.

"Is that all you got?"

Chin felt shaken. He suddenly realized that the promotion was not a done deal. It might well rest on what he said next. Caesare watched him frown and smiled to himself. He was getting through to the younger officer.

"I think it goes deeper than that, General. Probably not as sinister as the pundits suggest."

"Oh?"

"I think the new regime is, well, *embarrassed* at the regime they just replaced. Like the Germans after the war, perhaps. I think they see themselves as worthy partners with the civilized industrial nations. They want respect."

"Respect."

"Yes, respect. And they realize they have to earn it."

"Colonel, do I detect a note of admiration in your voice? Because I would like to remind you that officially, Persia is just another fancy-fucking-name for I-ran. We may not have been in a shooting war with them, but things have been pretty damn tense. Do I hear you admiring our enemy?"

"No, sir, not at all. I do *not* admire them, Iranians or Persians or whatever the hell they are. But I do remember, way back in my childhood, that Iran was once our best ally in the region. Better than Israel by a long shot. You recall, sir, my dissertation was on this very subject."

Caesare smiled. This was the *real* reason he was talking to Chin in the first place.

"How could I forget, *Doctor* Chin? And?"

"I think they could be our ally again. A *better* ally, not run by a dictator like the Shah. We're already seeing signs that the Hamas-Iranian alliance is breaking down. If we offer support, we have a chance of regaining them as an ally. But if we keep acting like bullies in the hood, sooner or later, the hood will gang up on us and kick us out. What's the good in that?"

"What good, indeed, Colonel. Maybe we should just give you your star now and put you in the National Security Office."

"General, I'm at your disposal. But I would be sorry not to get a chance to work under you."

At that, they both smiled.

"Just a thought, Colonel, just a thought. I want you on my team. In fact, I already have an assignment for you."

3

PROTESTS

The next day began ominously, as heavy, roiling clouds gathered over the capital city. A tropical storm had threatened serious rainfall but at the last minute had scooted off to the east. The thick humidity, unusual for early spring, added to the drama. There might not be rain, but there would be plenty of political thunder and lightning, beginning with the pickets. Storming back and forth in the free speech area in front of the White House, conservative protesters railed against the President's speech. The word RINO dominated most of the signs.

They showed up at dusk, emerging from a caravan of Lincoln and Cadillac SUVs, lined up for half a block near the White House. The Park Service guards in charge of White House security might have been worried if not for the quiet, orderly nature of the disembarkation.

The men were dressed uniformly in black suits and narrow ties with white shirts. The women wore long dresses of a similar design. They lined up at the rear of the third vehicle, an Escalade, from which picket signs were distributed.

The gentlest were of the "Bomb Bomb Bomb, Bomb Bomb Iran" ilk. The worst were removed quickly and quietly by the Park Service guards. A tall, gaunt man with an uncanny resemblance to the unbearded Lincoln bore a sign calling for violence against the Commander in Chief. As they dragged him away, he could be heard screaming, "But I'm a registered Republican! I voted for him! He betrayed us!"

His comrades supported him and took photos on their cell phones but did little else. Caught between support for their fellow and absolute obeisance to uniformed police, the police won.

• • •

The next day, having been given extensive media coverage, they had company – and not from supporters. By then, the storm clouds had moved on, burned off by the intense morning sun and leaving in their wake a steamy haze. A series of white panel vans with union stickers dropped off cadres of a different type: large men bearing signs made of heavy wood, not the light balsa wood that was typical in pickets. They did not act friendly or orderly; they were clearly belligerent. Under the direction of a leader with an electronic bullhorn, they quickly formed an elliptical picket line mirroring the first one. By directing his people to march clockwise, when the bomb-Iran crowd was marching counter-clockwise, the new leader quickly produced a confrontation between the two groups. In short order, the new group, carrying signs of pacifism and support for the President, had begun beating the first group, and a full-scale riot was underway.

• • •

On the third day, similar pro-Davidson and anti-Iran confrontations flared up in a variety of venues – Jewish community centers, Persian embassies, and Republican Party headquarters, among many others.

Charley Davidson knew his decision would raise a ruckus, as he thought of the first day's demonstration, but the extent and virulence of the protests caught him by surprise. The midterm elections had been kind to his party and his agenda, so he assumed initial protests would die out quickly. By the third afternoon, he realized it could no longer be taken for granted and called his Cabinet in to discuss it.

"See what this has gotten you, Mister President," said the Secretary of Labor, one of Davidson's two Democratic Cabinet appointees. Danny Hedron was a labor leader who compensated for his lack of street cred with histrionics. To him, there was no finer stage than the middle of the Oval Office, with a captive audience. Hedron was big and tall, as the expression went, and sported a full head of hair reminiscent of college in the 1970s. He waved at the others with his right hand as he spoke, showing his disdain for the actions displayed on the screen embedded in the wall.

"What? Unqualified union support?" said the Secretary of Commerce with his usual deadpan look.

"Hardly," the Labor Secretary said. A hiss sibilated through his teeth with the words. A physically small man, he had adopted the mannerisms of the weasel more than the rat. "The Israelis insist on action. It's not this simple."

Davidson looked at him sharply. Hedron was a personal friend, but not a completely reliable ally; in this case, he had hoped for more.

"Middle Eastern affairs have never been simple, Mister Secretary," the President said. "It would be a mistake to cast this as another Arab-Israeli conflict. Especially since the Persians are *not* Arabs and have their own agenda." Davidson's anger was obvious to the rest of the group, who knew he and Hedron were old friends from the California days. Normally he kept Hedron on a first-name basis. Not today.

"It comes with the territory."

Everyone turned and looked toward a back corner. Secretary of State Cameron Romulet was known for being seen more than heard, but when he *was* heard, his solid voice cut through the chatter. Romulet preferred to listen, let others hang or at least expose themselves, and move only at the most auspicious moment. His Yankee patrician heritage gave him a sense of security and quiet self-assurance that required no bluster or outward pretense to gain acceptance.

"The President has made the right decision for America. These other countries have their own reasons. Any complaints or attacks he receives are a reflection of their agendas, not ours. He can only prevail by holding firm and not showing weakness by making excuses."

"Thank you, Cam, I appreciate that," Davidson said. He looked directly at Romulet, who nodded in reply but said nothing.

"Just send them a *sign*, Mister President," Hedron said. The energy in the room had changed subtly; he knew Romulet had stopped his momentum. "A sign."

Davidson just sat there, mute, staring into space for a moment.

"Mister President?" Hedron said. He waved his hand in front of Davidson's face, trying to break him from his reverie.

"I will give it some thought," Davidson said. In politics, he had long believed, a pretend concession went a long way.

● ● ●

With the Senate out of session for the moment and no pressing overseas funerals or coronations requiring her presence, Vice President Joan Queenan allowed herself unstructured time to catch up on national and world events.

Not that her time was truly her own. Although she did not work *for* the President, she chose to work at his direction when he chose to direct her. Charley Davidson had scaled back the scope of her office to something closer to the traditional role. Davidson felt strongly, or so he claimed, that previous vice presidents had been allowed to creep into a chain of command where the vice president had no constitutional role. At the same time, he did not want to risk her becoming another Harry Truman, who was unaware of the Manhattan Project when he became President.

At least, that's what he claims. Does he think I'm a dumb blonde the way most of the world does? Even with my ten years in the Dome House and two years in the White House, he still seems uncomfortable with me. Is it because he's attracted to me? He's not a young man, but old habits die hard, especially if you have a Hollywood-sized ego. But who is he to judge me for my hair color? Him and half of Washington. Half his votes came from people who rooted for the killer robot in those stupid movies of his. He's lucky to be here. Me, twelve years without a husband or social life, not so lucky. Life has not handed me the deck of cards I expected. Albert. Dead. Horrible. I got here due to horrible events, but now that I'm here, I wouldn't have it any other way.

It's not too soon to start thinking about my future. Charley Davidson might be bodybuilder-buff, but he has heart problems. Steroid use during his weightlifting years. We're already halfway through the term. You'd think I'd have several years to worry about the future, but the future has a funny way of slamming you when you least expect it. I already see signs of politicos turning their sights away from Charley and toward me. Makes me feel like Sarah Connor. Some of them want to destroy me as a possible presidential candidate before I even become one.

Joan often spent her free mornings reviewing critical wires and meeting notes from the National Security Office. Queenan was well schooled in politics at every level, but often felt, sitting in the NSO meetings, like she thought Lincoln must have felt in his first Cabinet meetings. She knew she was completely out of her depth, at least at first. Her saving grace was twofold: there was no international crisis, and even if there were, her response would not be called for in any case.

She flipped through papers. One of her aides had organized them, for her convenience, by region and country. Joan was more of a hands-on person than a computer person, so to organize her thoughts, she arranged and rearranged the stacks of documents – first by region, or by issue, or by nuclear status, or by rogue or terrorist status. On more than one occasion, she had organized her information by oil, coal, or natural-gas status. Nuclear was a category all its own, because it involved weapons as well as electrical generation.

Somehow Persia keeps floating to the top of the stacks. Three dozen years it was a rogue state. Its only ties were to other rogue states, or states it could manipulate into opposing American policies. Particularly the policy of unconditional support for Israel.

But after the Persian Revolution, there was a significant change in attitude. It didn't last long enough. As soon as the new secular president was sworn in, we found out that he'd just detonated Persia's first test nuclear device.

From where I sit, I see them dancing near the edge of the cliff, but there is great clarity at the edge. On the cliff, you can see the enemy approaching from any direction and turn to face it as quickly. In the old regime, Iran's old rulers played that game like chess masters. Pretending to be suicidal fools. Puh-leeze! Nixon and Kissinger taught them how to play that game and they did it much better with the Soviets.

Charley Davidson is no diplomat, but he's understood this from the beginning. He uses his strongman's psychology to make his opponents feel weak and insecure. Two decades on the Hollywood A-list will do that for you. His confidence is unstoppable! If I had that kind of confidence, I would be Pope by now. Charley has no doubt he can overcome anyone with the sheer force of his presence. So he saw little need to provoke the Persians on the national stage. A pacifist Republican among warmongers. He's fought unflinchingly against what seemed to be the prevailing national headwinds.

I agree with Charley: War with Persia is not necessary. But he's letting them off too easy. Look at Roosevelt at Yalta. He was so sure he could win over Stalin with the sheer force of his personality ... just like Charley today. Roosevelt was wrong. Truman paid the price. Charley's wrong, too, but I'll stay out of it; nothing to be gained by mixing it up with him in public. The stakes aren't that high. Persia doesn't really want to wipe out Israel, it just wants to balance it. It wants Israel to know it cannot attack with impunity. Pakistan and India have kept a nuclear peace for more than forty years. Israel and Persia can do it, too.

Tired of arranging and rearranging data that were days and days old, ancient in these days of Big Data, she turned her attention to the pouch of overnight notices about army and fleet movements around the world.

Joan was surprised to see a steep increase in movements of all types, even though no provocations were at hand, not even the Persians. Fleets near Taiwan, Hong Kong, Shanghai, the Strait of Hormuz, the Suez Canal, the Black Sea ... all across the board, she saw stepped-up activity. Nothing in the South China Sea, which was what the Chinese Navy cared about most these days. Anyone watching her could have seen it in her face, screwed up in puzzlement, but she worked alone. While her staff handled her external affairs, Joan Queenan did her own thinking. She was determined to find out what the military activity was all about.

4

PROJECT MAY DAY

"**W**e have a military exercise set in the Middle East for May first, May Day," General Thornton said. The audio and visual reception for the videoconference was not very good, so as a result, his face appeared laced with static and his voice sounded a little like a voice synthesizer.

"You see?" President Davidson asked. He looked to his Vice President, sitting there in the room, for acknowledgement. "I'm sorry we didn't keep you in the loop on this, but it didn't seem important."

Queenan nodded, not fully buying it.

He keeps me out of the loop because we run in different circles. He's a Hollywood Republican. That means for him, drugs, abortions, and homosexuality are as common as church attendance in the heartland. I'm a Texas conservative. I'm liberal when it comes to justice and fair play, but that's about it. Just as long as he doesn't treat me the way the Kennedys treated LBJ, I'll be okay. So far, no complaint.

"What's the purpose of this exercise, General? Are you trying to anticipate a world war or something?" Queenan stared at him intently while she spoke. She noticed that Thornton looked down, then to the left, before looking her in the eye and speaking.

Built like a fireplug, Thornton had a physical presence that made it clear he feared no one. At his nicest, he tended to look like a pit bull ready to take a bite, just for the fun of it. His video presence, though, was less than intimidating. Queenan had been around power players long enough, starting with her late husband Albert, to know the type. Knowing this, she found it easy to take him on.

"Absolutely, Madame Vice President. We can anticipate, or we can capitulate."

Queenan tilted her head to the left with her trademark quizzical smile, captured on more than one magazine cover. Thornton knew the look but had not worked with her enough to use that knowledge.

"Capitulate to–?"

"Right now, the focus is on the Persians, wouldn't you say?"

"But the Chinese and Russians are sending them arms and supplies, so I doubt it's that simple, General."

"Zackly so, ma'am. These maneuvers are for their benefit as much as anyone," he said. He finished with the briefest of nods, perhaps a fraction of an inch: for this warrior, a major concession of place and respect.

"Do you anticipate taking on the Persians, Russians, and Chinese all at once, General?"

Thornton, a man with an inexplicably Levantine complexion and white hair, straightened as if a steel rod had vertisected his spine.

"No, ma'am," he said. The stiffness of his feelings was apparent in his voice. "I leave the guesswork to the politicians. It's my job to make sure that if called upon, no guesswork is required. We simply do what must be done."

"I wish politics were so simple," Queenan said. Her words were a quiet murmur spoken to no one in particular.

"Is that what you think, Mister President?" she asked. She turned toward Davidson, who sat up straight at his desk, head erect, staring off into the distance. He gave the appearance of daydreaming, but in a strangely vacant way.

He said nothing. His vice president and general waited patiently in deference. The silence was thick.

He continued to say nothing. There was no explaining this odd deviation during the conversation.

Thornton looked at the Vice President and raised a lone right eyebrow in question. He looked like he wished he was chewing on a cigar, but his face was screwed up as if it were right there in his mouth already: *his* trademark look.

"Charley?" Queenan said to Davidson, reaching out.

Davidson looked at her.

"Yes, Joan?"

Joan dropped a little, relaxing.

"You had me worried there for a minute. Is everything okay?"

"I'm fine. Why shouldn't I be? Now, where were we...?"

"We just finished up with the Vice President's briefing on Project May Day, Mister President."

"Yes, yes. If you have no further questions, Madame Vice President...?"

Queenan turned to Thornton.

"No questions at the moment, but I would appreciate being kept in the loop. I'm fascinated by these types of plans and would like to learn."

"By all means," the general said with a grunt, still trying to chew on that phantom cigar. He turned his head to the big man. "And now, Mister President, if you have no further use for me right now, I have an exercise to oversee."

Davidson and Queenan said their goodbyes and waited for Thornton's connection to end before speaking.

"Why do I think there's more to this exercise than flexing muscles?" she asked the President.

"Because there *is*," Davidson said. The vacant look was gone, and a twinkle had returned to his eyes. "Don't you get it? He wants a fifth star."

"Well, duh!" Queenan said. They both laughed.

"I know, all four-stars want a fifth star. It's human nature. They talked about it for Colin Powell, you know."

"Oh?"

"When he retired. Sometimes an officer is boosted up a grade for retirement, for a better pension, but it would have set a precedent."

"In what way?"

"Five stars is a big deal in the military. We don't have field marshals, but a five-star is bigger than a field marshal. Think about it. Our four-stars have *command theaters* – entire regions, plus four specialized commands with global reach. The main reason to have a five-star is so he can command many armies and navies in a single theater. The last time we had five-stars, it was during a world war, and eight men – admirals and generals – got a fifth star at the same time. Marshall. Eisenhower."

He stopped for a minute, staring blankly again. Queenan worried he was going off into Never-Never Land again. What was wrong with him?

Davidson came to with a start.

"Christ, why can't I remember the other two?"

"You mean the other six? Like MacArthur, Bradley, Nimitz, Halsey, and so on?"

Davidson grunted and once again seemed to trance out as he had earlier. Twenty seconds passed. Then he continued as if nothing had happened.

"It's the only reason Patton got his fourth star."

"So the general's ambitious. Not many ambitions are left to a four-star general. Those who have tried running for president haven't done so well."

"Sure," the President said. He nodded his head. "Just look at Wes Clark. A good man. A good general. He made the mistake of running in the Democratic Party, where generals are routinely despised."

He leaned forward across the desk, as if to take her into his confidence with a big secret.

"That's what they wanted me to do, you know? Run as a Democrat. Because of Hollywood. I couldn't do that, you know? It just wasn't me. I believe in business."

"Looks like you made the right decision, Mister President."

"Anyway," he said, standing to signal that the meeting was over, "Truman handled MacArthur, and he was a national hero. Stormy's itching to be MacArthur, but I met Douglas MacArthur, and he's no MacArthur. I can handle Stormy just fine."

● ● ●

"Is he even old enough to have known MacArthur?"

"Oh, sure. MacArthur died in 1964. Charley would've been in his late teens, early twenties. Don't ask me how they would have met, but it's chronologically possible. For that matter, don't make more out of it than it is. He was just paraphrasing that old quote that Lloyd Bentsen made about Jack Kennedy in that 1988 debate."

"Dan Quayle shit in his pants when the Iceman said that. Did you see the look on his face? Priceless." Mary Driver laughed loudly and repeatedly, slapping her knee. A laugh led to choking, which led to a coughing fit. After several moments, she recovered well enough to talk again. Joan laughed along with her, in her characteristically restrained fashion.

Driver was her chief of staff, her mentor from the Houston days, and closest confidante. Back when Queenan was a member of Congress, they had developed a weekly social hour with wine and back-home gossip. Now, working in the White House, they usually had the Rose Garden to themselves.

Like Queenan, Mary was a childless widow whose only family was her work, but that was where the similarity ended. If there was such a thing, as a Renaissance woman, Driver might have been it. An autodidact by nature in spite of her college education, she stayed up to date on trends, fashions, and modes of thought that usually left her generation behind. A ghost legion of hackers was at her command, conducting all types of targeting, publicity, and even occasional dirty tricks. She was also, like Davidson, a fitness nut. Now in her early sixties, she had developed a bit of a reputation as a cougar.

"Tell me more about this military exercise, Joanie," she said. Driver traced her finger lazily around the rim of her wine glass, now sweating in the humid afternoon sunshine. Her puzzled frown was a far cry from the happy warrior persona she usually projected.

Queenan described it quickly.

"Let me ask you something," Driver said.

Queenan gave her an inviting look.

"What's the purpose of military exercises like these?"

"Well, he said it was to flex some muscles in order to remind the Persians and their friends of our capabilities."

"Think about this: Is that really the purpose of a military exercise?"

"What are you getting at?"

"Well, don't forget Artie was a teacher at the War College. We used to talk about history, especially military history, all the time." Arthur Driver, her husband, had died years earlier in the crash of a small plane.

"In general," Mary said, "the idea is to test the ability to deploy effectively. That usually means rapidly, but as you know, the logistical challenges are enormous."

"If I recall, that was Eisenhower's specialty," Queenan said. "Logistics. Schwarzkopf's, too. And Petraeus'."

"Not Schwarzkopf—that was just good PR. Anyway, Thornton is giving you a political reason for this exercise," Driver said. "Not military. Don't you think that's odd?"

"Maybe," Queenan said. "All the generals are politicians, especially the four-stars."

"Think about this," Driver said. "Thornton is commanding forces across such a wide region, spanning so many theaters, that it's not a big leap to justifying a fifth star."

"Oh, but that opens a can of worms," Queenan said. "You make him a five-star, you have to give a fifth star to the Chairman as well. His superiors have to have equivalent rank or higher. And it raises the question of the other chiefs."

"True, unless they make him Chairman, which I don't think he's in line for, since Admiral Bana's the Vice Chairman. Anyway, my real point is that I'm a bit worried. Who's the real instigator of this mission, the President or the General?"

She watched the Vice President stand up and start walking around the patio slowly, washing her hands over each other.

"Joanie, are you okay?"

"Fine, fine, my skin's just feeling a little clammy."

Driver peered at her through slitted eyes and waited for Queenan to continue.

"Now that you mention it, ole Stormy did most of the talking. In fact, part of the time the President seemed to be tuning out, thinking about something else. I'm not at all clear on how important this is to him."

"That's worth knowing. Because a military exercise is only a single order away from becoming an invasion force."

5

QUEENAN'S QUESTIONS

"**Q**ueenan is starting to ask questions about Project May Day." Stormy Thornton let that thought hang while he began to bench-press another set.

"The Old Man didn't keep the Queen Bitch in the loop?"

Finished with the set, Thornton chuckled and stood, letting the younger officer replace him. Under the gym's harsh ceiling spotlights, his shiny scalp gleamed from beneath the military-severe haircut.

"Guess not. He's a little old-fashioned that way, which is one of the reasons our operation will be a success." Thornton watched the officer, Colonel Trent Oliver, as he completed his set. He knew that Oliver, fifteen years younger, could press a lot more than he but noticed Oliver downplayed it, presumably as a courtesy.

"What should we do?" Oliver just sat on the bench, not even breathing hard, waiting for his next set.

"Not much. Thinking of this as a problem to solve would be a flawed approach. Check around on your end while I touch base with the commanders."

"Got it. What are we looking for?" Oliver leaned back onto the bench for another set.

"Any signs of hinkiness? Someone who seems not completely with the program – hesitant, asking questions, that sort of thing. It is now the seventeenth day of April – my birthday, as you failed once again to notice. We have two weeks, exactly fourteen days, until May Day. Let's just keep the machine moving. Events will take care of themselves."

Thornton paused to look more closely at Oliver. The E-ring was filled with private gyms that allowed such conversations; using his clout, Thornton made sure this one was available exclusively to him.

He liked Oliver because he was *simpatico*. Natural rapport like theirs was a rare asset, especially since most general officers found it safer to keep their own counsel. Oliver had been a young captain serving under Thornton when he received his second star, causing him to be reassigned. When they next crossed paths, Oliver had already seen enough distinguished combat to receive two Silver Stars and a Purple Heart. After a hip injury took him out of combat for good, he ended up as Thornton's personal assistant. Strom Thornton relied on this young colonel to take his back when needed. Though he had yet to realize it, he was about to rely upon his young protégé more than ever before.

The ghost colonel smiled with a small smile that suited him. Along with his haircut, longish by military standards – which is to say, short, but not severe – he projected a soft, lemony look. Although not short at five eleven, his slender, wiry frame gave him a non-threatening countenance. On occasion, that misunderstood appearance had given him an edge in a sudden confrontation and saved his life.

"I'm on it, General."

"Do I need to spell it out? Absolute secrecy is a requirement."

"Always a requirement, General. Spell it out if you wish, but I know what's required – as well as what's not." Oliver finally realized he had been hogging the bench and got up for the general, who quickly took his place.

"Exactly so," Thornton said. He dropped down to the bench and prepared to lift the barbell. "After all, this is the Vice President we're talking about. There are limits to what we can and cannot do." Turning his attention to the lift, he let Oliver speak.

"I used to think that until the first time I saw *Apollo 13*," Oliver said. "The way those engineers went about solving problems, dealing strictly with what was available, was impressive. Made me think of dropping a naked SEAL into a swamp with only a buck knife, and having him fly out in a man-made hang glider."

"Using a motor, he machine-tooled with the knife, running on kerosene personally brewed in a still," Storm said. Lying on the bench between sets, he smiled slightly, a crooked smile that frightened most who saw it. "Did you see that movie before or after Afghanistan?"

"Actually, between my first and second tours, when I was home on extended leave. You look at my jacket, my first tour wasn't very impressive. I barely made it from first light to captain. But my second tour – wow! I went in with a totally different attitude, a total can-do attitude."

"Which is what I always need and rarely get," Thornton said. "So what are you saying?"

"I'm saying there is a creative solution to anything. Let's see what's what and go from there. Mind if I do another set?"

$$\bullet \ \bullet \ \bullet$$

"Comin' home late tonight, Carol," Oliver said. He had connected to his wife on his cell phone, via Bluetooth, as he drove from the Pentagon parking lot.

"Again?"

"Again, yes. I told you I'm on full alert for two weeks. Don't make me the bad guy here, Carol."

"I know, I know. A girl can hope, can't she? I miss you, Trennie." As she spoke, Carol Oliver pulled on a party dress, preparing for a night on the town. "It's worse when you're overseas on assignment, but it's still frustrating. Please tell me you'll find some time for us soon."

"Count on it," Oliver said. He spoke tonelessly, with no serious intent.

I warned her when we got married what it would be like. Guess I didn't spell it out plain enough. One of these days, I'll have to change that.

$$\bullet \ \bullet \ \bullet$$

The young woman stood at the maitre d's station, looking about anxiously for her date.

"Over here!" She heard the words for a moment without their registering. Looking around, she saw an older woman – fifteen, perhaps twenty years her senior, and showing it – waving at her, a folded linen napkin serving as her flag. Cindy Wilson pursed her lips together and scurried over to meet Belle Lafontaine Thornton, as the maitre d' turned to assist the next patron.

When the invitation came via a third party, Thornton's social secretary, Cindy, wondered whether a military wife really could have a social secretary. Puzzled by this unusual approach, Wilson had felt a bit put off, but you don't say no to the wife a four-star general – not if you were engaged to marry a colonel with his own dreams of stars.

"Ms. Thornton?" she asked. The brightness in her voice emphasized her relative youth, and their age difference. Belle stood up and stuck her hand out prominently as a woman might, with her fingers pointed downward from a crooked wrist.

"Belle," she said. "Cindy? May I call you Cindy?"

Cindy smiled and nodded. With a slip of the shoulder she let her purse slide down gracefully into the seat opposite Belle's.

"Chardonnay?" Belle asked. She held up her own wine glass, already half emptied.

"No, I'll take the house Cab," she said. The waiter, who had hovered at her elbow before she was properly seated, nodded and moved off. Cindy looked around her, taking in the ornate fixtures and upscale dress of the clientele. She felt her plain suit was barely adequate; she would have to enhance her wardrobe if she was going to be associating with a better crowd.

"So I hear it's official," Belle said. She hunched her shoulders, leaning forward as if they had an exciting new secret to discuss. Her tone was hushed and almost conspiratorial.

"Yes, it is," Cindy said. She couldn't restrain the grin on her face. "Sammy and I are getting married in just three months. He's asking the General to be his best man."

"Which, of course, he will do," Belle said. "I just wonder what the *quid pro quo* will be." She leaned back in her chair with a satisfied smile on her face, fingering the string of oversized pearls around her neck.

Cindy looked at them, barely registering the thought that the pearls made her look matronly.

"What do you mean?" Cindy asked. She was shaken, exactly as Belle intended.

"Stormy gives nothing for free. Everything's a deal with him. So when a former officer of his, Colonel Samuel Chin, asks him to be best man, that's a matter of prestige. That will actually go in both their files, and it will make them both look good. Stormy would avoid your wedding like the plague if he saw a downside. I guarantee he gets something out of it, or thinks he does."

"Wow," Cindy said. "That's pretty mercenary." She emptied what was left in her wine glass with a quick gulp, then signaled the waiter with the empty.

Belle nodded, still playing with the pearls.

"Welcome to My World. Welcome to the U.S. Army. The good news is, their frequent and sometimes extended absences mean we get a *lot* of freedom. How wisely you use that is up to you, but we do have options."

Cindy looked sobered by Belle's flood of words, but she was starting to put more distance from her sobriety.

"I thought being a military wife was mostly about the travel," she said. "Was that so wrong?"

"Not so wrong, but not necessarily reliable. Mid-level officers succeed partly by hitching up to successful generals. If they find a good one, they stay in the elevator with him and ride to the top, if they can."

"Are you saying that with Sammy working for General Caesare, we're stuck here in the District? I'm supposed to be a Pentagon wife for the rest of my life? I'm not even thirty-five, for cryin' out loud!" Her indignant pose amused Thornton.

"You'll have to figure that one out for yourself," Belle said. "When Stormy met me, he thought he was getting a petite Southern belle. That's because I was introduced to him as a debutante from old-New Orleans high society."

"Being named Belle probably didn't help any," Cindy said. She spoke into her wine glass, not facing Belle directly; they both laughed. "But you weren't a deb?"

"Oh, I was, or at least what passed for it in the late twentieth century. I speak French with a glahriously Nawlins accent, dontcha know? That's all Stormy and his general friends and politicians see, or hear. That and my mahh-velous Continental manners."

They both laughed at her exaggerated accent.

"But otherwise I do as I damn well please. When the cat's away, the mice will play."

When Cindy flashed her look of surprise, she laughed.

"Not *that* kind of playing, darling. At least not me, though Lord knows the opportunities are always there. But I have my freedom and I've learned to enjoy it."

"I don't mean to pry," Cindy said, "but what about children? I know you don't have kids. Don't you have any regrets?"

Belle looked at her sideways, out the corner of her right eye. She tightened and loosened her lips several times as she considered her reply. As she did, Cindy suddenly noticed how much makeup Belle was wearing, and how it cracked with wrinkles whenever she smiled or frowned.

"Some," she said. "I admit it. But it's not like you might think. I don't sit around moping all the time about what might have been. I grew up wanting kids, but you know what? I saw Stormy's fellow officers all around him with really messed-up kids. Boys whose self-esteem was ruined by having an important father who never gave him the time of day. Girls emotionally wasted by the disinterest of the most important man in their lives.

"But I was like you, sweetie. I just wanted to get away from home. Marrying military seemed like a small price to pay. An' since I was pretty sure Stormy was goin' to go all the way, I didn't see much downside. Worst case scenario, he gets blown away in Asia while I'm sitting here raising rug rats."

"But it worked for you. No rug rats, and he made it back from Afghanistan in one piece. They even call him the Hero of Afghanistan. You must be proud."

"Proud enough," Belle said. "But in an odd kind of way. Daddy was a CEO and he wanted me to marry a corporate guy. They pretty much look down on military. I guess some of them respect the power of the

military, but money-wise, they're all so rich they don't see much difference between what a buck private and a full general make. For me, it
wasn't what I wanted. Wasn't worth it."

"What wasn't worth it?"

"Basically, being on call 24/7," Belle said. She made a face by drawing down on the corners of her mouth. "For the wife, the corporate lifestyle is far more rigid than in the military. They have watchers. The
watchers watch the wives and kids closely and judge with a harshness
worse than any desert winter. Send your kid to the wrong school and
you may as well live on the far side of the moon. Join the wrong club
and you might as well retire.

"So I married Stormy. Were there compromises? Sure, but aren't
there always? Stormy has this very powerful, compelling style. In a *good*
way. He makes it easy to go along.

"And three months after we got married, Stormy was off to
Afghanistan for what turned out to be triple-deck tours. When it was
all over and he came home for good, he came home with a star on each
shoulder, a limp from a damaged knee, and a thimble-sized office in the
E Ring of the Pentagon. Now he's Chief of Staff. Short of an assignment
to the Asian or European commands, which would be a demotion, I
imagine we're here for good."

"I didn't know they did demotions at that level."

"They don't; not really. A demotion means retirement. Sometimes
they do, though, if circumstances warrant it. If we got into a shooting
war, as they call it, and they needed a good battlefield general, Stormy
could be the man. The way the world is these days, you never know."

The waiter delivered refills, for the second time. As they drank,
both found the words flowing a little more freely.

"Do you think Sammy's here for good?"

Belle looked up at her over the tops of her eyes, thinking. Her fingers continued to toy unconsciously with her pearls, but now much
more slowly, as if the fingers were confused.

"Is that what you want?" she asked in return.

"Not necessarily. I was really wondering what's best for Sammy's
career."

"Good question. Once he gets his star, he'll probably get assigned overseas. That's probably what he wants. That's where the promotions are."

"He can get his stars in the Pentagon, can't he? Like a staff general. Don't a lot of them do that?"

"Don't count on it," Belle said. The wine was slowing down her speech as well as her fingers. "Look, I'm no expert. I don't do it for a living. I just know what I hear. I think I know about the Pentagon's pecking order. What these guys respect the most is a fighter. They call themselves warriors. It's all about fighting. That's what soldiers do. So between shuffling papers and commanding troops in the field, you can expect your husband to want to command in the field. If I were you, I'd plan my life accordingly. It's not too late to have some kids to keep you busy. Don't get me wrong—I didn't do it, and I'm not miserable. I just think if I *had* had kids, I'd be a whole lot happier. So don't kid yourself. Pun intended."

Cindy smiled; she almost giggled but caught herself.

"Look, Belle, I really appreciate the advice. I gotta go. I haven't heard from Sammy, and I want to be ready in case he makes it home at a decent hour tonight."

Belle stayed behind. Once Cindy had disappeared from view, Belle waved to the waiter and switched to Glenlivet. Her body's instant response to the harsh assault of scotch on her senses never failed to please her. As the familiar numbness infiltrated her gums and sinuses, she smiled a secret smile to herself.

"Bel-la! Bel-la!"

Belle jerked her head toward the familiar voice, the twin feelings of delight and dread marching together into her life again.

6

OLD FLAMES

"Hello, darling," she said. She lifted her cheek for a kiss, and Colonel Samuel Chin leaned over. He kissed her far more enthusiastically than might be expected of a colonel with a general's wife.

"I just missed her, didn't I?" Chin asked. He aimed a broad smile at her. His dimpled chin glistened with his happiness at finding her alone.

"Yes, you did, and you don't fool me one bit," she said. She patted his arm patronizingly.

"Have you been drinking alone?" he asked her. Looking more closely, he noticed her bobbing and weaving in her seat.

"Not really, darling. Only for a moment after your precious left. Whatever will I do once you are married, darling?"

"The same as always, sweetheart," he said. The twinkle in his eyes and in his smile subsided as he took on a more serious mien.

"Now, look, Belle, let's be serious for a moment. It was all over between us a long time ago."

Chin took a good look at her for the first time in a long time.

She's older than I remembered. A dozen years older. I guess I chose to forget it.

He smiled, realizing the need for a modern context for their relationship.

She's a cougar—isn't that what they call it when the woman is older? What we used to call a Mrs. Robinson. She was a lot more attractive when

I was younger and she was more worldly. Now it looks like the years of Scotch have taken their toll. Am I just noticing? Was I blind to it?

He realized it didn't matter anymore.

"It's just common sense," he said. "Cindy and I are getting married. From now on, we have to be more formal."

"Yes, dear," she said. Failure to get her way tended to engender a stolid woodenness apparent to anyone who knew her. "I'll pretend to believe it as long as you want to pretend to believe it." The alcohol was grabbing hold of her. Instead of animating her, it cemented her in place, taking her to a trance-like state that might easily segue to unconsciousness if allowed to continue. Weaving silently in her chair for a moment, she dropped abruptly to the table, her head making an audible *thunk* as it hit.

Belle was not nearly as drunk as she wanted Chin to think. She noted this with satisfaction as he rushed to her side to assist her. He struggled to get her sitting upright while she pretended to be passed out. Mumbling occasionally to show she was not comatose, she waited for Chin to pay the waiter. After much maneuvering he got her to walk to the valet parking area on her own, but it was touch-and-go. The valet delivered Chin's car, then helped him get her into the front passenger's seat. He tipped the valet with a ten and drove away.

"Where we goin'?" Belle mumbled as they pulled away.

"We're going to get you home," he said.

"Don't wan' go home," she objected, with no sign of sobriety remaining in her voice. "No one home."

"No one home?" Chin asked. He was surprised. "I was under the impression the General had no plans to travel today."

"Sudden trip," she said. "Somethin' 'bout May Day."

Both fell quiet while Chin absorbed this information. When they arrived at the general's home, Belle tried to get him to come inside with her.

"Jes for a minute," she said, still slurring her words. "Make sure no one broke in or somethin'."

"Break into Stormy Thornton's house? Who would ever be that brave, or that stupid?" Chin asked.

"The District's full of the stupid ones," she said. "Just come in for a minute." She pulled on his arm with both hands, as a child might. "Pleeeeze."

"I'll come in," he said, "but only for a minute. This is *not* a good idea."

"You won't be sorry," she promised, but he was. As soon as he closed the front door, she turned around on him, threw her arms around his neck, and tried to kiss him passionately. She was a little too drunk to register his total lack of response, so he grabbed her arms by the wrists and pushed them down to her sides.

"Bel-*la*, my dear, no means *no*. No more. Why can't you do yourself a big favor and divorce the guy?"

She sniffed as if she was about to start crying.

"Oh, no," Chin said. He put his hands up in the universal signal for *stop*. "Don't start crying on me, Bella. I didn't create this situation. I just moved on."

"I can't leave him, Sammy," she said. She was now sobbing with abandon, which made Chin even more uncomfortable. "You know that. I've got nowhere to go. I've got nothing but a big empty zero of a marriage. Stormy's so dedicated to his job, he doesn't even cheat on me."

"You don't think he's–?" Chin let the unspoken question hang.

"Stormy? Oh, hell, no," she said. "He likes women. Just not that much. Unlike most men, sex is nowhere near the top of his priorities."

"I guess that's served him well," Chin said, "considering his rank." He withheld his next thought, which was that he would be smart to do the same if he ever wanted stars of his own. Stars were tough to get for a bachelor, especially a man never married at all. While he kept his counsel, he also observed that Belle, or Bella as he used to call her, was suddenly acting far less drunk than only moments before. He knew her well enough to figure it was all an act, but he let it play out anyway. Long after he had gotten over her, he still had a big soft spot for her, big enough that even her unappealing drunkenness did nothing to harden it.

They sat in silence for a few moments. With perfect timing, just as Belle started to try to kiss him again, Chin stood abruptly.

"Time to go," he said. "My fiancée is expecting me home at a reasonable hour tonight."

Belle nodded abjectly, staring at the floor in stony silence.

"My time is past, I know," she said, her tone now weary. "You still have your life ahead of you. Just leave this old woman to mourn."

Chin got impatient when people felt sorry for themselves. He hated it in his men, but he hated it in his women even more.

"Good night, Belle," he said. He turned sharply and walked off, his hard leather soles clopping with small reverberations on the flagstones.

• • •

The buzz on her iPad told Joan Queenan she had received an e-mail, so she made a quick check to assess its importance. She furrowed her brow and tossed her head in the signature move known to millions of voters as she puzzled over the message. The e-mail address was unfamiliar and it contained an attachment for some kind of file. Mary had warned her never to open attachments from unidentified or unexpected sources, so she left it alone until she could get her friend's help.

An hour later, Mary took a look and immediately recognized the video format. As she did so often when confronted by a mystery, she smiled and started bouncing up and down in her chair as if bopping to an internal beat. Driver transferred the file to her laptop, scanned it for viruses, and set it up in front of the Vice President's seat. She stood behind Queenan and watched over her shoulder.

The video clarity was substandard but viewable. Queenan thought it came from a camera behind the head of a general, who was holding a videoconference with other generals. Was that the back of Stormy Thornton's head that looked so familiar? Soon the voices and intonations made it clear whom they were watching.

General #1 (back of head in foreground):

"As we all know, the military is the only professional class in government today. I think that shows in some of the recent, er, decisions we have seen. Any concession of any type that weakens our resolve as the world's leader threatens to dangerously destabilize this country."

General Wildfire:

"We owe you a debt of gratitude for taking this bull by the horns, Stormy. In a very real way, you are putting your entire career and everything you've achieved at risk."

General Behrsberg:

"Not that much risk, not really. If we let things go the way they're goin' now, the whole country is at risk, not to mention Israel. And with the top guy asleep at the wheel, we're in greater danger than anyone ever imagined. Anyway, these fleet movements are pure theater. As long as no one gets an itchy trigger finger, most people will never even know something happened. As long as they have fantasy football and Facebook, no one will notice the difference."

Stormy:

"We're set. It's a go. I've held back a lot of details on a need-to-know basis, but it's smooth sailing. The main thing to watch out for is folks asking questions and sticking their noses where they don't belong. So get in touch at the first sign of snoops."

"A bit odd, don't you think?" Driver said. Joan noticed Mary was wearing a low-cut dress that showed a lot of cleavage. It irritated her, but while Mary went through this change in her life, she preferred to play along as if nothing was happening. Maybe after a few months her older friend would tire of the game she was playing. Driver straightened up and began pacing around the room, since she preferred to think on her feet.

"Hard to say. Who knows what passes for ordinary conversation among the top brass?" Queenan said.

"True, but think about this: How often do theater commanders get together like this?"

"You may be right. Each one operates in a theater so different from the others ... the real question for me is, what is Stormy doing that's so risky? These guys don't get to the top spots by taking risks. Project May Day, which you never heard about from me, Mary, since Stormy and the President told me about it in confidence, is an over-the-counter operation."

"I know. We talked about this before, remember? But these jock-straps act like they're doing something that's a big secret, and risky to boot. Help me understand: Why is May Day necessary? Persia already knows what we're capable of."

"True, Mary, but it never helps to remind them."

"What if it's more than a reminder? Aren't exercises like these often used as a smokescreen for real military maneuvers? Is there any chance that Charley's planning a sneak attack?"

Joan Queenan stared hard at her friend, who waved her arms theatrically as she walked and talked. Charley Davidson was not her friend, or even a close associate. Before the campaign, they had never met. Joan was too professional to take it personally, but he had taken significant steps to reduce the role of the vice president in government operations, based on his own interpretation of the VP's limited constitutional job description. She did not really know the man or his ethos. She knew only what he had done, and where he had come from: Hollywood, the only realm of greater fantasy than Washington, D.C. Was it possible Charley was putting one over on everybody? Was Charley about to engineer a sneak attack on Persia?

7

WHITE HOUSE GAMES

Chin's early morning arrival at the office was met by a captain who grinned big as they saluted.

"Out with it, Captain," Chin directed. "Let me in on the joke. I could use a good laugh."

"If you wanted laughs, I'm surprised you joined the Army," the captain said in response. "Sir."

Chin appraised him, taking a closer look at his face. He and the captain were new acquaintances, so much so that he had yet to give the young officer's file a proper reading. He would have to change that. A man with his wit showed promise.

"I'm impressed with your ability to sidestep a direct question," he said. "I hope you'll be equally impressed with my ability to redirect you back to the question. Now, what's so funny?"

"Not really funny, sir," the captain said. He was tall, thin, and so young it was hard to believe he was anything but a second lieutenant. "But, well ..."

"Well, what?"

"You have an invitation, sir," the captain said. He rocked back on his heels and smiled, satisfied for a reason that had yet to reach Chin, who stood there running his fingers through his hair. He had allowed it to grow more than an inch long, which made him practically a hippie in the Pentagon's short-haired culture, but the slightly longer hair was appealing—the appeal of a change that massaged his ego. Soon his imagination wandered to an image of himself as an older man with long, white hair and a stereotypical Chinese mustache with goatee; it was funny to think about, but he was sure it would appeal to his uncle.

Returning himself to the moment at hand, Chin leaned forward to peer at the man's nameplate, trying to cover the fact that he had already forgotten his new aide's name.

"Yes, I know, to the party at the Persian embassy," he said, already losing interest.

"No, sir, I mean a *social* invitation," he said. "Sir." He was biting his lower lip, as if suppressing a laugh.

Ah, to be young again, Chin thought.

"Yes, yes, Captain – Reading. And?"

"You are being asked to play tennis, sir. At the White House."

"At the White House? Since when does Charley Davidson play tennis? And why would he ask me if he did?"

"Not the President, sir. The Vice President. Queen Joan."

Chin's jaw dropped down.

"And, oh, the Chairman's in. He asked to see you as soon as you arrived."

After trading salutes at the door, Caesare waved him in. Chin could not believe it: his boss sported the same silly grin as his aide.

"I hear you're scoring in the big leagues," he said, grinning like a dumb schoolboy who had just seen his first *Penthouse.*

Chin groaned.

"It's not what you think," he said. He felt weak.

"Oh, and what do I think? If you know what I'm thinking, perhaps I can safely infer a high probability of validity for my assumptions."

Chin finally broke down and grinned back.

"All right, all right," he said, waving to the nation's highest ranking general. He walked over to the nearest wing chair and dropped into it.

"Just between you and me," he said.

"Oh, right, total secrecy," Caesare promised with a mocking grin. Chin noticed that Caesare's left hand flopped down in a weak-wristed pose he had never seen in public.

"My first assignment after being promoted to major was liaison between the House Armed Services Committee and the Army. Joan was a member of the committee from her very first term."

"Joan, ay? And from there, nature took its course."

"I *wish*. No, she was still getting over her husband."

"After two years?"

"Some people take longer than others. You have to admit, the circumstances were extreme. Having your husband gunned down right there in front of you – some women would never recover from that."

"But instead, she picked up a gun and shot back."

"That she did. She's a tough cookie, I guess. More like a tough nut – too tough for me to crack. To the best of my knowledge, no one has ever gotten to first base with her."

"Well, she's no dyke. I'd a known it the first time I met her," Caesare said. "She probably just needs someone to help her find the 'on' switch. Might that be you, young colonel? You can't be more than a couple of years apart. There's more than one way to get that star, I guess," he said.

"I doubt it, sir. If I was the one, I think I would have found out a long time ago. But we did get along well enough. We just never clicked in that way."

"Whatever's going on," Caesare said, "I want the full scoop. There's no such thing as an innocent game of golf or tennis in this town. She has an agenda. Go, play, return – and share." With that, he picked up a nearby golf club and began practicing his putt.

• • •

When Chin was escorted to the White House tennis court, Joan Queenan was already there, practicing serves. Only her Secret Service bodyguards stood nearby, at a discreet distance, looking outward. She wore a white tennis outfit that highlighted her high degree of physical fitness. She was what, forty-five? Forty-six? He was impressed; not many women took care of themselves at her age, especially in politics. His own choice of a wife barely this side of thirty was no accident. Vice President or not, he admitted to himself that he liked what he saw.

"I can't believe it," he said. He approached her with a handshake, but she turned it into a quick hug. Such closeness was new for him; he took in her scent, a combination of the office, a light perfume, powder, and something – something Joan. He realized that, one baby step at a time, he was finding himself closer to her at a time that he was questioning his engagement to be married.

"Can't believe what?" she asked, smiling at him, remembering their work together a decade before. "It's good to see you."

"It's good to be seen," he said. It was a standard reply he had copied years ago from a governor he had met. "But my God – it's been ten years, and you look like you've actually gotten younger."

"Careful, Colonel," she said, laughing. "Last I heard, you're actually engaged to be married."

"That I am," he said. He laughed back, enjoying a brief respite from real work. "But every engaged bachelor has a longing for one last –"

"Watch it!" She laughed again and wagged her index finger in his face. "Or I got three guys who will wrestle you to the ground."

"Okay, okay!" he said. He held his palms in front as if to hold her in abeyance. "So you really invited me here to play tennis?"

"I really invited you here to play tennis. I told Kevin, who schedules the tennis court, to find me someone I could beat. Somehow, unbelievably, he came up with your name."

Yeah, right, Chin thought. That answer was so transparent, he knew she wanted him to see through it. In a moment she would get around to telling him what was really on her mind.

Transparent or not, the Vice President proceeded to thrash the colonel in a series of matches just close enough to be interesting, but decisive enough to forego the chance of a rematch changing the balance. He had been prepared to throw the games to her as a courtesy to her office, but he was dismayed to discover she did not need it.

By the time they were done, Chin was out of breath. He hadn't noticed the Potomac humidity earlier, but now he was sweating heavily; his uniform showed sweat stains under his armpits and across his chest. Queenan, on the other hand, was breathing normally and showed only the slightest sheen of sweat across her brow and upper lip. They met at the net while he worked to catch his breath.

"Out of shape there, Colonel," she said. He recalled that she could be a tease. "They must be keeping you behind a desk these days."

"I have a feeling you know exactly where they're keeping me," he said. "And starting tomorrow, I am back in the gym. The E-ring gym is out of this world. It must have been built by NASA."

"So is it true what they say about Chazz?"

"Who?" he asked. He pretended innocence but knew exactly what she was asking, because it was the first thing everyone wanted to know about Caesare.

"You know what I'm asking. Is it true?"

"Well, there's only one way I could know for sure," Chin said. He tried to act like he was laughing it off, waving at her and backing away slightly. He preferred to dodge the question but doubted he could get away with it for long.

"Yeah, yeah. Say it ain't so, Joe. Half the women in D.C. already say it ain't so."

Chin grinned.

"Yeah, well ..."

"Yeah, well, nothing," she said. "Is he?"

"Like I say, I can't know for sure, but short of that, I'd say hell, yeah."

She laughed. Chin wandered back until less than a foot separated them.

"He lets his hair down with me just a little more than he does in public. I think he secretly wants to be out of the closet but can't afford to lose the respect of his men. That is, of course, the men who don't already have it figured out."

"We're long past the days of Don't Ask, Don't Tell. It's not only okay, it's *in* to be gay. Why not him?"

Chin, who was still holding his racket, bent over to pick up a tennis ball. He began batting it against the ground with his racket as he spoke.

"Gay in the general public, among twenty-somethings, is one thing. Among the middle-aged general staff, something entirely different. Maybe it's all in my head. Maybe it shouldn't matter. Who wants to find out the hard way that it *would* matter? You can't put the genie back in the bottle. The stakes are too high."

"I'm glad he understands that. How do you like working with him?"

"He's actually a great boss, except that I'm basically his boy. The only time I have any freedom is when he's in an executive session I don't have privy to."

"Seems like a great opportunity, just the same."

Chin kept batting the ball against the ground but continued to move back from the net.

"Theoretically, yes. It puts me in a good position in case lightning strikes. But without the lightning, it's a nowhere job. The goal is to punch my ticket one more time and take a star with me."

"Of course it is," she said. "And why not? With your file, you have every reason to expect it in a two- to four-year time frame."

Chin was impressed. He had expected her to read up on him, but it was clear she understood how the promotion calendar worked at the Pentagon. Right – ten years on the Armed Services Committee. *Doh.*

"You're no dodo, Sam, so I know you know I asked you here for a reason other than tennis."

"Unless you really are that desperate to find someone easy to beat," he said. "But with your game, you don't seem desperate." Before she could respond, he whacked the ball straight at her.

She laughed and easily returned the serve to the opposite side of the court, which he did not even try to chase.

"It's a military question," she said. "I need you to treat this is with the highest possible confidence. That means only you and me, not even your boss. I know he's going to grill you on this conversation. You can't tell him what I'm about to ask, not unless I say it's okay. Can you do that?"

Chin paused. This was not a casual question. At the War College he had learned that all decision-making is treated like a chess move. Deep insight would come only from tracing all the possible event-path combinations and assessing their probabilities. Any event was the result of a long chain of events, each link of which was a step with a probability.

Though he had a prior relationship with Queenan, enough that they liked and trusted each other, she was not his superior. She was not in the chain of command. Without a doubt her influence could not be overestimated, but neither could that of Gus Caesare, the military's boss of bosses. Caesare would write his next efficiency report, which would either boost or end his career. Chin gave her a hard look to make sure she knew this conversation was all business.

"What you're asking is potentially dangerous. Quite possibly a violation of my duty as an officer," Chin said. "Are you sure this is a good idea?"

"I'm sure about nothing," Queenan said. "I admit it. Which is why I wanted you. I trust you. That's a precious commodity. In very short supply these days."

"Tell me about it," Chin said. "But then again, in our business, was it ever any different?"

"Probably not. Here's the deal: I think Stormy Thornton's up to something. I need someone on the inside who can gather a little information and tell me if I'm full of shit or not."

"*Full of shit?* Wow, Joanie, Washington has certainly changed you. What is it you need to know?"

"Have you heard about this Project May Day?"

"May Day ... May first. Less than two weeks away ..."

"I know, I know. What do you know about the operation?"

"Isn't it a regional fleet exercise of some sort?"

"That's what they're saying, but something doesn't seem right."

"That's what this is all about? Something doesn't seem right? Somehow I don't think you'd drag me here just because something didn't feel right."

"And it may be nothing, but I want to be sure. I don't trust Stormy. I think he's holding back from me. In fact, I think he's holding back from Charley. You've never met him before, have you?"

"What? Who? Me? The President?" Chin put his hands to his chest, almost flustered. Military men, other than the top generals, rarely associated at that level.

"Yeah, well, he's acting different."

"Different how? How long have you known him, anyway?"

"Not that long. Just since he picked me for the nomination almost exactly three years ago. The campaign was pretty intense, but we were separate ninety-five percent of the time. That's why I want to be careful enough to go slow, but also thorough enough not to miss anything."

"I still don't get what you're worried about, Joanie. What's the scoop?"

8

SUSPICIOUS VIDEO

After watching the e-mail video a second time, Chin shook his head and grimaced. Queenan, who had been watching over his shoulder, stood there in her tennis clothes as if she always came to the office in such attire.

"Damn suspicious, no doubt about it, but they're all smart enough not to come out and say what it is they're thinking. One thing I notice, though, is who's *not* in the videoconference."

"Who?"

"The global commanders. Everyone here has a theater command, such as Europe, Asia, and so on. But the global commanders – Forbus in CyberCom, or McGee in SpaceCom, or my boss – none of them are here."

"Is that important?"

"We'll see, Joanie, we'll see. What's the bottom line for you here?"

"I think Stormy's planning an Operation Persian Storm. That's probably not what he'll call it, but I think he'll do it. With or without the President's approval."

• • •

Sam Chin had attended embassy parties before, but the Persian affair was one of those rare events, a coming-out party for an entirely new government and regime. Unlike most officers he knew, he enjoyed the rare chance to wear his best dress uniform. He briefly wished he could have brought Cindy, to impress her, but quickly disposed of the thought. Any baggage at all would make it impossible for him to operate, he figured. Before the night was through, his figuring would be validated more than once.

Chin had no idea where to begin. He was on a fishing expedition, but a big party was not a bad place for anonymity, or so he thought. Before he could verify that theory, he was recognized. Standing on a step high enough to give him a good strategic view of the room, he saw a familiar face cutting through the crowd, followed by two Persian officers in uniform, struggling to keep up.

"Reza! What are you doing here?"

The two men met and clasped in a bear hug, each trying to outdo the other. At five-six, Reza Lavi was built like a small bear, with a black curly beard that enhanced the resemblance.

"Me? What about you? I thought you were still in Afghanistan."

Chin shook his head.

"I'm back for good, I think. Unless I get my star. Then who knows?"

Reza Lavi nodded his head and smiled. His eyes were lively, not those, Chin thought, of a man who had seen warfare firsthand.

"A general can do anything he wants. Then I will definitely want you for my friend."

"What, a colonel's not good enough for you?" Chin asked. He smiled to show he was kidding.

"In your case, yes, my friend, but a general is even better. What's this I hear about your new assignment? Star or no star, you are an important man now. Allow me to introduce you around."

With that, Lavi took him by the elbow and guided him toward a row of Persian generals standing more informally than Chin would have expected. For one thing, he noticed they were all drinking wine or, in one case, scotch or whisky of some sort. He was amazed at this display of secular disdain for Islam, which must have been approved at the highest levels of government. When he had heard their claims on television at a press conference, he was skeptical. Now he was amused to realize that drinking actually gave them credibility.

Lavi addressed the general standing closest to them. The Persian was a three-star, only slightly taller than Lavi, with only a spot of gray at his temples and a gray mustache thick like steel wool on his upper lip.

"Sam, I'd like you to meet Lieutenant General Fahr Arkhami, commander of our nuclear forces."

Arkhami did everything but salute. He clicked his heels together and stood straighter. The Persian general looked at Chin. He held out his hand, which Chin shook with warmth.

"Colonel, it is a distinct pleasure. Please call me Frank."

Chin stared at the man, who had spoken to him with impeccable English, if perhaps with a bit of a Boston accent.

"Harvard?" he asked.

Arkhami smiled.

"Exactly? And you?"

"The Point," Chin said.

"An Academy man," the general said. "Regrettably, we have nothing equivalent for training our own officers. We are working on it, but after more than three decades in the wilderness –"

"I'm sure you have a lot of catching up to do, General," Chin said. "You say nuclear forces? I am amazed to see you over here. If there is any chance at all we could get you together with General Caesare, it would be my honor and privilege to make the arrangements."

With that, Arkhami took Chin by the elbow and guided him to a quiet corner of the room. Chin discreetly looked around to see who might be listening. He confided to him in a quiet voice.

"When the time is right, I certainly want to meet with your commander," he said. "But there is protocol. I cannot just talk to people here and there. Everything must be arranged."

"Of course, General. I just want you know that a lot of us in the military, not just the politicians, hold out a lot of hope for your Persian Dawn, as some people call it."

"Back home we have discussed this at great length," Arkhami said. "Even my brother."

"Your brother –?" Chin looked puzzled.

"My brother, the new President? You didn't know?" the general said. He chuckled and looked at Chin with bemusement.

"Oh, damn," Chin said. "Well, who better to trust with the nuclear football?"

"Football?" Arkhami looked puzzled.

"Er, uh – football. That's our, uh, nickname for the briefcase with the codes to our nuclear missiles. Who better to trust than your own brother?"

"Exactly so," the Persian officer said. "And for this reason I can tell you, in confidence for now, that when the time is right, we will be happy to negotiate the Middle East's first strategic arms treaty."

"With Israel?" Chin asked but found himself talking to thin air. No sooner had he heard the words than their source disappeared.

"Well, Colonel, I was going to ask you to introduce me to the general, but he seems to have vanished into thin air." Chin heard the words as he looked around, mystified at the Persian's disappearance.

"Indeed." He turned to see an old acquaintance, Senator Benny Gritman of Oregon. Gritman had the Tip O'Neill look down to a T, starting with the bulbous, bloodshot nose. His face lit up when he recognized Gritman.

"Benny! How long's it been?" Chin started to give him a bear hug, but he stopped short as he remembered the formality of the occasion. He reinforced the handshake with his left palm to the senator's right elbow.

"I don't think I've seen you once in the ten years since you left the Armed Services Committee," Gritman said, "and I'll never forgive you for it, you sunuvabitch. You were my eyes and ears in the House." The goofy smile on his face gave away the intent of his words. From the cut-crystal tumbler of whiskey in his hands, he proceeded to empty the contents with what seemed like a single gulp. No sooner was it gone than he reached out and waved to a passing waiter, who quickly departed with a new drink order.

"Excuuuuse me," Chin said, "but if memory serves, it was you who left, when you flaked out on us to join your new buddies in the Senate."

"Oh, yeah, maybe that was it," Gritman said. "But you were gone pretty quick after that anyway, weren't you?"

"Yeah, off to Afghanistan, like everyone else in this man's army. Now I'm back and working for the Chairman."

"What's it like to be the bend-over for the Army's number-one faggot?" said a crude voice, interrupting. With this diversion, Gritman received and consumed another double Scotch on the rocks.

He and Chin turned to see another colonel, Trent Oliver. To Chin, Gritman was an old-school rock-heart conservative, but Oliver was two bridges too far: a power-hungry man looking for a chance to be dangerous. They had clashed sporadically since their West Point days in the same class. Chin was easygoing and less judgmental than most high-ranking officers, but to him Oliver represented everything that was wrong with the military now or in the past.

"Excuse me?" Chin said. He tried to make his words as cold as possible. "The birds[1] I see come from an officer, but the words I hear come from a toilet."

"I'm a fighter, not a lover, lover-boy," Oliver said.

"They need you in Afghanistan," Chin said. Try as he might, he had trouble suppressing a tight grin. "Why haven't you volunteered to go back?"

"After three tours, they value my experience here," Oliver said, but he answered defensively, edging back a little. "Not my fault all the staff generals have forgotten what it's like, if they ever knew in the first place."

"I'm sure Stormy appreciates having you around to remind him," Chin said. "In case he forgets." He let the words drop and land, flat. Oliver looked unhappy at where things stood but made no further effort to improve his position.

Gritman reacquired his attention.

"Tell your boss we're with him," he said. "Come May Day, we're looking forward to some changes."

Oliver watched them as the senator spoke.

"*With* him?" Chin asked. "What's that supposed to mean? Stormy's –"

---

[1] The insignia of a colonel is an eagle, hence the common reference to a full colonel, as opposed to a lieutenant colonel, as a "full-bird colonel" or simply a "bird colonel."

At that moment, a young captain grabbed Oliver and whispered into his ear. Oliver listened. Glancing at Gritman and Chin, his eyes flitted back to his aide. He nodded and followed the young officer away from the group without a single goodbye or other acknowledgement.

"Saved by the lamb," Chin said. Gritman laughed, a little too loudly. He looked around for another drink.

"Son, I just want the General to know that we are behind him and SubCyberCom one thousand percent. Come May Day, we're looking for some changes around here. No more pacifists, pantywaists, faggots, or women."

Chin peered at Gritman, confused by the juxtaposition of sentiments. Something did not add up, but when it did, he worried what it would add up to.

"Senator? Stormy's in charge of May Day, not my boss. I work for the Chairman, now, remember? Gus Caesare?"

Gritman, now working on his sixth double Scotch, finished it with a gulp and stared at the ice, puzzled.

"I – I gotta go," he said and then lurched away.

Chin was having trouble processing this conversation. He considered following the influential senator, but before he could, he felt a feminine tug on his left arm. Turning to see Belle Thornton, he also saw an empty cocktail glass and behavior that suggested prior consumption of at least a couple more.

Overdrinking seems to be in vogue tonight.

"J-Sammy?" Belle looked unsteady on her feet.

"Belle, what brings you here? I heard Stormy is *in absentia*."

"In absentia? Who talks like that?" she asked. She struggled not to slur her words, unsuccessfully.

"I do," Chin said with a grimace. "Tell me you didn't come alone."

"Course not, silly," she said. She brushed his arm with her hand, without a great deal of subtlety. "Stormy's 'round here somewhere. Only problem is, I don't know where." She giggled like a drunken schoolgirl, with her hand covering her mouth.

"Come with me," Chin said. Taking her by the arm, he guided her to a side room and onto an unoccupied sofa. Nudging her with one hand to her elbow, he sat her down gingerly, as if she might break, but she plopped down in an overstuffed pile of cushions.

"How will I find Stormy if I'm stuck over here?" she asked. The subtle hint of a whine crept into what had started as a sultry voice.

"Let Stormy find you," Chin said. "I'll look around to see if I can dig him up. You stay here."

"You want to dig him up, you better get a big shovel," she said, giggling again. "A biiiiiig shovel." Belle spread her arms wide to demonstrate her point. Losing her balance in the process, she fell back onto the amply cushioned sofa.

"You wait here," he said, with a new grim note in his voice. He looked around for a moment to get his bearings. Satisfied, he walked off looking for Belle's husband, General Strom Thornton.

The party had a lot of life left in it but was clearly in decline. The line of dignitaries no longer came in from the outside; it was gathered near the door, as attendees began to leave.

Discovering the trend, Chin followed the path of least resistance by trailing a line of British diplomats to the front. He used the motley banter of the Brits to cover his visual search for the senator. He soon found his target, who seemed far more alert than before. In fact, he was steady enough on his feet that Chin briefly wondered whether the senator had been testing him but quickly dismissed it. If he had any liberal instinct at all, and he was often accused of quite a bit, it was his idea that while most successful power players acted rationally and with forethought, a large minority of them were lucky, stupid, and weak. He saw no accounting for their success other than the grace and higher purpose of God. Chin did not himself call this liberalism, but instead a simple recognition of his experience and observation.

Chin planned to drift slowly to the door with the Brits, but Gritman disappeared so quickly that he had to double time it to keep up. He took a chance and bolted to the front, cutting through the middle of several startled but acquiescent groups. Not a moment too soon, he saw the senator step into the back seat of a one-stretch Lincoln limousine.

Thinking of his promise to Belle, Colonel Samuel Chin hesitated only briefly as he considered the choice between sentiment and duty, so briefly that no one watching would recognize it. Then he bolted for his car.

9

CHASING CONNECTIONS

*W*hat am I doing? What do I expect to accomplish? The senator's probably headed home, but all my success has come from following instinct and seizing the moment. I learned that in high school football. It's worked for me ever since.

Chin settled quickly into the drive. While not trained for inconspicuous tailing, he knew Benny Gritman to be an armchair warrior without an ounce of self-awareness. Soon it became apparent that the senator and whoever accompanied him were headed toward the Capitol, perhaps to the senator's office.

May Day. First Joanie, now Benny. If they came up in random conversation, no big deal, but Joanie just asked me about it. Now Gritman's saying things that make my skin crawl. Things that point to Stormy. What's old Stormy up to? Is this what Joanie is worried about? She's got me seeing spooks behind every bush.

In the end he was not required to be a conspiracy theorist. Gritman pulled into underground staff parking for the Russell Senate Office Building, where Chin assumed he kept his office; not knowing for sure, he figured he could verify it later. Chin could not follow inside without a pass card, so he was done for the night. But having parked across the street from the underground entrance, he only had a moment to consider his options before a Park Service police car arrived. Its bubblegum machine lit up the nightscape like a mobile theme park.

Attired in a dress uniform, Chin relaxed as the police officer approached. He looked to the driver's side window, but he forgot that police procedure had changed in recent years. He felt more than saw the officer's flashlight splash on his right side. He turned without thinking and was blinded by the light for his troubles. He blinked while his eyes tried to adjust.

"Can I help you, sir?" the cop asked. His voice was firm but deferential. He could tell he was talking to an Army officer but was not schooled in the markings of rank.

"Colonel," Chin said. He had learned in his first tour of duty to take the dominant role when handling a figure of authority; polite correction was a good way to do it, if done in the proper context.

"Colonel, how can I help you tonight?" the cop asked. Now he was even more deferential than before.

"No need, Officer," Chin said. "The senator asked me to make sure he made it back to his office okay. I think maybe he had a couple of drinks in him. Probably I should have driven him myself, but try telling that to a U.S. Senator, right?"

"Right," the young cop said. He touched his fingers to the brim of his cap in a cop salute. "Have a nice evening, Colonel."

Chin nodded slightly, pulling away from the curb slowly, making sure his left turn signal was flashing to keep the cop happy. He was ready to head home. His thoughts flashed on Belle, and how he had left her behind. He was sorry, but that had been his good guy kicking in, the good guy who had never helped his career one iota. The rational officer in him recognized that his past with Belle was best left in the past. Soon he would be a married man.

Preoccupied by encroaching thoughts of marriage and family, he almost missed Trent Oliver. Sam watched his fellow colonel with silent contempt as he parked in a side above-ground parking lot. Oliver scurried over to the front entrance of the Senate Office Building, which was the only entrance available at eleven at night. Oliver was in full operational mode. He scoured the area for witnesses but missed Chin's car, perhaps because by pulling away, it seemed to pose no threat. Turning to his own Lexus, he did not notice Chin's car as, shielded by the shadow of a building and a fog that was rolling into the area, it turned around to wait. One thing Sam Chin knew how to do was wait, and watch.

● ● ●

When he walked into the office back at the Pentagon the next morning, Chin greeted Captain Reading. Reading usually gave him a rundown of the day's events before he even made it back to his office, but this time Chin took the lead.

"I need you to call Fort Meade and see if General Forbus is available."

Reading nodded.

"Shall I tell them what it's about?"

"Not this time," Chin said. "Since I've never been to CyberCom HQ before, I thought I'd pay a courtesy visit to the commander."

Reading nodded again, absorbing the fact that Chin had completely avoided giving him a straight answer. Secrecy and misdirection were common in the military, especially in the upper brass, but it was a first for his new boss.

A few minutes later, Chin had his answer.

"He's in," Reading said. "But you'll have to hustle. He's leaving at three."

Chin ran into his office, grabbed his jacket, cap, and briefcase, and headed for the door.

"On my way. Have a car meet me at the front door."

"On it."

During the drive to Fort Meade, which was two-thirds of the way to Baltimore, Chin played catch-up on wires and internal memos. He stayed so absorbed in his work that he barely noticed the drive until they pulled up to the front gate. From there they discovered the security procedures – first at the front gate, then at the front door, and again getting off the elevator – were so onerous that they almost doubled the total travel time.

By the time he actually got to meet the general, Chin was not only anxious but a bit pissed off as well. That changed fast. Forbus strode through his door without making Chin wait. Chin hopped up and stood straight at attention, saluting.

Forbus saluted back.

"Good afternoon, Colonel. Looks like you made pretty good time getting here. Come on in, I won't keep you waiting. I bet you've had plenty of that already."

"Thank you, General," Chin said. He felt grumpy but didn't want the general to catch him acting that way. "I don't think we'll need much time, but I needed to ask you about this in person." He waited for Forbus to sit down before following suit. As Forbus walked around his desk and took his seat, he tried making his measure of the man. He had seen plenty of photos of him but never saw him in person before, never heard him speak, never saw how he treated subordinates or superiors. Forbus was a moderately light-skinned black man, about six feet tall and thin. Chin found himself wondering if Forbus, who must be in his mid-fifties, was naturally lucky to have no gray hair, or if he dyed it. Having asked, he realized he already knew the answer.

"How's the General doing? How do you like your new post?" Forbus asked these questions casually but watched Chin intently as he spoke.

"I trust the General knows the General far better than I," Chin said. He had a tendency to speak circuitously until he had the measure of a man and his intentions. "I've barely been there a week."

"And? What do you think of life at the top?"

"I suspect life *near* the top is far different from life at the very top, General," Chin said.

"That it is," Forbus said. He laughed, almost but not quite self-consciously. "And I'm starting to see how you got the job. You avoid questions quite well."

"I had actually come here in the hope of asking *you* a question, General," Chin said.

"There you go again! But ask away."

"My question is this: What is SubCyberCom?"

Forbus stared at him, stoic except for the slightest hint of puzzlement.

"SubCyberCom? That some kind of joke?"

"No joke, General. I'm trying to track down some loose ends on a conversation I overheard at the Persian embassy party last night.

I don't want any loose talk, so I came to ask you directly. I hope you don't mind, sir."

"No problem, no problem," Forbus said. His growling voice reminded Chin of Stormy Thornton. Forbus lowered his eyelids and looked away, clearly deep in thought. "Look, I'll do some checking around, but this doesn't ring a bell. Can you give me some context?"

"Nothing that probably doesn't sound obvious. I get the impression it could be related to control of vital communications links in case of a national emergency."

Forbus stared at him, this time not looking away.

"I think I would be aware of that, son," he said. "And I am assuming that if you are asking, then Gus doesn't know either. So I will check up on this and get back to you toot sweet."

"Thank you, General." Chin exchanged a couple more pleasantries, saluted, and left. Before he even made it to his car, Forbus was on the phone with his assistant.

"General Fuchs is traveling today," he said to his captain. "Where can I reach her?"

"She's billeted at Nellis, sir," the aide said. "Let me get her for you." He turned to his phone panel and began punching numbers as he listened over a headset. After a moment he spoke quickly, listened, and punched another button. He turned back toward Forbus and lifted his head slightly to address him.

"They say she's incommunicado, sir," he said.

"How can that be?" Forbus asked. "She's got a mil-spec certified satellite phone with her. She can take calls anywhere in the world."

"Almost anywhere, sir. They say she's underground doing some kind of testing, in an electronic quiet room that doesn't let any signals in or out."

Forbus nodded and stalked back into his office. Less than a year as Commander in Chief of the Cyber Command, he relied on Fuchs, a three-star and his top commander, almost completely for technical understanding of the cybersphere. Not that he was incapable, but he had never been more than an executive; Fuchs had grown up eating, drinking, and sleeping the cyberworld even before the Internet. She was from an entirely different generation.

• • •

Lieutenant General Claudia Fuchs loved the desert. Despite what Forbus' assistant had been told, she was not actually underground, not yet. Early that morning she had driven straight out of Nellis Air Force Base in Las Vegas, where she had arrived in a CyberCom jet that was effectively her personal airplane. She could have flown directly into Area 51, but she enjoyed the drive that most found barren.

Claudia loved the desert because she grew up in it. She had never learned to enjoy the District's winter snows or summer sweat. In Las Vegas, her hometown, the air was so dry that sweating was rare unless one wore a hat; in the dry air, it just evaporated. But she did wear a hat, and she did chafe under it, but only to herself. She would never let her driver, a skinny sergeant in his twenties, see her sweat. The fact that she was a stocky woman over six feet tall made her even more determined to look in control at all times.

It was a bright, sunny day, the kind that Claudia had grown up with but her driver would never get used to, since the sun always seemed to hug the horizon.

As they drove north out Highway 95, past Indian Springs, past the world's largest drone command center at Creech Air Force Base, they drove a bit longer. North of Las Vegas is the country's largest military reservation, Nellis Air Force Range. Home to many controversial but normally well-shielded activities, the Yucca Flats range had seen dozens of above- and below-ground nuclear tests that only ended in 1992. Sin City's nuclear lawn parties were long gone, but a vestige of that age still remained, and it was hers to command.

Eventually they turned onto an almost invisible dirt road off the highway. Discerning the cues was difficult even after dozens of visits, so they needed a GPS to be sure of the location. Rocky washes common in the areas made the turnoff barely distinguishable. Only a few times of year did these dry creek beds flow, but on those occasions, spot flooding was common. At times the large rocks caused the driver to slow almost to a crawl, as his Humvee tilted dangerously to one side or the other.

After a while the ground flattened out and got smoother. Fuchs was reminded by the terrain that most officers went in by helicopter, as she could if she chose. Despite her Air Force heritage, she liked to get the lay of the land. Nothing could be seen above ground anyway, so there was nothing special to be gained from an aerial view. She liked to keep an eye on security and make sure nothing out of the ordinary was taking place at ground level. "I'm a hacker, not a flier," she used to say when she thought she had to make an excuse. Now, with three stars on her hat and shoulders, no excuses were required, ever.

The barely perceptible road was mostly flat rock that wound around the mountain until they arrived at a semicircle of steel tightly fitted into its side. The door was accompanied by no guard shack and had no apparent knob or method of opening – because none was needed, as long as a soldier held an encrypted military-grade garage-door opener and knew the thirteen-digit pass code. The sergeant punched the code into the opener. Once he saw the code was confirmed, he looked up.

The metal door, little more than two sheets of half-inch plate armor, parted in the middle as they slid away from each other on tracks, into the mountain. When the opening was wide enough for the Humvee and no more, the driver shot through as if being chased.

He slowed down instinctively, because he never could get used to driving indoors. From previous visits he knew that the pavement was smooth, non-porous cement that was easy to skid on, especially if even a dab of water, oil, or grease had strayed onto the pavement.

Five hundred feet inside, he pulled up next to a line of vehicles he thought of as a hitching post. Anyone heading down into the cyber bunker, buried for security under a mountain that was otherwise unused, had to stop here for the final step of the journey.

Fuchs left the vehicle and walked over to a maglev car, where she was met by a colonel and a squad of NCOs accompanying him.

"General," he said, "welcome back to Area 53."

She smiled and nodded.

"Let's get going," she said. "We have thirteen days and counting."

10

SUBCYBERCOM

After several hours, Forbus was fuming. He had not heard from Fuchs, nor had there been further reports of her whereabouts.

"I can't believe I haven't heard from her yet!" he raged at Captain Hambor, his aide. "It's been hours!"

"In the old days you could go days without knowing where your top staff was," Hambor said.

"Huh?" Forbus turned around and stared at the young man. "What's that supposed to mean?"

"You know ..." the captain said. He immediately felt defensive and intimidated. "The old days. Nam. World War II. Before we had world-wide communications and GPS."

Forbus snorted.

"Is that supposed to help? Because these damn well aren't the old days. I should be able to find out where she or anyone else is anytime I need them. The minute they think they can hide from me is the minute they stop thinking of me as God.

"Get me the base commander over at Nellis. What's his name?"

"I'll find out, sir. But if she's gone out to the Area, don't forget it's attached to Edwards," he said, referring to Edwards Air Force Base.

"Call 'em both if you have to. Just find her."

After a couple of quick queries on his computer screen, he looked up at Forbus.

"Colonel Joshua Crockaday, sir. At Nellis. She almost always flies in to Nellis."

Forbus frowned.

"Why? With the airfield they've got at the Area, she could go straight there."

"Yes, sir. You'll have to ask her why, but that's the way she does it. Some of the boys have a bet going that she's a secret gambler, so she maybe likes to sneak into Vegas."

"Hah!" Forbus said. "As long it's a secret, who can collect on the bet? Not much of a bet!"

"Yes, sir," Hambor said. "Shall I get Colonel Crockaday on the line for you?"

"You do that," Forbus said. He turned his attention to a special military-grade iPad that he favored for much of his work. A moment later his assistant had the answer.

"Sir, Colonel Crockaday is on secure line 3."

Forbus hurried into his office. He punched the button that brought up Crockaday's face on the middle panel of his media wall. Crockaday was a sharp-looking man of about forty-five, with slightly wavy blond hair quickly going to gray.

"Colonel, I hope your day isn't as fucked up as mine is turning out to be."

"Good, good afternoon, General," Crockaday said. He spoke with a characteristic stammer that flared up under unexpected pressure. "To what, what do I owe the pleasure of this call?"

"I hope to God for your sake that a call like this is not the best you can do for pleasure," Forbus said. "But it's very simple. I'm trying to track down General Fuchs. I know she's out there, but I can't get her on the phone."

"Honestly, General, I don't know. She blew, blew in on her jet and headed straight out into the desert in the Humvee I arranged for her. We have not been notified of her intention to actually bunk here, so I'm assuming that if she's staying, she'll stay at the Area."

Forbus paced around as the colonel spoke but stopped and stared at him each time he spoke himself.

"Fuck! Don't you have any way to track her?"

"Not at all, General. I may, may be in charge of this little old Air Force base, but I have no authority over the Area. General Fuchs tells,

tells me nothing of her work other than when she will be arriving, and when she will be departing."

"That can be changed, Colonel, and maybe it should. Maybe a base the size of Nellis needs a brigadier running it, not a bird. Why don't you put out some feelers and see what you can find out?"

"I might be able to do that, sir, but how could you help me? I'm in the Air Force, not Cyber Command."

"We need officers with initiative, Colonel. It's that simple. On the general staff you can go to any command that wants you. Do you have what it takes to take it to the next level?"

"Yes, *sir*. I'll get, get with my men and get right back to you."

As soon as Forbus disappeared from his screen, Crockaday pulled an unregistered cell phone out of a drawer. He used a broadcast text message to his top commanders, requesting an immediate face-to-face with each of them, outside in a small pocket park. Crockaday knew that everything he did, said, or wrote in his office was monitored, but he had made special arrangements for his sanctuary; he used his burner phone for making them. White-noise generators were hidden at each corner of the park. Another was stashed beneath the base of a trash can in the middle. No electronics could be used in the park or penetrate anything that went on there – nothing short of lip readers with binoculars, which is why he chose an area with a grove of Joshua trees that provided visual cover as well.

An hour later Lieutenant Colonel Thomas MacArthur, commander of the Seventh Experimental Air Wing, approached the grove on foot, as he had done before. Before he had walked ten paces, he observed a figure emerge from the grove, headed in his direction. In only a moment he recognized the shape and movement of one of his peers, Lieutenant Colonel Travis Santana, an incongruously named Texan from San Antonio. As they approached each other, MacArthur raised his hand. Santana nodded and stopped.

"Mac!" he said. "The old man's in rare form today. Another secret session in the sanctuary." His mocking tone was not lost on MacArthur.

"What's up this time?" he asked the broad-shouldered Tejano. "Or is it a *secret*?"

They both laughed.

"Naw, he's just trying to track down the general, and no one seems to know where she is."

"The general?"

"You know, Fuchs. The one running SubCyberCom."

UNREACHABLE

Inside the mountain, Fuchs' iPhone beeped at her. The ringtone told her it was a text message, so she thumbed it open. Reading the message to contact Forbus, she swore softly and pocketed the phone. Thinking again, she pulled out the phone and sent a quick message back to him.

In his office Forbus received the message and swore again.

"Damn bitch is going into the quiet room without talking to me first," he fumed to no one in particular.

Under the mountain, Fuchs faced the team she had put together over more than a year's time.

"All right, gang, this is what it's all about," she said. Fuchs was not a very passionate leader, nor was she much of a team builder, but she had plenty of training. She knew the theory.

"We have firm intelligence that a major cyber attack will come in two weeks. Everything we can do or think of to do is what we need to be doing right now."

"Have we confirmed the source of the attacks?" one of her leaders asked.

"Anyone and everyone," she answered without answering. "We believe it will be multipronged, from a number of sources. The Chinese, most definitely; we think they're launching the attack. The Russians. And yes, the Persians. In fact, we think it's all about Persia."

"Are we playing defense, offense, or both?"

"Defense," she said. "Purely, strictly defense. I expect to have confirmed shortly the President's authorization for full commitment to Operation Intangible."

Everyone on the team gasped.

"Intangible?" the leader asked. "Are we going long or short?"

"Be prepared to go long," Fuchs said. "We're expecting the worst." As she stepped away from her podium, the room broke into groups of excited chatter. The general headed briskly for the exit. She believed in short, high-impact meetings. Let her staff sort out the details. She could monitor them from afar, while they got the benefit of thinking they were acting freely. She found that the illusion of freedom enhanced productivity and team cohesion. *Real* freedom produced chaos.

As she walked Fuchs sent another message back to Forbus signaling her availability. His response seemed to come back faster than the message could have been sent: Call back on a secure line.

Moments later Fuchs had a secure conference room set up for a videoconference with Forbus.

"What the hell is going on out there?" Forbus griped. "When I call, it shouldn't take hours to reach you."

"Sorry, General," Fuchs responded. "But I'm not sorry we have secure facilities. We've been doing unit and system testing on the President's Executive Order."

"Pertaining to...?"

"Pertaining to Operation Intangible, sir. As part of our ongoing mission to preempt any hope of attack on the Cyber Command mission."

"Which takes us back to why I called. General, I've been getting a lot of queries about something. I'm sorry to say I don't know the answer, so I'm hoping you can tell me."

"Yes, sir, of course." Fuchs stood there, almost at attention even after being put at parade rest. She waited.

"I have to say, it doesn't make much sense. But the more I think about this executive order, the more I wonder if someone's doing an end run around me."

"Yes, sir. And?"

"So, General, tell me: Have you ever heard of *Sub*CyberCom?"

• • •

Fuchs stared at her commander, thinking furiously. Though she had tried anticipating this moment, she had never arrived at a satisfactory reply. Now, needing one, she focused carefully to avoid sounding interested in the subject.

"Sir, it's nothing."

"Nothing? I just heard about it for the first time – from a colonel who heard it from a senator. A United States senator! Even if it *wasn't* something, it's something now! So tell me, General, what *is* that something?"

Fuchs snorted.

"It's just the unit I've been at all day, sir. *Sub*CyberCom. *Sub* for subterranean, that's all. That's the testing I was telling you about."

"What's your timetable for going live?"

"For the ability to go live? April thirtieth. But as you know, actual usage is limited to direct presidential order."

"That's the idea. Come the first of May, I want a live demonstration of your capability. Can you do that?"

"Yes, sir."

"Will you *commit* to that?"

"Yes, sir. Well…"

"Well *what*?"

"Well, I'm not sure how to demonstrate the live capability without actually *going* live. Did you have something in mind?"

"If you can't demonstrate it, how the hell can you test it? Show me a test, General. I'm sure your geek squad can find a way to do that."

"Yes, sir." They both disconnected at the same time.

Fuchs was on her iPhone again before the connection was even cold. After listening just long enough to confirm the voice that answered, she spoke.

"Remember that problem you warned me about? The time you said that was coming soon? It's here. He knows."

12

SUDDEN DEATH

"**G**eneral, ever since we installed the secured videoconferencing network, I can't *tell* you how much I've missed the presence of warm, physical bodies in the same room when I talk to them."

Forbus grimaced inwardly as Caesare spoke. He knew it was probably his imagination, but he *thought* Caesare had just leered at him. They traded salutes. Though Caesare was not his commanding officer – that privilege was reserved for the Secretary of Defense – he was nominally Forbus' senior.

"General, if I may," he said.

"Gus," Caesare said. "It's just us boys here." He shook his shoulders in an affected manner.

"Gus, if you don't mind, let's turn on your white-noise generators," Forbus said.

"Oh, *that* kind of meeting?" Caesare walked behind his desk, leaned down, and flipped an unseen switch.

"Yes, sir. Some things going on back in Nevada have me a little concerned. Among other things, I'm not sure of the security of our own electronic communications."

"What do you do over there at Fort Meade, George, if you aren't securing our e-mail? For God's sake, what else is there?"

"Quite a bit more, Gus. There's the entire Internet, including our own separate intranets, security of the banking system, ongoing cyber attacks from Eastern Europe and Asia. The list just goes on and on."

Caesare waved what seemed like a limp wrist at him.

"I know, I know. I'm just bustin' your balls. Sit down and tell me your story. Can I offer you a drink?"

Forbus gave him his first smile of the day and ordered a Makers Mark neat. He began talking.

"Gus, are you familiar with Operation Intangible?"

Caesare looked off in the distance as he considered the question. Forbus could tell he was drawing a blank.

"Should I be?"

"*Yes*," Forbus said. He mustered as much certainty and authority as he knew how. "It's the standing order to be activated in the event the President declares a national emergency and takes control of the Internet. It provides the protocol for limited or complete shutdown or control, depending on the order."

"Sure, sure," Caesare said. "Thank God it's never been needed. There'd be hell to pay if we ever used it even for a day."

"Exactly my point. Have you ever heard of *Sub*CyberCom?"

"No, George. If I had, I'd probably come ask you what it meant."

Forbus gave Caesare a long look. The senior general looked at him quizzically, waiting.

"It's not my doin'," Forbus said. "But *someone* has created this unit called SubCyberCom. I didn't create it. I've never heard of it before. *That* gives me a damn funny taste in my mouth."

Caesare made a face as if imagining the taste.

"Who's behind it?"

"Hard to say, but General Fuchs is my feet on the ground out there. I asked her about it and she said it was no big deal, just an underground unit. *Sub* for subterranean."

Caesare nodded.

"Sounds reasonable. But if you thought it reasonable, you wouldn't be here. Am I right?"

Forbus nodded back with a grimace.

"You are *so* right."

"What do you propose to do?"

"I'm bringing you into the loop because I'm not sure where this will lead. But any time I have questions for a three-star, even my own, I want my ducks in a row. And it may lead nowhere. That would be ideal. But I've got to know why we have an active unit out there that I've never even heard of before."

"You know about all your units everywhere?"

"Damn right, I do. At one time or another, I've visited every one, sometimes even broken the dirt for a new facility. Or I did, until this SubCyberCom came along."

"We'll have our own little recon mission," Caesare said. "But first, I'm going to talk to the President. Something doesn't smell right. We need to keep him in the loop."

Forbus visibly relaxed. He sat higher in his chair, as if a weight had literally been lifted from his shoulders.

"Sounds great," he said. "Would you like me to accompany you to the White House?"

"Naw, I got it covered," Caesare said. He used a trademark gesture of his, holding his left hand with the index finger extended and the thumb making like a cocked pistol, winking, and pulling the trigger. "I'll get back to ya."

• • •

"Stormy, what the *hell* is going on over there?"

Strom Thornton looked at Caesare patiently, as you might an untrained and not very bright pet. He raised an eyebrow in question. The two watched each other on video monitors as they talked.

"You know damn well what I mean," Caesare said. He made two small but menacing steps toward Thornton, who stood slightly straighter, as if anticipating an assault. "Those morons over at CyberCom may not be able to connect the dots, but I damn sure can. SubCyberCom is part of Project May Day, isn't it?"

"That's need-to-know, General." Thornton spoke plainly, with a blank look giving away nothing.

"What?" Caesare said, almost spluttering. "I'm Chairman of the Joint Chiefs. I damn well need to know about my own military's operations."

"Your military, General?" Thornton asked. He arched his left eyebrow for emphasis, as if questioning his credibility. "I remind you once again, you are not in the chain of command and hence have no need to know."

Caesare fumed.

"We'll see about that," he said and cut the comm.

"Indeed, we will," Thornton said to the blank screen. He walked over to his desk and pulled open a lower drawer. Reaching in, he pulled out an unused prepaid phone. After punching in eleven digits, he listened. When he heard the expected voice, he spoke.

"I have a Level Eight assignment for you," he said in a crisp command voice. He listened for a moment.

"I'll see you there," he said as he disconnected.

• • •

Like a lot of top brass, Caesare kept a secret bungalow for privacy – privacy for activities best left off base and away from the official residence, which he knew to be monitored for security purposes. Unlike the other top brass with similar hideaways, he never used his for female companionship. When he did use it, he always went alone. He knew his driver had suspicions, but it was better for him to suspect than to know.

After punching in the personalized security code at the gate, he drove up to the townhome, where he breathed a sigh of relief at the familiar black Cadillac already parked in the second slot. He felt the familiar stirring. Oh, why did life have to be so complicated?

After using his remote to open the garage door he drove in, closed the door, and entered the residence from the garage. Unlocking the door, he opened it with care.

"Palsy?" he said, suddenly unsure of himself; they had not been together in more than a year.

"Right here, Chazz," he heard and spun around to the familiar smile, the slight musky scent, and strong chest.

• • •

"It's a crazy new job I've got, Palsy," Caesare said.

"I figured," the dark-featured Sicilian-American said. "I'm surprised they let you away without bodyguards. If I was doin' your security, you wouldn't go out the door without half a platoon at least."

Caesare laughed. He always felt comfortable leaning back in his old friend's arms.

"The president has to put up with it, but I don't. Not as long as I'm discreet and as long as I'm packing." He nodded to the holstered Colt .45 semiautomatic lying on a nearby table. The .45 had not been standard issue for decades, but a four-star general had a way of getting past petty rules.

Paul "Palsy" Palmio pulled back slightly on the pillow, as if assessing Caesare.

"There's talk in the hacker community, Chazz," Palmio said. "Pretty high-level stuff. I'm wondering if you can tell me if it's true."

"Hacker community?" Caesare asked, turning around to look at his lover. "Since when?"

"Since ten years ago," Palmio said. "Not me personally, of course, but I gotta a crew. I got lotsa crews, but this one is special. They know how to break into other people's computers without havin' to be there."

"And?"

"And there's talk about something called Operation Intangible."

"Operation Intangible? What do you know about that?"

"Me? Nothin'. At least nothin', and now somethin', 'cause I can tell from that look on your face that I hit pay dirt, didn't I?"

Caesare's face turned dark. He crossed his arms and rose from the bed.

"Need to know. And now it's time for you to leave."

• • •

Palsy's got no idea just how sensitive this subject is. If I hadn't known him all my life, I would be having him hauled in and interrogated right now under the Patriot Act. With his Mafia background, he might never see daylight again. But we don't have to do that ... I can track this down on my own. Time to talk to the President. After that, a talk with the Chiefs about some protocol changes, and an investigation to plug these leaks.

As Caesare drove, he started paying more attention to his navigation. For some reason, the steering wheel was responding sluggishly, as if attached to the wheel assembly by a rubber band. How much wine had he drunk? Not that much, but the way the Town Car was behaving, he thought *it* must have had a whole case.

He started to have that thought, but it was never completed. Without warning the car seemed to jerk, sliding as if on glass. Not a good sign! Given the warm weather, the only explanation was an oil slick or grease spot. He tried to respond without over-responding, but the car skidded, unheeding of his efforts.

The road was a small state highway, divided by decrepit fencing that separated the opposing lanes by mere inches. The terrain on each side was not particularly treacherous, but neither was it perfectly flat. The lanes were divided by two-foot-tall posts connected by rusted metal stripping with fluorescent beading to catch headlights at night. Even when new, the fencing was more cosmetic than functional, as Caesare found out.

The car swerved inward and scraped against the fencing. He expected sparks but saw none; instead, he felt the grinding jolt as the car door scraped against it. He was surprised there was no inside shoulder, but then he was back in the lane, skidding again. He tried tapping the brakes and turning the wheel in the opposite direction of the skid, but he might as well have been tap dancing, for all the response he got.

The general now realized something was wrong, wrong beyond the ordinary difficulties of night travel on the road. He regretted the folly of not using a driver. Caesare was not a fearful man or a coward – his courage had been proven more than once on the battlefield – but he had a sudden chill, like death looking over his shoulder. As he turned to look, the car skidded again, into the divider and through it, as rust and rotten wood gave way to the commanding force of thousands of pounds of metal hurtling at more than seventy miles per hour. The end came too quickly to register, when he was swept away by an eighteen-wheel fully loaded tractor-trailer roaring down the road in the opposite direction.

PART II

13

FUNERAL FOR A GENERAL

"When I was younger, so much younger than today..."
Insightful words from a twenty-five-year-old drug addict half a century ago. I wouldn't mind being twenty-five again. What would I do with it? I was already a hot-shot lieutenant getting his ass shot off over there. What would I do differently? Not a damn thing, but Cheezy's dead. There are no coincidences; hence, he died for a reason. Hence, someone had a reason to kill him. Who would that be? What would that be? Something he knew, or something he planned to do. Maybe both.

Colonel Samuel Chin watched the funeral ritual. The weather was one of those Potomac rarities, golden sunlight but low humidity, reminding him of the California coast, but he felt separate from it, detached. The last time he felt this way was the day his father died. He had led a battalion of Marines and spec ops warriors to clean up a small army they had flushed from nearby caves. It was a hot day, a real scorcher that sent the natives scurrying for shade. Using a tank as a forward post, they lured the enemy into a box canyon, a trick straight out of America's Old West. After the first ten minutes it was more of a mop-up than a fight. An hour later, as they finished securing the canyon and adjoining valley, one of his staff officers approached him, an experienced man, but at the moment his youth betrayed him. Chin thought he looked like a kid about to confess a broken glass to his mother. His arm was outstretched. A major at the time, Chin saw he was holding a hardened satellite phone.

"Sir, we have a message for you from D.C. They couldn't find you on your phone, so they called me."

"Who, General Thornton?"

"Yeah, right, Stormy hisself! Hell, I don't know. Take the call and find out."

Chin nodded and took the phone.

"Major Chin here," he said.

"Major Samuel Adams Chin?" the commanding voice asked.

"Yeah, that's me," Chin said. "Who's this?"

"Sorry, Major. I have some bad news for you. This is Dan Bradley with International Red Cross. I've been asked to convey a personal message to you."

"Red Cross? Personal message? What –?"

"Major, your father passed away this morning."

"Passed away?"

"General George Marshall Chin died of an apparent stroke at 6:59 a.m. Central time. It was quick, probably instantaneous, and by all accounts painless. Please let me offer my profound sorrow at your loss."

Chin just nodded. Dazed, he handed the phone back to the captain. Dirt, wind, and machines blew past him as his awareness faded; the sights and sounds around him registered in only the most remote sense. Quietly, respectfully, his men gave him space; his officers took over for him. While not as legendary as his namesake, General Chin had his share of accomplishments. More than his share of respect.

General Chin's son stood there, immobile, his eyes fixed ahead as he struggled to accept the reality of losing the realest man he had ever known. He decided not to mourn his death but instead to honor his life.

Sam's father died an old man; he had been almost fifty before Sam was born. After retirement General Chin had returned to what he called his ancestral home, just outside New Orleans. In that community the Chin clan had lived and grown for six generations, with influential members in law enforcement and local elected office, while maintaining its Chinese ethnicity. As a youth Sam watched the General turn into a local godfather. Like Michael Corleone, he went away to college, and then war, to flee the depravities of his father's second vocation. Unlike Vito Corleone, his father lived for many decades, allowing him to pursue his own dreams without fooling himself about the need to care for the family's worst traditions.

Chin brought his thoughts back to the present.

Changes are coming. First an investigation. What are the chances Cheezy had an accident on that back road? Too unlikely, but so far, neither the Army nor the FBI has found any evidence that it was rigged. It happened in a spot notorious for nighttime collisions, and with a high casualty rate. Law enforcement sees nothing unusual, other than the victim's identity, so the Army won't touch it unless there is a good reason.

More importantly for me, my boss just died. The best, purest ticket-punching opportunity of my career, gone just days after I started. There was no down side until now. Now there will be a new Chairman, who will want his own man for the post. I'll be on my way out the door before the ticket ever got properly punched. Due to no fault of my own, my record will carry a question mark that no one can erase – no one except a new "rabbi." That's what they call it in intelligence. The guys I've worked with, they all had mentors they called rabbis, who turned them into protégés. Troops, really. I'm a good Catholic, but the idea appeals. I need a new rabbi.

Sensing a change in the energy of the crowd, Sam awoke from his reverie. A sudden rustling emerged from the gathering's nearly total stillness. Looking around as if recovering from a daze, he realized the outdoor service was over. Most people headed for the parking lot, but he stood in place. Trees and hedges cast shadows that struck sharply through the sunlight; he watched people walk in and out of the umbrageous areas without anything actually registering. Politicians and generals streamed past him, like water around a rock in the middle of a stream. He knew most of them and recognized even more, but he failed to notice the man who tapped him on the shoulder.

"Colonel?"

Chin whirled, startled. He saluted quietly when he saw George Forbus standing before him. Forbus waved to show it was not necessary.

"My condolences on the loss of your commander," the general said. "I know it must be hard on you. If not personally, then perhaps professionally."

"Well, General," Chin said. He started to say more but was lost for words. He knew it would be a sign of weakness to admit to any problem, but then, wasn't it natural to be out of sorts after your boss had died an unexpected, violent death?

"Yes?"

"It's certainly true that I'll need a new assignment, unless the Vice Chairman wants to keep me on."

"If I know the Admiral, he'll want to bring his staff with him, but you never know. I certainly have room on my staff, if the Cyber Command appeals to you. You strike me as more of an action-oriented guy, I admit, but cyber is the future. It couldn't hurt your career to cyber-up."

"General, I appreciate the offer. I may have no choice but to take you up on it. In fact, you and I have some unfinished business – *SubCyberCom*?"

"Exactly so, colonel, exactly what I want you to work on for me."

"Sounds attractive, general, but –"

"Then do it, son. No buts." Forbus appeared to stare at him, probably was staring at him, but with his aviator's sunglasses on, it was hard for Chin to be sure.

"I do wonder, General, if I would be more effective checking this from the outside. Once your staff knows I'm working for you, they'll shut down. If there's anything for me to discover, I won't be able to discover it."

Forbus pulled off the glasses, peeling them to the side with his left hand. He pulled up an inch or two closer to Chin and looked him directly in the eye.

"You think it will be any easier with folks knowing you're attached to the Chairman's office? I don't see how that could be so."

"Perhaps you're right, General. But right now I don't have to answer to anyone. If I'm working for you, I imagine you'll be getting phone calls the minute I start poking around. This gives you cover, and when I do come on board, you can make it look like you took me in to shut me up." Chin smiled as he said this.

Forbus pinched his face up on one side as he considered the proposal. He looked at Chin, thinking it over. Finally, he nodded.

"I'll give you three days to get this sorted out. No more, because this offer comes with an expiration date. You can take an easy path to a star, or a hard path to nowhere. It's your choice." After Forbus stared directly into Chin's eyes for a brief moment, he stalked off.

• • •

Sam Chin did not drink often. When he did, he had two rules that he followed without exception: never be seen drinking in an Officers' Club except in the company of a general, and stick to beer.

After the funeral he dressed in civvies – polo shirt, cargo shorts, sandals, and sunglasses. His yuppie disguise. Not far from Fort Meade was a neighborhood bar where he decided to sip on a beer and consider his next steps. Failing to say yes to Forbus immediately could be a big career boo-boo, he realized, but among four-stars, he thought he saw in Forbus something he had never seen in a full general before: understanding. A guy he could get through to. But the best way to help was to go in under the radar.

Lost in his thoughts, he failed to notice the dark-haired man who sat down next to him.

"Let me have a Jack and Coke," he told the bartender. Chin turned his head to look at the man, who nodded at him. After Chin put his Budweiser up to his mouth and took a swig, he set it down again and kept looking into the mirror behind the bar.

"Shouldn't you be drinking Sam Adams?" the man asked with a crooked smile. His pockmarked skin suggested terrible childhood acne, or worse. Sam smiled back. He paused long enough to let the remark sink in. The man saw the question marks in his eyes as he jerked around. He looked pretty sinister but opened up with a big smile that rarely failed to win over his targets.

"Relax," the guy said. "I'm here to find out what really happened to my best friend."

"Oh?" Sam asked. "And who would that be?"

"Gus Caesare."

14

SURPRISE VISIT

Chin moved to a back corner booth without saying a word, sitting down and waiting for the man to follow. When he did, Chin just looked him in the eye.

"Like I said, pal, relax," the dark man said. "Or should I say Colonel Chin?" His greasy grin turned Sam's stomach. Struck by the odd smile, he had a sudden feeling. Where had he seen a smile look like that before? On Cheezy himself. Were these two guys *really* good friends?

"And your name is...?" Sam asked.

"Oh, sorry. Paul. Paul Palmio," he said. Palmio stuck out his hand for a shake. Chin took it carefully, regarding him as one might a rattlesnake.

"And how did you know the general, Paul?" Chin asked. Sam eased himself into the booth seat opposite Palmio but never stopped watching him.

"Oh, Gus and I, we go way back to the old neighborhood," Palmio said, getting comfortable.

"*Old* neighborhood?"

"Back in Brooklyn, growing up. We was kids together. Popped our cherries together," he grinned. Chin's stomach turned a little more.

"You're not a military man, are you Paul?"

Paul just grinned.

"God help me if I am. God help the whole fuckin' country, for that matter." He knocked back the second half of his drink and waved at the bartender for another.

"You know, Paul ... can I call you Paul?" Sam looked at Palmio for affirmation. Palmio nodded.

"Sure thing, Sam."

"Paul, the Army was the general's entire life. Since you've known him for so long, you know he never married or had kids. So I'm feeling a little protective here. I buried a good boss today, and I don't know you from Adam. What is it you want, anyway?"

Palmio's face changed to dead seriousness.

"Ok, Colonel, you don't know me from Adam, and I don't know you, either, but I asked around, and you're the guy I dug up. You're the guy who should care about Gus' murder if anyone should."

"Murder?" Sam had been looking down at the table but jerked his head up at that.

"Yeah, murder. Let me be painfully honest with you. To tell you the truth, bein' honest is almost always painful for me, but just this once I'll give it a shot. I'm gonna tell you two things, neither of which might surprise you by itself, but put together, well, you may be pretty surprised.

"Colonel, in my job, I'm in upper management. I help oversee an ethnically based family organization with a wide array of business enterprises. Does this help at all?"

"Ethnically as in..."

"As in a little town outside Palermo."

"Sicily?"

"Unless maybe you know of some other Palermo, which I don't. That's factoid number one. Factoid number two is, I was with Gus Caesare the night he was killed."

Sam stared at Palmio.

"'With Gus' as in...?"

"Yeah, as in that," Palmio said, nodding his head. "I'm countin' on you to be the soul of discretion here. I don't know why, but I got a feelin' that's the least of your concerns. But we met at his in-town condo that night. I had a bodyguard with me, but he stayed out in the parking lot, you know? The guy's been with me a long time and I know I can trust him or else I wouldn't, right? But the next day, Gus is dead and Jacky Minora, the fuckin' Jew bastard, has disappeared. I put the word out on him but he musta skipped town and contrary to popular mythology, I don't have eyes and ears everywhere in the country."

"Okay," Sam said. He tried to take it all in without being distracted by the lurid details. "Why come to me? What do you think I can do about it?"

Palmio smiled.

"I thought you'd never ask."

15

OVAL OFFICE

"**S**o you see, Joanie, we have a hell of a mess here. A hell of a mess."

Chin watched the Vice President closely as she rocked back in her executive chair. She twirled a Mont Blanc pen in her fingers as she considered the situation.

"Sam, the problem we have is Charley."

"Clearly we have to speak to the President. Chances are he's the only person who can tie all these strings together in a neat package."

"What do you mean, Sam?" She leaned forward over her desk as she spoke to him. As she did so, a blond curl drooped over her face. She brushed it back with a practiced sweep.

"I mean, chances are the President already knows about these things we've discovered. Chances are he already knows how it's all tied together. I'm not even sure what the benefit is of going to him. He just tells us he's already got it under control and to let him handle it, right? Chances are, if he wanted to share this with us, or at least you, he would have done it already."

Queenan stuck out her lower lip in a studied frown. She picked up a heavy law book that had been resting on the edge of her desktop. Joan did not pay attention as she flipped through the pages; instead, she looked at Chin.

"That's assuming a lot, Sam. It's no big deal if a colonel in the Pentagon doesn't know about all this, but I'm the Vice President and I'll be damned if I'll be cut out of the loop on this. I'm going to see Charley, and you're coming with me." With that, she slapped the book onto her desk, the snap-shot sound lending power to her words.

• • •

"Tell me about yourself, Colonel."

Chin fidgeted slightly in the seat, which was unusual for him. But then, he had never met the President of the United States before. He laughed, certain that his unease showed.

"I'm surprised you have to ask, Mister President. I know you have a whole staff devoted to digging this stuff up. I bet you have a file on me this thick," he said. He spread his left thumb and index finger to demonstrate.

"Perhaps so," Davidson said. He cocked an eyebrow at Queenan as he led Chin on. "But who has the time to read it? I'd rather hear it from you."

"Well, sir, as you no doubt know, I got a poli-sci degree from the Point, and later, while I was captain, the Army encouraged me to accept an offer from Oxford to pursue a PhD in Asian economics."

"Focusing on Chinese, I assume."

"Yes, sir, for obvious reasons. But then as soon as I got back, some-one decided it was time for me to earn my salary. I got shipped off to Afghanistan."

"Where you ended up earning your Medal of Honor."

"I don't know about earning it, sir, but yes, I did see some action. And I guess you've been reading my file after all."

Davidson broke into a grin.

"Got me there. So how is it I get the impression you and Joa-, excuse me, the Vice President, know each other?"

Chin smiled and looked at Queenan, who smiled at the President.

"We met while I was in the House, Mister President," she said, answering for him. "When I was on the Armed Services Committee, Sam, I mean, Colonel Chin, was assigned as an Army liaison."

"After you returned from Afghanistan?"

"Correct, Mister President. But as you probably know, I didn't get a chance to stay before they sent me back again."

"The first time you came back a major. The second time you came back a light colonel. Now I see you're a full-bird colonel. I guess the war's been good to you, yes?"

Chin frowned and shook his head.

"War's not good to anyone, Mister President. Can I be frank?" He paused.

Davidson nodded perfunctorily.

"I'll be glad when we're out of there, Mister President. And I sure as hell hope we don't turn around and send our troops to Persia. This man's army could use a couple a years of R and R."

"Okay, fair enough," Davidson said. "And what do you have for me today?" he asked, looking at Queenan.

"Mister President, I appreciate your agreeing to meet with us like this, especially my request to leave the generals out this time."

"Who needs a general when we have a hero like Colonel Chin?" Davidson asked. He smiled his Hollywood smile at Chin, who turned beet red.

"Yes, well, after our last conversation about Project May Day, I didn't want to raise anymore alarm bells until we had a better handle on what's going on." Queenan paused in case Davidson wanted to interject, but he said nothing, so she continued on.

"But Project May Day is just part of the picture, Mister President. We've spent the last week tracking down a secret unit called SubCyberCom." She continued after a momentary pause. "Does that ring a bell with you?"

A voice interrupted from the side of the room. "Of course it rings a bell."

The scoffing words came from Tammany Dreidel, the President's chief of staff. His completely shaven head and walrus mustache made him look more the ward heeler he once was. Chin and Queenan swung their heads in Dreidel's direction. Queenan's own chief of staff, Mary Driver, continued watching the President.

"Is that all you got?" he asked.

"Madame Vice President—" Driver began, starting to turn toward Queenan.

"Yes, Mary?"

"I think there's something wrong with the President."

16

FUGUE STATE

The room became deathly quiet as all four turned to look at Davidson, who had not said a word in several minutes. In fact, as they quickly saw, he had apparently not even *moved* in several minutes. He stared ahead with a blank expression, as if completely engrossed in a movie only he could see.

"Mister President?" Queenan said, as much a statement as a question. She got no answer.

"He's been like that ever since the Colonel stopped talking," Driver said. "I've been watching him."

"You know, this happened before, when Stormy and I first met to discuss Project May Day with him," Queenan said. She looked at the others. "Tam, have you seen this happen before?"

Dreidel looked uneasy, like an overweight kid caught with a chocolate bar.

"Certainly not," he said. His body language said something else; he clearly felt defensive as the other three looked at him. "He just gets wired up from all the stress."

"He doesn't look wired to me," Chin said. He stood up and walked to the side, as if examining the President from another angle. "In fact, he looks downright relaxed. If I could relax like that, I wouldn't have any problem sleeping at night."

"Meanwhile, we're sitting here talking about him like he isn't even here, and he isn't even noticing," Driver said.

"Tam, I'm really worried," Queenan said. "Let's get some medics in here and have him checked out."

"Right away, Madame Vice President," Dreidel said. He rose quickly and slid out the door.

"I'm still waiting," Davidson said suddenly. He stirred just enough to make it clear he had returned from his inexplicable reverie.

"Waiting?" Queenan repeated.

"Waiting to hear what brought you here," Davidson said. Queenan and Chin exchanged nervous looks.

"We're just following up on Project May Day, Mister President," Queenan said.

"Mister President, with General Caesare out of the picture, General Forbus has asked me to transfer to his staff," Chin said.

"Such a shame to lose a good man like the general," Davidson said, glancing off to the left. Queenan recognized it as the onset of boredom.

"Before the Chairman died, I spoke to him about a secretive unit that General Forbus and I have investigated. It's a unit called SubCyberCom."

"What about it?" Davidson asked. His voice was duller than usual, and his eyes had lost a lot of their famous twinkle.

"Well, I, uh, I don't know. I've reached a dead end, but there's something damned peculiar going on here, Mister President. SubCyberCom is apparently a secret unit in CyberCom that even General Forbus doesn't know anything about."

"No doubt the General will communicate with the President when he feels the time is right."

All heads but Davidson's turned to the door, where Dreidel stood with a paramedic and a naval officer, who hustled into the room. They started toward Davidson, who looked at them sharply, so they stopped and looked at Dreidel. His bushy mustache often concealed his smiles and frowns, making him hard for strangers to read.

"Mister President, we think you've had an episode," Dreidel said. He seemed to be trying to sound soothing, but the tension underlying the words were anything but. Dreidel nodded to the paramedic and doctor, who walked behind the President's desk. The doctor checked his pulse while the paramedic inserted a digital thermometer into his mouth.

"Episode?" Davidson started to ask a question but was silenced by the thermometer. Queenan, Chin, and Driver watched from the front of the room, concern etched on their faces. While the doctor and medic did their work, Dreidel pulled the others over to the front, by the door.

"I think we need to shelve this for another time," he said. His voice was hushed in a modular tone he often used to downplay an event. "Will it hold?"

"Probably not," Chin said. The grim tone in his voice was unmistakable. Dreidel looked at him sharply.

"But it will have to." Queenan said this with a soothing tone in her voice. When she spoke, she touched Dreidel's shoulder as if confiding in him. "Let us know when you think he's up to another meeting."

"Of course, Madame Vice President," he said as she, Driver, and Chin filed out the door.

The three of them walked silently for a moment before they stopped.

"Wait a minute," Queenan said. She put one palm to Chin's chest. Mary stopped at the same time. Chin, smelling her perfume, looked at her and noticed her provocative clothing for the first time. He smiled.

"Are you thinking what I'm thinking?" Queenan asked.

"I don't know," Chin said. "But I'm thinking we can't wait another week."

"Exactly," Queenan affirmed. "Only seven days until May Day."

• • •

"I didn't hear everything they said," Dreidel said defensively to the voice on the other end of the line. "POTUS had another one of his zone-outs. I had to go for the doctor. No one said anything of substance while I was there, but I had to leave. I think they know about May Day."

"They saw it?" the voice from the grave asked.

"They saw it all," Davidson's chief of staff said in confirmation. "The cat is out of the fucking bag."

17

NEW ORLEANS BOUND

Chin made the arrangements to fly without fanfare from Andrews Air Force Base. Instead of the Chairman's plane, which would send a lot of unwanted eyes looking in his direction, he arranged for a flight on an old two-seater. The pilot was happy to get some authorized air time for the jet, as a recent overhaul had added ten years to its lifespan. He got a chance to check it out while he took Chin to the Gulf Coast.

By the time they flew in to Biloxi Air Force Base, it was well past nine, but Chin had napped on the flight and was now wide awake. Once he was assigned an unmarked car from the pool, he headed west on Interstate 10. He had a two-hour drive ahead of him and ten hours of thinking.

Chin always enjoyed this stretch of road toward home, even as a teenager. Whenever he needed to get out of the house and away from his family, he would hop in his car and head down the coast toward Gulfport and Biloxi. Back in the day, they were still quiet little coastal towns, unsullied by the casino invasion, but except for the still-evident ravages of Hurricane Katrina, the drive had changed little.

Tonight, with a full moon shining up high over the coastal area, he could see its reflection in the sea. The silvery orb cast a bluish-white light in a long trail toward the coast. The Mississippi coastline was steady and even, hardly a surfer's paradise, but its quiet regularity always calmed Sam's nerves. On his right he saw the empty foundations of houses never replaced in the decade since Katrina. On a whim, he parked the car. He removed his shoes and socks to carry and began walking in the sand. He felt the balmy breeze, smelled the clean salt air, and felt at home, as if a day had passed instead of a decade.

The president has a problem. In addition to all this May Day and SubCyberCom nonsense, he may be seriously ill. Who decides that? When does it become a matter for the Vice President to handle?

SubCyberCom is somehow tied up with Project May Day. But how? What does a cyber unit have to do with military maneuvers? Are they incorporating cyber attacks into the exercise scenario? I need to ask Forbus. He should know. Better yet, I can take his job offer and find out for myself. That's probably why he offered it to me.

But if SubCyberCom is dirty ... and God help me, I think it is ... I need help. Outside help. Someone that Stormy and his storm troopers can't get their hands on.

Eventually he returned to the present and aimed himself back in the direction of the car. As soon as he did, he saw the silhouette of a police car. Its searchlight beamed into his car. Any police officer could easily discern the subdued military markings.

Sam approached the vehicle, allowing the searchlight to change direction and spotlight him. He put his hand up to shield his eyes from the bright light. When he got to the car, he sat on the hood to pull on his shoes and socks. As he brushed the sand off his feet, the police officer approached.

"I take it this is your vehicle, sir?" the cop said.

"It is for the night anyway," Chin said. "I just flew in to Biloxi and I'll be flying back out in the morning."

The cop just nodded, noting the medallions of rank on each tip of his collar.

"You haven't been drinking, have you, sir?"

This time the officer flashed his big Maglite into Chin's eyes.

"No," Chin said, indignant. His interrogator paused for a moment.

"Well, I'm going to have to ask you to move your car," the cop finally said. "This is a no-parking area."

"So it is," Chin said. He noticed the street sign for the first time. "I have to get going anyway."

"Take your time," the officer said. "But next time, try to look out for the signs."

There are signs everywhere. But where do they point?

18

ANCESTRAL HOME

Despite arriving after midnight, Sam awoke early, a habit adopted on the first day of boot camp. As always when waking up at home, the bright rays of sunlight splashed through the open second-story window to make sure he arose in a timely fashion. Stretching, he pushed the lightweight comforter back from the bed. Through the window he saw the low-slung buildings of the French Quarter.

Although the view of the aging structures was a familiar sight, enough years had passed that he saw them with fresh eyes. He had forgotten how small and parochial the old neighborhood was. Had it become small, perhaps since Katrina, or had it always been that way? Was his new perspective a function of the international vistas available to him in his work? He supposed it was. Everyone knew a child coming home saw things differently, but he was no child.

Sam looked down into the courtyard, where the sun and shade changed quickly throughout the day. His father's only surviving brother, once a violent youth, slowly performed the gentlest of martial arts, *taijiquan*, in the middle of the square formed by the surrounding buildings. The elderly man, who at five-nine was tall for his generation, sported a Buddha belly that gave him a sense of gravitas in his casually measured movements. He was surrounded by a group of eight whose ages appeared to run the gamut, including two teenage boys who displayed a weight-trained musculature.

Smiling, he quickly donned sweat pants, a T-shirt, and some Chinese slippers that remained in the closet for him ten years after he last wore them. Within moments he had joined the group in the smooth, flowing movements of the Yang style of *taijiquan* as it had been practiced in 1900: sometimes fast, sometimes slow, sometimes with flashes of quicksilver power, sometimes gentler than the slightest breeze. While the older practitioners did not make the effort, the four youngest included the jumping kicks that had once been a hallmark of the style. Chin made the effort but discovered his forty-something hips were stiff and needed loosening; if anyone noticed, and he was sure his uncle had, they did not let on.

When they finished, they stopped and held a standing pose of utter stillness for another twenty minutes. Staring into a water fountain, Chin lost himself in a deep meditation until he heard the sound of a gong. All around him, the students slowly returned their minds to the present and moved out of their stances, all toward Sam, welcoming home the uncelebrated hero of New Orleans.

After only a moment the crowd parted. Sam saw his uncle approach, walking with deliberation but not difficulty as an old man might. Their eyes met. Sam raised his right fist and covered it with his left palm, wrapping the fingers loosely. He rotated his hands so that the palm of the clenched fist faced outward.

"Lao shr," he said, bowing deeply.

His uncle, Ling "Leonard" Chin, grunted and nodded his head a fraction of an inch, at the same time casually returning the kung fu salute that meant *I greet you as a friend, my weapon sheathed.* Then they embraced in a deep hug. Sam tried to wrap himself around the older man but found himself grabbed and held like a hungry bear. Sam could tell from his uncle's movements that, while pushing his late eighties, he had still not become a truly old man. The strength of the clutch surprised him. Smiling, he started to tear up, so he broke the grip and held his father's brother at arm's length, looking at him.

The family patriarch broke out into his own Cajun Mandarin dialect. Sam was rusty, but he followed along as best he could. Soon they were chatting away in a family language few in the world spoke.

"Rusty, I see," Ling said.

"Who could I practice with?" Sam asked.

"No one, I hope. We speak privately to be safe, not obscure."

"True. How is your health?"

The old man hesitated but kept a blank look on his face. Sam saw that as a bad sign, since he had never known him to hide his good feelings. He waited without saying anything. Ling put his hand on his nephew's shoulder and guided him to one side of the quadrangle. A table and four chairs sat in the shade beneath an overhang. As they took their seats, a woman of Chinese descent came out a side door. First she looked at the two of them. Then she turned to Ling.

"Are you ready?" she asked.

He nodded sharply without saying anything. She scurried off. When she was out of sight, he answered the question left hanging in the air.

"Nothing to say except the continual movement toward oneness with the Tao, which may not be too far away. I can still punch, I can still kick, I can still sit, and I can still push my *taijiquan* students. But each day as I move, my body feels less and less my own. More and more a thing over which I have less and less control."

Sam nodded. He waited for a moment before continuing.

"I visited my father's grave this week."

Another pause. The old man looked up at him, into his eyes.

"The memorial was very difficult without you. Even worse than having him buried far away, instead of with his family."

Sam nodded again.

"It was difficult for me, too. Difficult and impossible. Out in the wilds of Afghanistan, it was impossible to make it back in time. But since he is buried at the Arlington National Cemetery, I go to him often. I talk to him. The things I see happening in my job ... I wish I could get his advice."

"You could still come to me for advice if you would treat me with the respect an old man deserves," Ling said.

Sam blushed. His head pointed down, he looked over the tops of his eyes.

"I'm sorry. Even after several years, my father's death has been difficult. After missing the memorial, I was embarrassed to come home. So I buried myself in my work."

"But now that you need my help, you're not embarrassed anymore, neh?"

Sam picked up his chin and looked straight at the man, who looked every bit as strong as the generals he served.

"That's right," he said. He switched back to English. "It's high time I turn back to my family."

"Good," said the patriarch of the Red Stick Tong. "Let me show you something."

19

TRIAD BUSINESS

S am drove as his uncle directed, trying to suppress his discomfort at driving a U.S. government vehicle, military no less, into
what he was sure was an illegal enterprise. The situation was awkward,
but he had asked for it. He knew that his great-grandfather had started
the tong with the unlikely assistance of Dominic Troscante, son of the
founder of the country's first Sicilian Mafia gang. Troscante had used
the Red Stick Tong to engineer the execution of the New Orleans police
commissioner in 1890. They had a strong affiliation that lasted many
decades, but the alliance slowly drifted apart as the Mafia lost influence and the Chin family wove its way into the fabric of the southern
Louisiana power game. Although Chin and his father had rebelled
against the family business by making careers in the military, there
were plenty of uncles, brothers, and cousins to keep things going. Sam
knew his curiosity was unhealthy, but he reminded himself he was here
on a mission.

They drove for less than fifteen minutes, through a variety of neighborhoods that kept him guessing where they were heading and what
he would see – but almost all reflecting the uncorrected desolation
that had followed Hurricane Katrina. Privileged neighborhoods had
repaired themselves, where necessary – in the French Quarter, it was
not – but these neighborhoods had been stagnant even before the storm.
The tong, like most underworlds, thrived in the shadows of such places.

When they entered a warehouse district, Sam was sure they were
near their destination, but soon he realized they were taking his uncle's
version of the scenic route. Finally they drove into an upscale shopping

district, where Sam saw a familiar eMart logo on a big-box store up ahead of them. Ling grunted, pulled Sam's right shirtsleeve, pointed to the store, and signaled to go around back.

As they pulled to a halt in a parking spot and emerged from the car, more than a half-dozen ethnic Chinese men approached from several directions. None looked savory to Sam, who would have been reaching for a sidearm by now except for his uncle's lack of concern.

"What have you gotten us into now, Uncle?" he asked, bitterness tingeing his voice. His uncle muttered a Chinese phrase in a dialect he did not recognize, but by now he could tell the approaching men were friends. Several of them broke into smiles as Ling made introductions. Soon Sam was shaking hands with everyone. They turned to head into a door by the loading dock. In an ordinary worker's break room they sat, drank coffee, and talked. Finally Ling made a gesture with his hand. Everyone melted away like fog on a suddenly breezy night.

Only with the others gone did Sam feel comfortable talking.

"Does this mean what it looks like, Uncle? Have you really made the family legitimate, like they talk about in the movies?"

Heavy-lidded eyes appraised him. Ling had been a lean man most of his life, but in his dotage, his face had taken on extra skin and wrinkles that seemed to create a burden far greater than the weight of his karma.

"America truly is a land of opportunity," he finally said, drawing out the words. "Perhaps not in my grandfather's time. Perhaps not in the Troscante's time. Now, yes, certainly, there is no reason to go against the law in America. But in China ... "

"You do business with China?"

"Everyone does business with China, my nephew. Like a great tsunami, it scours everything that goes before it. And like all the communists, all the tsars, all the emperors, there is no law but the law you can make of it. My friends in Texas have a saying: 'In Texas, everything is legal, as long as you don't get caught.' Maybe once, but no more. But in China, certainly. If we can do it, then it must be legal. In a sense, we create the very law through our actions."

Sam scrutinized his uncle with care. Now an experienced warrior himself, for the first time, he saw the family patriarch as an aging warlord incapable of retirement, capable of surviving only by making every game his. Until this moment, he had been unsure whether to ask what was most on his mind, but now there was no doubt. Events in Washington were spinning out of control. The colonel had no choice but to use friends and alliances where he could find them. *Who better than the patriarch of a six-generation New Orleans crime family?* he asked himself ironically.

"Lao shr, when was the last time you had dealings with the Troscante family?"

The old man started to frown but caught himself. Sam knew he prided himself on his inscrutability, which was not nearly as common a trait among Chinese as believed by non-Chinese.

"Business or personal?" he asked, but Sam laughed.

"Since when was there ever a difference with the Italians?"

"Once there was a difference," Ling said. "But not since I was a young man. It is only one of many reasons to avoid business with the lowest of the low Europeans."

"They don't mind you going legitimate?"

Ling gave him a sideways glance.

"They have enough competition without me," he said. "But just to be sure, I help them on the back end. Importing."

"Not –?"

"No, no. But just like everyone else, they like to acquire goods at unusually low rates. Then they sell them below street prices and make a profit."

"Oh, I get it," Sam said. "You're the Chinese connection."

"There is good money to be made just getting people together with a common interest," Ling said. "And it is a much more friendly business than getting into territorial disputes."

"Well, in that case, I can breathe easy," Sam said. "Because I need a favor."

● ● ●

Flying back to Washington that afternoon, Sam's iPhone buzzed him with a text message. Smiling, he recalled his grandfather's next-to-the-last words: "You will have your answer before you arrive home." Then he smiled again, remembering the very last words: "Don't be a stranger!"

He sobered up quickly when he read the message.

Palmio is a friend but always demands full payment for a job well done.

As he flew home, Sam considered his situation. The last couple of days had brought back a familiar feeling, the feeling of being on his own in the field, forced to cope without a massive support structure behind him. He enjoyed it but still felt a little out of his element. Returning to the field with a mission was one thing, but right now he had no idea what his objective was. Should he keep tracking down this elusive SubCyberCom? If he did, what was the possible outcome? More to the point, what was the best possible outcome? What was the worst?

As long as he was an officer without portfolio, none of the possibilities looked promising. Good or bad, working for a four-star again, he would have cover. Before he made this decision, though, he had one more stop to make.

20

PERSONAL SECRETS

"Caesare had a secret gay lover who's a Mafia capo? Wow." Vice President Queenan sat in her second office in residence at the Naval Observatory. At one time it had been a vice president's only office, but her portfolio in the White House had relegated this office to a lesser status. Mary Driver, sitting in a corner in a tight-fitting yoga outfit, whistled.

"You can't make this stuff up, folks," Sam said. "Truth can teach fiction a lesson every time."

"It all revolves around SubCyberCom," Queenan said. "We're getting plenty of tantalizing clues, but it doesn't feel like we're getting any closer to the core truth."

"What we need is some serious e-tel," Driver said.

"E-tel?" Chin repeated.

"E-tel. E-intelligence. Time to get online and start gathering raw data. Isn't that what the Cyber Command is for?"

"I don't think we can count on the Cyber Command until we know who's doing what with who," Chin said.

"You mean *with whom*," Queenan corrected, smiling. She stood up and began pacing behind her desk.

"Yes, *Mommy*," Chin said. Driver snickered.

"Don't take it personally, Colonel," she said. "Joanie loves correcting people's grammar."

"I don't love correcting it," Queenan corrected. "I just can't stand to hear bad grammar. It's like fingernails on a chalkboard."

"Haven't you heard? *Who* is the new *whom*," Chin cracked. "At any rate, I'm worried about who we can trust. Or is that *whom* we can trust? Anywhere we turn we could be setting off alarms."

"Maybe that's not a bad thing," the Vice President said. She walked over to the huge three-foot globe standing in one corner of her office and began revolving it slowly, playing with it like a large ball.

"How do you mean?"

"Isn't it a classic setup in detective stories? An investigator starts shaking things up by asking questions. Pretty soon, someone gets pissed off, I mean, upset, and things start happening."

"Things like someone trying to kill the guy asking the questions. And we may be faced with that situation right now, Joanie," Chin said.

"*Joanie?*" Driver asked. "Getting a little familiar, aren't we?"

"I mean, *Madame Vice President*," Chin said. He hissed, glaring at Driver. Queenan and Driver traded knowing smiles.

"You're right, of course. And what we lack right now is official standing."

"The Vice President's office isn't official enough?" Chin asked.

"Yes and no," Queenan said. "Mostly no. Recall the classic definition of the vice presidency as, and I quote, 'not worth a bucket of warm spit.' You'll be happy to know that that little gem came from Thomas Marshall, my predecessor under Woodrow Wilson. If Wilson had had his stroke in today's political world, Marshall would have been Acting President within twenty-four hours. Instead the country struggled through eighteen months of political chaos – remember the Red Scare? That was J. Edgar Hoover's entré to political law enforcement. Possible only because Marshall didn't have the balls to do his job." She began twirling the globe slowly, as if studying it, which she was not.

"Maybe there *is* something we can do," Driver said.

"Like what?" Queenan asked. She turned to look at her mentor.

"Think about this: Maybe it's time to use my hacker platoon for something more than social media and campaigning."

"Your *what?*" Chin asked.

"Oh – my hacker platoon. It's not really hackers, but we call it that because it sounds neat. I have a squad of a couple of dozen social media,

SEO, and microtargeting experts. We can get pretty much whatever we want out of the Net. It's not like we really have to hack stuff, because it's all there if you know how to look."

"And you know low to look?" Chin asked.

"She knows how to look," Queenan said, "but let's consider our position. If it ever got out that my political consultants were hacking, or even investigating, military affairs that involve security clearances, there would be hell to pay. Justifiably so. We just can't do an end run like that without getting our asses, I mean behinds, handed to us in a sling."

"Not to mention the ammunition it would give to Stormy if he ever found out."

"God help us if he did," Queenan said.

"So it's time for me to take General Forbus up on his job offer," Chin said.

"Sounds like a plan."

"If you can't get the info you need running the Cyber Command, you're hopeless," Driver said with a smirk.

"Well, first off, I won't be running the Cyber Command," Chin said. "I don't know *what* I'll be doing. For all I know, he'll send me on a world tour of remote listening posts."

"Not likely," Queenan said. "They replaced them all with satellites years ago."

• • •

"I'm all yours, General."

"Smart move," Forbus said. From behind his desk he squinted up at Chin as if seeing him for the first time. He had papers in his hands and a large stack in front of him. He wore narrow reading glasses over whose top he peered at Chin. The combination of the glasses and the tight gray hair against his dark skin made him look older than Chin remembered.

"Realistically, my only move," Chin said, "since I'm not ready to retire."

"I like working with realists," Forbus said. He smiled, more like a grimace, as he removed his glasses. "You'll find we have more action in this command, right now, every day, than all the other commands combined." Standing, he clasped his hands behind his back and began strolling around the perimeter of the room, deliberately avoiding the colonel's gaze. He knew it would make Chin uncomfortable, which he enjoyed. A man off his best game is easier to assess.

"How so, General?"

"America has been at cyberwar for years."

"With China?"

"With China, with Iran, with Eastern Europe, with Russia, with all our enemies who never had the courage to face us down like men," Forbus said. "Think of them as ninjas sneaking in the back way to Oda Nobunaga's castle fortress."

"I'm not up on medieval Japanese military history, sir, but I think I get your point."

"Colonel, I'm sure you're wondering why you're here and what I have in mind for you."

"The thought did cross my mind, General. To be honest, I'm still dizzy from the events that got me here. There are a lot of questions about the Chairman's death."

"Don't you think it was an accident?" Now standing in front of Chin, he paused momentarily, then began walking in a circle again.

"One thing they taught us at the War College, as you know, sir."

"Yes?"

"There are no coincidences."

"And what is so coincidental about General Caesare's death?"

"Sir, I have information about his death that has a direct bearing on this question. I've had a rather unusual visit from a man who claims to know—or, rather, knew—the Chairman well."

"By which you mean?"

Chin, who had been standing at parade rest in front of Forbus' desk, shifted uncomfortably on his feet and looked down at the floor.

"Sir, I'm sure you know the rumors about the Chairman's personal life."

"Not rumors. Fact. I'm sure General Caesare was aware that at our level, there are no secrets. No privacy. We've known since he got his first star. What do you know about it?"

"I received a personal visit from a man claiming to have been with the Chairman during his last hours." He went on to relate everything he had heard from Palmio.

"Holy cow," Forbus said.

"It all comes back to SubCyberCom. Even this Palmio guy thinks so."

"Your first priority is check this guy out every way to Sunday," Forbus said. "I don't like the Mafia having access to the nation's top secrets. Let's find out about this cyber initiative of his that he's so proud of. And let's find out about SubCyberCom once and for all."

"Will I have a command, or will I work directly at your discretion?"

"Both. As of this moment I am giving you command of the Seventh Regiment, Second Brigade, First Division, First Corps, of the Cyber Command. This regiment is devoted to digital forensics. Are you familiar with the field, Colonel?"

"What I don't know I will learn, General."

"I'm counting on it. I know it's unusual, but you will report directly to me, not the brigadier. Your mission is to leverage this regiment's capabilities to get to the bottom of SubCyberCom and General Caesare's death, among other things. And whatever you can dig up on Palmio. With Project May Day coming up in less than a week, we have a lot of work ahead of us. Come over here, I want to show you something."

With that, Chin turned and walked in the direction of the general's voice. Forbus stood in front of a glass display case with a single ceiling spotlight showing off a satellite, one which did not look familiar to Chin.

"One of our latest C3I satellites. As you may know, our newest nuclear destroyers to come online all have extensive automation and remote-access capabilities. This satellite is the key to control and coordination. Right now, it only handles three destroyers, but it has the capability to handle as many as one hundred, depending on data-traffic volumes. Project May Day will be the first real test of these babies."

"I've heard very little about the Project May Day exercise, General. In what way are we involved?"

"CyberCom has a general mission of protecting America from cyber attacks, Colonel, but that's really a dual mission."

"How so?"

"Obviously we are dedicated to protecting the American public from cyber attack. But we also have to protect the American military. If a cyber enemy ever found a way to take control of our toys, it would be a disaster beyond measure."

"Our toys? You mean –?"

"Our ships. Our subs. Our planes. Our missiles. Some of our drones have already been commandeered by the Iranians. And if they can do it – hell, they did it with twenty-six dollars' worth of parts from Radio Shack. A bright high school kid could do it. If our enemies could take control of our weapons, even if all they did was destroy them, it would make the sack of Rome look like *Mister Roger's Neighborhood*."

21

TENNIS WITH CHARLEY

"I felt a little strange asking you for a game of tennis, Mister President."

Davidson gave her his Hollywood grin, that one that once won him millions of adoring fans, and tens of millions of dollars in personal wealth. They stood at the White House tennis court in summer shorts and T-shirts. The day was partly cloudy with a big dose of humidity, but the sun was low enough in the sky to cause problems, so each wore a ball cap with their respective emblems of office. More than a dozen Secret Service agents had spread out in a wide circle around the court.

"Worried about how badly I will beat you? You look kind of pale. Did you sleep well last night?

Queenan laughed. She was well versed on his tactic of making people feel weak or insecure next to him. In her case, it was unnecessary: She could see that even at seventy-five, his bulging calf muscles alone made her feel weak. The rest of him was even more fit.

"If I was worried, I wouldn't have suggested it, Mister President. Fact is, I find it hard to get a good game out of anyone at the White House. If you can even score off of me, I'll be happy."

The president laughed back.

"It will be my pleasure to make you happy," he said. He was also big on harmless innuendo. He walked over to a stand full of tennis racquets, so she followed him. Soon they were both trying out all the racquets, swinging them for the feel, as they talked.

"Funny," she said. "Suggesting tennis made me feel like a teenage girl asking a boy for a date."

"We aren't teenagers," he said. He gave her a rueful smile. "And I'm afraid we're both way past the dating game. But it sounds like you need to get out more, Joanie."

She laughed at that.

"*Me?*" she said.

"*You,*" he said with emphasis. "My spies tell me you have not had a single social engagement since Albert died. And that was how long ago?"

"Oh, Charley," she said, sighing. "More than a dozen years. I was so young. It seems like a lifetime ago. So much has changed."

"Don't I know it? I've been through quite a few changes in the last few decades, too."

"But your changes were mostly by your own devices, Charley. Mine mostly just happened." They both settled on racquets, so she began walking to the opposite court to try a few serves.

"Give yourself credit," he said. "Sure, you didn't have the family you wanted. Sure, your husband was gunned down by terrorists. But you started making your own choices the minute you picked up that body-guard's gun and fired back at the men who killed your husband. You've been controlling your own destiny ever since. From now on, to keep moving forward, you have to pick a prize and keep your eye on it. That's what I have done. And I think you have, too, in your own way." He gave her a knowing, almost fatherly look.

"Now if you don't serve," he said, "I will."

Queenan laughed.

"Okay, okay."

Queenan looked closely at him again; he knew what she was doing, she could feel it. His personal charisma drew her in, making it almost impossible to believe that this intelligent, engaging man could be developing some sort of cognitive disorder.

Davidson won the first match, but not by much. Stopping for water, they met at the net for a moment. Neither was breathing hard but Davidson, a quarter of a century older, had a look to him that Joan found odd. She often forgot how old he looked now, but she had recently watched a rerun of his earliest movie, *Sacred Steel*. The difference in age shocked her. Now she found herself watching him much more closely than before. *Watching for what? Signs of incapacity? Then what?*

"I know we're not playing just so you can get a good workout, Joanie," he said to her. He looked deep into her eyes as he said it. She looked back and saw the same clear, sincere face she had known for three years.

"You're right," she said. "I just don't like having these talks in a room wired for sound." She said it as he had started walking away; he stopped and turned halfway, giving her a sidewise glance.

They noticed at the same time. Without warning, almost without a sound, the entire Secret Service squad headed to them at a dead run. Queenan looked at the President and could tell that even he was startled.

As the agents approached, they spontaneously broke into two groups, one for each of them.

"There's been an incident, Mister President," the lead agent said. The senior man on site, his dark-black hair was just long enough to cover his earpiece when the wind was still, as it was today. "Come with us." Burly men surrounded him and half-carried him at a quick pace into the closest doorway.

"Where are you taking the Vice President?" he asked.

"To a separate location, Mister President. In case of attack."

Once inside the doorway, which led to a small side room, some agents secured the outside door, while others examined the nearby hallway.

"What the hell has happened?"

"A sudden communications blackout, Mister President. Our entire security net went offline. I have no idea what is going on or if anything else is affected. It could be a national emergency or a comm glitch. Until we know for sure, we're keeping you secure."

"Don't you have cell phones?" his voice took on unusual emotion but quickly reverted to his command style.

"They're all offline. It could be a cell tower, it could be jamming. We don't know yet."

"If it's a national emergency, I sure as hell can't be standing here with my thumb in my ass," Davidson said. "Get me to the Situation Room pronto. We'll find out quick enough what we have on our hands."

Ten minutes later, Davidson was settled into his seat in the Situation Room, where he awaited word from the Secret Service and his staff. Within a few minutes, the agent in charge returned to the room.

"He-he," he laughed, his nervousness betraying him. "For a minute, it felt like something out of *Rise of the Eliminators*," he said, referring to one of Davidson's hit movies.

Davidson looked at him with a blank stare.

The agent looked back at him and saw nothing – no intelligence, no awareness. Nothing. He turned back to the outer office, where three more agents waited, expecting him to emerge with the President.

"Someone get the President's physician. Get Dreidel in here, too."

• • •

"Major, I'm still waiting on that preliminary assessment on the White House blackout," Chin said into his speakerphone. When he heard someone clear his throat, he looked up to see two thirtyish captains standing at attention, side by side. They saluted together. Almost unbelievably, one wore a name tag that said *Smith* while the other was named *Jones*. When he saluted back, they relaxed slightly but remained at attention.

"At ease, gentlemen," he said. "What have you got for me?" Both men relaxed in parade rest. Jones, slightly shorter but stockier than his companion, stepped forward.

"The man Paul Palmio was easy to check out, sir. The Justice Department would have stacks and stacks of file folders full of reports, if they had file folders or printed reports anymore."

"Moving right along..." Chin said, restless.

"Yes, sir. As he reported, he is a captain for the Banini crime family in New York. Caesare grew up in the neighborhood that Palmio's old man, Joseph Palmio, used to control."

"Any evidence that he ever worked for them?"

"None at all, and we looked *hard*. He grew up a friend of the family, but more like an older brother who went his own way."

"But not a brother, right? Not a blood relation?"

"Not as far as we can tell, and we used Italian sources to be sure."

"Very good, Captain. And what about Palmio himself? What kind of a man is he?"

"Not a button man, Colonel. He must have made his bones when he was young, but he's past all that now. He seems determined to drag the mob kicking and screaming into the twenty-first century. He has indeed formed his own little hacker brigade. They are certainly up to no good, but I see no impact on us at this time."

"What kind of stuff?"

"Mostly online gambling – rigged or semi-rigged games. We could get this guy's entire outfit up on charges in nothing flat."

"I hope I don't have to remind you, we're army cyber intelligence, not prosecutors," Chin said. "Plus online gambling will be legal soon, one way or another, in most states. Even if it weren't, there aren't enough hours in the day to report every crime we're going to run across."

"Yes, sir. So how do I know what you want me to report and what you don't?"

"It's my call, Captain. If I tell you to do something, do it. Otherwise, don't do it. Is that clear? This goes for both of you."

"Yes, sir. What are our orders? Shall we pursue this further?"

"You shall not. For now, this group remains our secret. Secrets can turn into assets, Captain. The sooner you can understand that, the sooner you can be called Major."

The Jones snapped off a salute and left the room, leaving his peer, who looked slightly nervous.

"And what do *you* have for me?" Chin asked.

"Report from the Walter Reed patient records," Smith said. "Eyes only." Chin returned the salute and dismissed him. Only after the captain had left the room and vanished from sight did he look at the envelope. He slowly opened it, carefully, as if fearful of damaging a fragile gift.

He removed the single sheet of paper. As always, he read it from top to bottom in exhaustive detail. Chin took in every logo, name, address, every detail until finally, the payoff: the text of the report. His smile of anticipation quickly turned into a deep frown at what he read.

Colonel Chin had no time to absorb the information before an unfamiliar but still highly recognizable figure came storming into the room. At six-foot-four and two hundred thirty pounds, all of it muscle, Brigadier General Jack Teegerblom always dominated the room he was in. His bushy walrus mustache, though mostly gone to gray, added to the effect.

"Who the hell invited you to my brigade?" Teegerblom said. His thunderous voice filled the room.

Chin jumped to his feet. He saluted rigidly.

Teegerblom waited a moment before answering the salute.

"I'm under order direct orders from General Forbus, sir," he said. Based on the general's intimidation tactics, he decided it was best to stay in stiff attention mode.

"In *my* brigade?" Teegerblom asked, incredulous. He walked around Chin in a tight circle, staying close, as if inspecting an unbelievable animal. "I don't *think* so. Not in *my* brigade."

"I asked him the same thing," Chin said. "Sir."

"You did, did you? And what did he say?"

"He said – and I'm quoting him here, sir – he said it's not *your* brigade. He says it's the *Army's* brigade."

"Hmmmph. I expect to be kept in the loop, Colonel." After Teegerblom stared down at the colonel for a moment, he stormed out again without another word.

• • •

"General, how did you come to be in charge of the Cyber Command?"

"Why do you ask, Colonel?"

Chin had gone to Forbus' office to discuss the new report from Walter Reed, but he felt uncomfortable with the subject. Forbus could see his discomfort. He waited to see how Chin would handle it.

"I know enough about your background to know you're not the original nerd or anything like that. So I just wondered."

Forbus laughed.

"Good question. I was drafted, like you."

"Just like that?"

"Not just like that. It was the result of some extensive aptitude testing, personality profiling, all that stuff. I was deputy director at NSA before I came here. Now, son, tell me what's on your mind. What has your staff uncovered so far?"

"Do you want to see the report, or shall I just tell you?"

"Hell, son, I get to read plenty of reports, and I can tell this one's a doozy. Just say it, straight out."

"Would you believe our Commander in Chief has Alzheimer's?"

22

HOT POTATO

Forbus stared at him. His mouth hung wide open for a moment until he caught himself.

"Say again? Are you shittin' me? Let me see that report!" He grabbed the folder with a grim look on his face that softened a little as he read it. After a moment, he looked up at Chin.

"Says they aren't sure. Aren't sure if the President has Alzheimer's or not. Isn't that a helluva thing! A hell of a thing!"

"Yes, sir. From what little I know about it, there is no established protocol for diagnosis. No way to be sure."

"No way to be sure? Goddamn! He either has it or he doesn't!"

"That may be, sir, but I don't think the doctors know how to tell which is which. All we can do is wait, and watch."

"Treatment?"

Chin shook his head slowly. Forbus stood up and started walking along the wall of his office. Eventually he came to an electronic wall map. He stared at it without really seeing it. The lights and images blurred in his unfocused eyes.

"This is not something we can ignore, but it's also not our job to sort it out. We just pass it along and let the politicians handle it." Forbus remained standing as he spoke, as if in a trance.

"Yes, sir, but pass it along to *whom*? Not the President. The Vice President? Isn't it kind of a conflict of interest, since she could be our next president?"

"Under the Twenty-Fifth Amendment, it's between the Cabinet and the Vice President. I'll take it to the Secretary of State and the Vice

President. They can figure out what to do with it, if they want to do anything at all."

As he returned to his office, Sam felt like he was being suffocated by a crushing weight. He had been working nonstop since Caesare hired him, with no relief in sight. He needed a break ... then remembered Cindy. Some fiancée he was. They had not spoken in days!

• • •

"You're just the tonic for me, sweetheart," Sam said. He was lying in bed next to his fiancée late that night. Cindy was a slender woman, but she had wide hips that could fill out as she got older. He wondered what her mother looked like. She sat up in bed and looked at him. He cringed inwardly; he knew a scolding when he saw it coming.

"You say that, Sam Chin, but you disappear for days at a time. Do you ever think to call me or even send me a smiley text message? Sometimes I think you aren't serious at all about our getting married!"

"Of course I'm serious! But there's a lot going on right now. First General Caesare dies. Now I get some sudden news about the President."

Cindy looked at him like the mother of a wayward boy who had not a clue how to handle the child. Her dark haircut, a kind of modified pixie cut, set off her face with almost heart-shaped curves.

"What *kind* of sudden news?"

"Oh ... I can't talk about it, not really. But if things go the way they're headed, we could see some astounding changes at the White House. Really astounding. I can't get over it."

Cindy stared at him as wheels in her head went round and round.

• • •

"Madame Vice President, it's come to our attention that Project May Day may be dangerous for America."

Joan Queenan sat behind her desk and stared, wide-eyed, at General George Forbus. Colonel Sam Chin flanked him on his left in a wing chair. Mary Driver sat in another chair in the corner normally occupied by the portable mini-bar, when it was in use. When she had heard the general was headed to the office, she had scurried into her office for a quick-change into a conservative ladies' suit. Knowing that Queenan favored cream-and-gold attire to highlight her blond hair, she usually stuck with continental blue or dark green.

"Could you elaborate?" the Vice President asked. No one could mistake the frostiness in her words.

Forbus exchanged looks with Chin. He went on.

"I understand you already questioned the President and General Thornton about Project May Day, but I wanted to make sure you understand fully what's in the works. I'm afraid there are some open questions that need to be answered before May Day, which is only five days away."

"I understand it's a military exercise to flex our muscles at Persia," she said. "That's not what we're saying publicly, of course. But isn't that what it comes down to? Moving aircraft-carrier groups around the Persian Gulf, protecting the Strait of Hormuz, that sort of thing. Top Gun exercises for the fighter pilots."

"True as far as it goes, Madame Vice President, but did General Thornton tell you about the cyber component to the exercise?"

"Cyber component?" Now it was Queenan's turn to exchange sideways glances with her assistant.

"It's a two-part drill. Both parts are quite ambitious. In Phase One, we're using a mobile cyber-comm platform in theater to identify and attack enemy weapons systems."

"Attack how?"

"A variety of cyber attacks, nothing physical. By now you must have heard of the Stuxnet virus' success in slowing down the Iranian nuclear program a few years back."

"Supposedly a virus infected some centrifuges and slowed down their uranium enrichment process," she said. "But also supposedly we had nothing to do with it."

"That's what I was told as well," he said. "I have no idea what the truth is. I only use it as an example of the value of such tools. We have developed an entire toolkit for identifying weapons systems in the field, and targeting them with cyberbombs, so to speak, specially designed for each type."

"General, I'm getting a funny feeling about this. Are you telling me this is more than a big exercise? Are you telling me this so-called drill is going live?"

"No such thing. It's a critical step in reaching Phase Two."

"And Phase Two is...?"

"I have a bad feeling about this, Madame Vice President," Driver said from her corner, speaking up for the first time.

"Phase Two is turning the same tools on our own military."

"What the fuck?" Queenan exclaimed. "Excuse me for that." Chin looked pretty startled, too.

"Not to *use* on our military, of course, but to anticipate our own weaknesses, for diagnostic purposes. After Project May Day is over, we will analyze the telemetry database to see where we might have been attacked. Then we'll use that information to patch over the holes."

"But if someone wanted to use that data against us...?"

Forbus looked at her, the gravity of his concern showing.

"There's no chance of that, Madame Vice President. But to change the subject slightly, let me ask you something. Where will you be on May Day?"

Queenan gave him a funny look.

"I'm scheduled to be out of the country. Attending a birthday party for the Pope, of all things. He's turning eighty next week."

Chin laughed. Forbus laughed. Soon they were all laughing.

"Oh, the envious, celebrated life of vice presidents!" Forbus chuckled. "And while you're out of the country, President Davidson will be underground somewhere in Area 53, monitoring the cyber exercises at our new facility there. Completely incommunicado. Not even Secret Service agents allowed. Doesn't that make anyone just a little nervous?"

"Well –" Queenan and Driver exchanged looks again. "What are you getting at?"

"What I'm getting at is we have a dangerous zealot running a regional military exercise with control of a large portion of our armed forces. He will be underground in a secure facility where he can, if he wishes, take complete control of the President. Control of the United States Government."

"Wait a minute!" Queenan protested. "It's a huge leap from *can* to *will*."

"I fully realize it, Madame Vice President. But so far you haven't asked me the most important question of all."

"What question is that, General?"

"That question is, why am I talking to you about this and not the President?"

Forbus said nothing more. He pulled out the folder with the Davidson diagnosis, walked over to her behind her desk, and handed it to her. Still wordless, he walked back to his chair while she opened the folder and read the news for herself.

"I'm afraid that Charley Davidson is no longer capable. We've all seen it in him. This report bears it out."

"This report bears out nothing," Queenan said. She shut the folder and dropped it on her desk. "There is no definitive test for diagnosing Alzheimer's. Hell, there's not even a *reasonable* test for diagnosing it. It's mostly watch and wait. I should know. Mother's daddy went through it."

"Well, apparently some of us have been watching a little longer than others," Forbus said. "Colonel?"

Chin nodded at Queenan.

"My diagnostics team has combed servers for e-mail from all the top general staff. We found correspondence between most of the theater commanders indicating a general, pardon the pun, awareness of his condition."

"Stormy knows?"

"Stormy knows, Wild Bill knows, I'm starting to think we're the last ones to find out. And from the tenor of the communications, I'd say they're taking full advantage of the absentee presidency."

Queenan set her mouth as if she had made a decision.

"General, you're starting to scare me. Do you realize you're describing the makings of a military coup?"

"I do, Madame Vice President. The only thing that's keeping me from screaming bloody murder is the almost total absence of physical evidence. God help me, I can feel it in my bones. Stormy Thornton wants to overthrow the mentally deficient President of the United States, but we don't have a shred of evidence to prove it."

23

THE STAND-IN

Cindy Wilson looked at her watch with studied impatience. Waiting was not something she did well. After pulling her phone out of her purse, a Droid model she chose just to thumb her nose at Sam's Apple obsession, she checked for text messages, to no avail. Sam was twenty minutes late for their happy-hour date, which was twenty-one minutes later than he had ever been before. An officer approached in uniform, but it was not Sam; she could tell that by his walk alone. The birds on his shoulders looked just like Sam's. Looking at his face, she saw him smile. He took her breath away.

"Are you Cindy?" he asked. "Cindy Wilson?" He held out his hand to shake.

"Er – yes. Yes. And you are?" Conservative by nature, she took his hand as if controlled by another person. Rather than shake it, she held on to it, almost intimately, until a wave of self-consciousness caused her to draw her hand away. Her new acquaintance gazed at her hand as if studying it. After the briefest pauses, which seemed like an eternity to Cindy, he turned his sly look toward her.

"Baxter," he said. "Colonel Bill Baxter. Colonel Chin got held up in a meeting with the Vice President. He texted me and asked me to cover for you."

"Texted *you*?" she asked, clearly dismayed. "Why didn't he just text *me*?"

"I'm sure I couldn't say, ma'am, but I think I got the luck of the draw, if you don't mind me saying so. Can I buy you a drink?"

"You certainly can," she said. Wrapping her hands around his left elbow, she offered her most inviting smile.

Moments later, he returned from the bar with Zinfandel for her and Maker's Mark, neat, for him.

"Thank you." Noticing that Cindy practically glowed as he handed over her wine, he flirted back without a hint of bashfulness.

"Do you work with Sam, Colonel Baxter?"

"Call me Bill, please, ma'am."

"Only if you call me Cindy. That ma'am stuff is so ... *stuffy*."

"You got it, Cindy. Yes, we've been working closely together, but he's more of the public face. I'm more of a behind-the-scenes kind of guy. Which is why he's stuck at the White House, while I get the pleasure of being here with you."

He smiled and clinked his glass to hers.

"Cheers." She smiled back and took another drink.

After a second drink, the colonel could see a noticeable sway in Cindy's posture.

"Can I get you another drink?" he asked her.

"I wouldn't mind another drink," she said, "but two's my limit for public drinking. I need to call a taxi."

"Can I offer you a ride home?" he asked. He took her elbow as if to steady her, but it was really to test her, to see if she would respond to the closeness. She did.

"Would it be too much trouble? I took a taxi because I thought Sam would be driving me home."

"That's what I'm here for. Wait for me in front and I'll drive around."

24

THE CHEAT

From the corner of the Oval Office everyone heard the non sequitur. "Oh, shit." The General, Vice President, and her chief of staff all looked at Sam Chin, who was looking at his watch.

"Oh, sorry," he said, blushing.

"Is there a problem, Colonel?" Queenan asked. The starch in her voice reminded him how much distance there really was between them, past friendliness notwithstanding.

"Nothing that concerns you, Madame Vice President, but I'm in hot water. I forgot and just stood my fiancée up for a date."

"No problem," Queenan said. Her tone was now several degrees lighter. "Just tell her you were with another woman."

• • •

As they walked into the outer foyer of her second-story condo, Cindy turned around and faced the colonel. For a moment her eyes changed focus and her awareness flew to her surroundings – the starkness of the cement-block architecture, the bleakness of an enclosed area with filthy linoleum and a cheap, scratched Plexiglas front window. She noticed a scrawny scrub of shrubbery that further saddened the ambience with the futility of its presence. She tried not to feel self-conscious as she focused on him; her intent of being held in his arms was clear, so he complied dutifully.

"Now it's *my* turn to buy *you* a drink," she said. "What'll you have?"

"What've you got?"

"Jack Daniels," she said. "That's all."

"Then Jack it is," he said, deadpan, and they both burst out laughing.

After she poured the drinks, she walked over to join him on the sofa, until she noticed his legs stretched out on the coffee table.

"Get your feet off the coffee table," she said. Her no-nonsense tone was serious.

"Yes, ma'am," the soldier said. After he scrambled to get his feet off the table, she handed him his drink with a coaster.

"I'll be right back," she said.

The colonel watched her retreat until he heard the sound of the bathroom door closing in the hall. He waited slightly longer until he heard the door lock catch.

With a sure, relaxed movement he slipped a finger-sized plastic pouch from his outside coat pocket. The tiny container was closed with a zip lock identical to those used for larger food-storage bags. Opening it, he shook the contents into her drink and swirled the drink around with his fingertip until the powder was dissolved. The whole process was complete in less than thirty seconds.

When she emerged, the colonel met her at the doorway, standing, taking her into his arms, hushing her uncertainty with his lips, sealing her desire with his arms.

Later, after he knew she was sated, he arose from the bed with purposeful moves, momentarily pausing to look back at her lying in the bed, naked and only slightly covered by sheets. Quite apart from his mission, Stormy Thornton's henchman, Colonel Trent Oliver, was quite satisfied with himself.

After Oliver found her drink and returned to the bedroom, he held it out in one hand. She stirred as he returned, admiring his wiry, well-muscled frame.

"What's that?" she asked. She was drowsy and relaxed, but by no means asleep.

"Your drink," he said, handing it to her.

"Thanks." Without hesitating, she gulped down half of it.

"Whoa!" he said. "I guess you needed that. Should my feelings be hurt?"

"Just thirsty," she said in reassurance, then gulped down the remainder. When done, she slapped the glass down on a side table.

"I don't know why I did this," she said to him. "Sam and I are engaged. I'm going to be married soon."

"I was raised with Southern manners," Baxter said. He gave her a shy, weak smile to suggest vulnerability. "A gentleman never tells. This will be our little secret."

"So you do work with Sam, right?" she asked. She hiked herself up just enough to rest on her elbows.

"Well, yes. Why?"

"It's just that he's been so ... I don't know, so caught up in his work. Ever since he went to work for those generals. Now he's in and out of the White House. This isn't the first time, you know."

"Oh, really?" When he turned around to look at her, she noticed the change in his attention. Encouraged, Cindy had an urge to try for a little more.

"Oh, yes, didn't you know? He and the Vice President are old friends from her Congressional days, when he was an Army liaison. I think they're worried about the President, but he won't tell me. Need to know, isn't that what they call it?" She smiled at him, a smile intended to project innocence, but Oliver took it much differently, as a threat, which he met with tactics never taught in War College.

Still wearing nothing at all, he walked up to her and took her in his arms. Instead of speaking, he nuzzled up close to her. She smiled and reveled in the attention.

"Even if they're friends, I'm surprised they have reason to talk these days. Are you sure you don't have reason to be jealous?" Oliver's wicked smile would have shaken her had she seen it, but his face was hidden as he nuzzled her neck.

She pulled back from him.

"Hey!" she said. "That's not fair at all."

Suddenly, her whole upper body jerked up, like a marionette pulled toward the ceiling. He watched her eyes dilate, cross, and finally close as she passed out in his arms. Walking her over to the bed as gently as possible, he dropped her onto the freshly mussed sheets.

Oliver watched her breathing, shallowly, for more than a minute. He had calculated the dose carefully based on her body weight but from experience knew it was impossible to be sure of the results. They would know soon enough; either way was fine. Killing her was not part of the game plan, but no harm would be done if she did not make it.

Thornton's fixer made a quick job of it. Having studiously limited his contact to a handful of spaces, he now wiped them down with a thoroughness borne of training and experience. From the trunk of his car, he retrieved a small hand vacuum, which he used on the sofa and bed sheets, to remove any trace DNA from hair or skin flakes. He knew there was one trace he could do nothing about, but that was no accident. As he slipped out of the condo building into a moonless night, he smiled, thinking of Chin's reaction when he found out.

25

THE SENATOR

Sam Chin sat in the meeting room of the Senate Cyber Security Committee, bored and restless. Forbus had told him to go to listen and learn, but he felt insecure about being there. He imagined that at any moment the entire committee would stop what it was doing, turn to him with perfect synchronicity, and ask him some burning question of cyber security that he was completely unprepared to answer.

His fears were groundless, as he went unnoticed. Instead some other poor fool was in the hot seat. Fortunately for the fool this was a closed session without media. Instead of a three-ring circus, this hearing was a quiet, almost private affair between committee members, senior staff, and the man testifying.

"Is it true, Mister Chairman, that the memory settings in your P39 series voting computers can be reset by simply flipping switches on the front of the box?" One of the senators on the committee was grilling a witness, who sat at a table in front. The witness gave all the appearances of an accused criminal being grilled by the police.

"No, sir, it is not. I can only imagine that you've been reading the maintenance manuals of some old, obsolete equipment. Our voting systems are completely secured against outside interference."

"*Completely* secured? Are you sure about that?"

"Yes, sir, completely. Our systems are encrypted with a dual-pass-key system that changes daily. None of our real-time voting systems are connected to any outside sources. They stand alone. They have no disk drives, Bluetooth, wireless, USB, SD, or FireWire connections. They are unimpeachable."

"Mister Chairman, I remember a time not that long ago when every criminal lawyer I knew was running around like his hair was on fire, because DNA evidence was considered absolute. Unimpeachable. Do you know what happened to DNA evidence?"

The witness, a fiftyish balding man who showed evidence of fighting the weight fight with limited enthusiasm, cringed under the interrogation. Small beads of sweat popped out on his wide forehead.

"No, sir, I do not. I'm not a criminal attorney. In fact, I'm not an attorney of any kind. I work for a living."

That drew a light response of laughter from the audience, but little from the committee table, where most of the members were themselves attorneys who had stopped working for a living the moment they entered the halls of Congress.

"What happened was, the chain of evidence got corrupted. From the time the evidence was bagged, to the time it was tested for DNA evidence, to the time the results went to the lab, to the time they were tested – in all those times, there was ample opportunity for the evidence to be mishandled and corrupted. As a result, defense attorneys discovered they could indeed fight DNA evidence. Do you follow me so far?"

"Uh, uh ..." the man said, mumbling, struggling to avoid having to answer the question.

"What I'm saying, Mister Worthington, is that your protocols may be just fine in theory. But in practice, there is ample opportunity for malfeasance. *Now* do you follow me?"

"I follow you just fine, Senator. And I agree those opportunities exist, in theory. Do you have any specific examples for me?"

"We have plenty of examples for you."

"I would like to thank the gentleman from Nevada, whose time has expired," the committee chairman said. Orange-haired and freckled, he spoke with a practiced drone acquired as a young man serving as bailiff in a municipal court. "Next is the gentlelady from Oregon, Senator Ostreng."

Chin paid attention for a few minutes, but at some point he stopped hearing and started thinking.

We need hard evidence of the President's illness, but who can provide it? The doctors can't diagnose it. A video of his trance would be attacked as fake. And who would we provide evidence to, if we had any? Politics drive me crazy. One thing I understand: fighting an enemy until it's dead or I am. Nothing like Capitol Hill politics. These half-steps are so inadequate. Is this what generals have to worry about? Am I up to it? Is this what I want? Eisenhower and Powell notwithstanding, a general is a man who leads an army in the field, like Thornton or Petraeus. Will I ever see a real battlefield again?

"A penny for your thoughts, Colonel."

Chin started as he heard the words, croaked out with a familiar lilt, but this time from behind. He practically jumped out of his chair.

The senator laughed. He laughed a big horselaugh.

"Senator Gaul?" Chin finally stammered.

"Fran Gaul, at your service," the man said, holding out his hand to shake. Chin took it and stared at the man making the offer. Somehow the infamous Nevada Democrat had left the committee table and approached from behind without his noticing. Chin nodded with a dumb look and shook. He felt foolish, but for some reason, all he could notice was the senator's professional perm. Although sixty years old, Gaul sported the hairstyle of a man much younger. Sam realized that the tight curls were intended to cover rapidly balding spots on the playboy's scalp.

"Still in prime military shape, I see," Gaul said, complimenting Chin's physique.

Chin gave him a crooked smile, looking Gaul up and down and noticing an entirely different physique, which Gaul noticed.

"Thank you," he said in a murmur.

"And thank you for not saying what you were thinking," Gaul said with a laugh. "I know I haven't kept up nearly as well since I retired. Now, Colonel, I hear tell from unnamed sources that you have some information that will interest me."

"Indeed I do, Senator. Can you suggest somewhere we can go that isn't wired for sound?"

"Even better. I have a very favorite spot that is *completely* wired for sound."

• • •

Chin let Gaul drive, which he realized was a mistake as soon as the senator started drinking. He knew Gaul to be a good friend of the President's, but he also knew from *Huffington Post* outtakes that Gaul was a pothead who favored Nevada brothels far more than he favored the minutiae of legislating. A block from their destination, Sam realized what Gaul had in mind; it boggled his imagination. In *this* town, where nothing was truly secret? And yet there they were.

Gaul turned to him with a satisfied smile.

"It's not Las Vegas, but they have some of the most beautiful, and most gen-u-wine, young ladies this town has to offer."

"Gen-u-wine?" Chin said. He stared at Gaul in amazement.

"Zackly." Gaul smiled and nodded in happy agreement.

Inside, they sat by the runway where the strippers pranced. The music and noise of the club provided protection from the bugs Gaul alluded to, but Chin had trouble keeping him away from the dancers long enough to relate his story. Gaul smiled and nodded, but whether he was patronizing or merely distracted, Sam had no idea. Worse, he was not sure which he preferred. When he was finished, or at least exhausted, he waited for a response from Gaul, but Gaul kept his eyes on the girls and his commentary on the utility of their attributes.

Chin tried to be patient, and it finally paid off. Gaul turned to him and spoke in his most matter-of-fact manner.

"Looks like I need to make a trip out to Area 53."

"Area 53?" Chin asked, puzzled. "How is that different from Area 51? And what gives you access?"

"Think of it as Area 51 for the Internet," Gaul said, grinning. "Out near the regular Area 51, but separate, buried in the side of a mountain, underground. Shielded from EMP, stuff like that. And I have access because I'm vice-chair of the cyber committee. I'm your inside guy."

• • •

On the way home, Chin checked his phone. Thumbing the call list, he saw a whole series of attempted calls, two or three minutes apart. They all came from the same number in the local area code, but he did not recognize it. Concerned, he called his voicemail.

"Colonel Chin, this is Doctor Morrissey at Washington General. We have a woman here in the ER who has your name and number on an emergency card in her wallet. Could you please call as soon as possible?" Chin heard him rattle off a phone number that he did not have time to memorize, so he played the message a second time. As soon as it finished, he called the number.

"Sam Chin here," he said as soon as he heard someone pick up.

"Doctor Morrissey," the man said. "I appreciate your returning my call, Colonel Chin. We have a Cynthia Wilson in our ER. She's about to be posted to ICU for observation. Is she a relation of yours?"

"Fiancée," Chin said. He could tell something was wrong. Tension ran through him like an electric shock. "What's wrong? Was she in a car accident?"

"Nothing of the sort, Colonel. Apparently she overdosed on some medication. We found a bottle of sleeping pills by her bed stand, and we know she had been drinking, so we're looking at a likely overdose. I know this is a tough question, but do you have any reason to believe Miz Wilson is suicidal?"

"*Suicidal*? Where could you get such an idea?"

"Just a possibility, but it has some of the earmarks. Not all of them, though."

"What does that mean? What are you not telling me?"

Chin heard dead air, a long, silent pause.

"I'm waiting," he said. "What's the rest of the story?"

"There's no easy way to tell you this, Colonel," Morrissey said. "I'm not sure I should say anything at all. But we may end up needing your help to get this sorted out."

"Get *what* sorted out? Just *tell* me."

"Colonel, Miz Wilson shows evidence of sexual activity this evening."

"She was *raped*?"

Morrissey cleared his throat and hesitated.

"Well, uh, no. There is no sign of tearing. We assume it was consensual. But it does leave open the question of whether she was suicidal, or something else."

"Something else?"

"You're the investigator, Colonel," the doctor said. "Not me. Part of me regrets giving you this information. But something tells me you needed to know."

• • •

Oliver relayed the new information to his superior.

"They know about the President, sir," he said. "It's just a matter of time now until they try to act on it."

"*Try* is the operative word," the gruff voice replied. "What else do they know?"

"Not much, but they are actively investigating SubCyberCom. If they keep it up, they're bound to figure it out. Forbus knows the most, but he hasn't tied it all together. What are our next steps, sir?"

"We want to end this, but we must be circumspect. With less than four days to go, it would be a mistake to overplay our hand now."

"Yes, sir. So we watch and wait?"

"Watch and wait. Focus on Chin. Like you, he has a lot more freedom of action in the field than Forbus does. He's the key to this."

26

FRAN GAUL

Francisco Gaul was a native Texan who had settled down in Las Vegas after retiring from the Air Force. Once a bomber pilot, he had been forced to desk duty due to inner-ear problems. Those were the days before Nevada became the drone capital of the world, so his aptitude for computer programming became the key to his future in the military. Eventually he retired with a respectable but not remarkable rank of major, having been held back by his developing avocations – first for gambling, next for women, finally for drugs.

The downward slide started within a week after he was stationed at Nellis Air Force Base, on the northeast edge of town. His wife of fifteen years, who had remained childless, had refused to move with him again, to Sin City of all places, and had hired an attorney to file for divorce. Fran was feeling sad, and lonely, and sorry for himself. Lately he had taken to playing Texas Hold 'Em online – not for real money, but to learn strategy. He realized that the hold 'em variations of poker, especially for tournament play, had reduced the game to something that could be beaten with the simplest mathematical strategy and the slightest of luck. At least, that's what he thought. After some online feature comparisons, he decided to try out a tournament at the Trapeze casino, with a buy-in of only one hundred twenty dollars.

His strategy required discipline but almost no luck at all. Unlike real poker, this tournament was won by placing in the top three finishers. Third place guaranteed a one hundred percent payout; first place, two hundred percent. He only had to place third to double his money.

To place third, he only had to outlast the people around him who were betting. The more they bet without him, the faster he could win.

His plan was simple: Fold almost every hand. Play and bet very, very rarely. He only *had* to play was when he was passed the boot; the game worked for him because of this very requirement. If he had to ante up with every hand, it would be hard to stay in the game for long. But since he only had to ante up with the boot, he only had to play those hands. And he refused to call or raise bets unless he had an extraordinary hand, with a high pair or trebles, a straight or a flush.

When he followed his rules, he won. Placing at least third, every time, was something he could do without too much trouble. That was good enough to turn a profit. Soon he found himself winning hundreds of dollars a night, playing in tournaments against inexperienced and gullible tourists. His nearly foolproof strategy guaranteed a steady stream of income, but it had built-in limits—nothing to retire on even when his military pension kicked in.

Only one feature of his strategy kept it from being foolproof: the requirement that he follow it with iron discipline. He must never make adventuresome bets, which he found increasingly difficult to do. Gaul's was a restless, creative mind. Only the rarest night failed to find him on the prowl for newer, better stimulation. Once he learned the trick of winning at Hold 'Em, he lost interest.

And when he lost interest, he started losing. Realizing his mistake, he went back to his strategy and began winning again. The pit bosses noticed. Pretty soon they were comping him a room and a girl. Soon all his free time was split between the girls and the game.

Gaul's work suffered, but he only had months to go until retirement and a twenty-year pension. Realizing he was losing interest and why, he made one final effort to pull his head back to his job and out of the casino. For a while the tactic seemed to work, but he had a fine tech staff that was happy to cover for him as long as he gave them great ratings. Soon he was past caring, and he was a retired major. He was happy to move on. He realized the Air Force was happy to let him, probably because a grounded pilot wasn't good for much at all.

Gaul also realized his steady diet of poker and women was not a great long-term play. At age forty-two, with a pension, he had tremendous freedom and no responsibilities. During a week-long hike at the Grand Canyon, he cleared his head and sorted out his options. By the time he emerged from the hike, his plan was set, although even he had no idea how far serendipity would take him.

Gaul had partied a lot and lost his fair share, but he had stashed away enough to finance his new project. He was only one man: That was the primary limitation of his poker strategy, similar to being an hourly worker. One man could only play so many games. The more he played, the more boredom worked against him.

So he started a poker workshop teaching his method. From a competition standpoint, he could teach as many people as he wanted, because so few amateurs had the discipline to follow it. What mattered was that tourists paid good money happily to learn insider tips that they thought would give them an advantage. The floor manager at the Trapeze gave him a free poker room to work out of.

His first couple of times out, he paid for the privilege, but soon the Trap's management saw the benefit of having a pro who cultivated the tourists. Through advertising they turned him into a minor celebrity, which allowed him to boost his rates to a thousand dollars a head. In an average week, he had two dozen paying customers, often more. With money like that coming in, he soon lost interest in playing for himself.

But he never lost interest in the women. Though nothing was ever said, they were assigned to make sure he never lost interest in the casino. High-dollar professionals, they did what they could to keep his interest, which was increasingly difficult to do. Gaul was a sociable guy whose attention and interests tended to wander. Eventually the girls escalated their own strategy, and drugs entered the picture—marijuana, methamphetamine, and prescription painkillers.

Fran's turn to political affairs seemed as unlikely as everything else in his life, but as usual he found a niche that worked for him and followed it all the way. When the casino's union, Associated Service Workers Local 327, threatened to strike over management's preliminary announcement that wage increases could not be up for discussion in upcoming contract negotiations, Gaul got involved. The threatened strike coincided with an attempt by management to revoke his own privileged status and make him pay for the use of facilities. Fran was confident he could take his show anywhere and be a success, so he was fearless. Taking up the union's cause, he quickly became a media favorite as its *de facto* spokesman– which did not thrill the union management, since he was not one of them and thus threatened their positions.

Upsetting the union applecart was the last thing on his mind: his vision had expanded to the national realm. Three months later, the sitting Democratic U.S. Senator, a married man with young children, was forced to resign in a prostitution scandal. The Republican governor, required to appoint another Democrat to replace him, appointed Gaul in the hope that the seat would be vulnerable to a challenge – a miscalculation that cost his party the next election. Gaul spent the entire year and a half building a national constituency around a semi-libertarian platform. Since then, Gaul had been elected twice in his own right. Somehow his personal foibles had stayed out of the public eye, such an open secret that his media opponents never saw an opportunity to hurt him. His national profile rose regularly as he lashed out against police and military intrusions against civil liberties. He supported legalization of marijuana at the federal level as well as in Nevada. He became a lone star among Democrats for his increasingly libertarian views.

Gaul had met California Governor Charley Davidson early after his appointment, when Davidson helped the Nevada governor host a week-long Governors' Conference at the Trapeze. Despite their lifestyle differences, Gaul and the Californian struck up a camaraderie that lasted over the years. Eventually Gaul had ended up being part of Davidson's "kitchen cabinet," a small, informal group of friends who could advise without fear of consequences. Davidson's libertarian leanings were often credited to the Nevada senator's influence.

● ● ●

After deciding his mission was too important to be sidetracked by fun or fundraising in Las Vegas, Gaul chose to fly directly to Area 51 by military jet. From there he was driven by Humvee to Area 53.

Inside the underground facility, General Fuchs prepared her staff for his arrival. Visiting politicians were given a snow job as much as possible, which was often quite a bit. Gaul's experience as a charter member of the Senate Cyber Committee, and his ground-level participation in building Area 53, put him in an entirely different league.

Fuchs' six-foot frame cut a wide swath as she strode from office to office, personally inspecting workstations and making sure all personnel got the word to secure their data against the senator's snooping. Most offices were already clean, but in one office she found three non-comms examining memos about the coming May Day plans. Rather than a small screen, they were examining them on a large, wall-sized Magic Glass display.

"I gave explicit orders to shut all this down," she bellowed at the group. All three cringed at her onslaught. They snapped to attention and saluted. She snapped back an angry salute.

"Shut it down now!"

The leader, a statuesque woman no more than thirty years old, nodded without a word and turned off the monitor but left the computer on. A moment later, after Fuchs left, she removed an SD card from the computer and slid it into her pocket.

Fuchs had everyone at the facility await Gaul's arrival in their small auditorium, where the room's multimedia capabilities were perfect for Gaul's presentation. Together the general and the senator strode out onto the stage. As they did, everyone present stood and applauded. Fuchs used her hands to wave everyone into their seats. The crowd grew quiet as Fuchs started the introduction. Standing military-straight at the podium, she cut an imposing figure, her profile almost iconic.

"You all know Senator Gaul here. He's the vice-chair of the Senate Cyber Committee, not to mention Senator from right here in Nevada. Some of you probably voted for him."

"Only some?" Gaul said with a smile. The crowd laughed, but now they were all on his side. Fuchs continued, determined as always to be unaffected by personal charisma.

"He's the Senate liaison designated to oversee implementation of our side of Project May Day, which is now only days away. Senator, would you like to say a few words?"

Gaul smiled and waved at the crowd, walked across the stage, and stepped up to the microphone Fuchs had vacated for him.

"Thank you, General," he said, looking at her. He shifted his gaze back to the crowd and scanned the room. He felt a momentary twinge of self-consciousness, knowing that everyone was watching him watch them. Although he was used to the attention, he would never forget a dark day in sixth grade when he froze in the middle of a spelling bee that everyone knew was his. Whenever he got nervous on a stage, he always managed to remember that day when he was eleven years old.

"I appreciate the hard work and patriotism of everyone in this room," he said. He laid his hands flat on the dais. Using his hands for support, he leaned forward, as if to connect more closely with the audience.

"Other than that, I have no special comments at this time. I'm here to see your presentation on your preparedness. General?" He nodded at Fuchs. Without waiting for a response, he walked over to sit behind a table designated for him on the stage.

"Senator, as you know, Project May Day is a war game scenario posited on a confrontation with Persia. The ground rules call for our forces to be uninformed as to whether the threat is potentially nuclear or not."

"Leaving open the possibility that it is," Gaul interjected.

"Leaving open the possibility that it is," Fuchs said, agreeing through repetition. "This means treating the situation with delicacy in order to assure that we do not rule out any chance of peace."

"Which is where our cyber intelligence capabilities can come in handy," the senator said.

"Can and do," Fuchs said. "Senator, if you don't mind letting my staff make its presentation first, there will be plenty of time for questions at the end." She gave him a questioning look.

"Fine," Gaul said. "I'll shut up." He smiled and nodded back.

Fuchs introduced a lieutenant colonel, a first-generation American whose parents were born in Iran before the 1979 revolution. The colonel began the briefing with satellite maps of the Persian Gulf region overlaid by blue avatars of the major ships that would soon be control-ling the Gulf of Oman, and hence the Strait of Hormuz and Persian Gulf. Gaul watched with increasing impatience but said nothing. When the colonel stopped to sip from a water bottle, Gaul spoke up.

"What about other militaries?" he asked. "What's Persia's navy doing in all this? How about China?"

Fuchs took the microphone back to answer.

"They're standing back, Senator," she said.

"Back? Not down?"

"Exactly, sir. There is a small Chinese contingency back in the Indian Ocean, which you can see here. They are clearly accumulating naval assets. But keep in mind, they have not even one carrier group that measures up to the least of ours." The display lit up red avatars. "And the Persians are all staying in port." The display lit up again, show-ing green avatars in Persian ports throughout the gulf.

"So no signs so far that they want a confrontation?"

"No signs so far. We've assured them this is only an exercise. It looks like they're taking us at our word."

"And if they decide to take a more active role? How prepared are we for that possibility?"

"Completely prepared, Colonel. Our listening capabilities extend to all signals from every ship in theater, whether friendly or unfriendly."

"And you have the means to process those data in real time?"

"As it happens, Senator, yes. Naturally, it takes significant personnel resources to staff this mission."

"I would imagine so. That's a huge undertaking."

"Yes, sir, it is. We've spent the last month running simulations to make sure we can handle it."

"Okay, let's war-game this a little bit. Suppose some crazy in Persia got a hold of their only mobile nuclear warhead, and they launched it at the *Ronald Reagan*. If that launch succeeded, it could take out the entire carrier task force. It would mean war. What are you doing to prevent that?"

"Not gonna happen, Senator. First of all, we'll know the minute they even *think* about it. The minute they start *talking* about it, we can shut down their systems completely. Lock everything down so they can't even drive their boats. They'll be back to rowing them with galley slaves."

"Do we *really* have that ability?" Gaul asked, dubious.

"Certainly, Senator. We've talked about this in closed hearings on more than one occasion," Fuchs said. She was starting to feel a little peeved and had trouble not showing it.

"*Talk*," Gaul said, wrinkling his nose. "If we have such a strong lock on the Persians, why is the whole world up in arms over their having a nuclear capability? What are we so worried about?"

"*We* are not worried, Senator," Fuchs said. "That's the politicians going at it. We stay out of it. We know what we can do. So does the President. I imagine that has a lot to do with why he's taken such a soft line in public. We have a stick so big even Teddy Roosevelt would be happy."

After the presentation, Fuchs accompanied Gaul from the auditorium. The senator felt an undercurrent of tension that made him nervous. Perhaps he was being too self-conscious, but this trip felt different from previous visits. Without knowing why, he felt like a lamb being led to the slaughter.

"We're not quite ready for your tour, Senator," the general said. "I've got some of our officers doing a final run-through to make sure we don't waste your time. Why don't you come to my office for coffee while you wait?"

"The break room will be fine," Gaul said, feeling a little grumpy. "If I drink too much coffee, it doesn't set well with my stomach. Maybe I can get a drink from a machine."

"Certainly," Fuchs said. "Sergeant? She looked at one of the female non-comms. On Gaul's previous visits, the general discovered it was easy to distract him with a pretty face. She had learned to accommodate his known proclivities for the statuesque – which is to say, tall and busty blondes.

The sergeant, Nancy Parkham, saluted the general and turned toward Gaul.

"Right this way, Senator," she said. She smiled, winked, and turned to lead the way down a narrow corridor. Because the space was so constricted, they walked closely together; no one could see them. Once she was sure they were alone, she turned to face him. Parkham started to throw her arms around his neck, clearly intent on an embrace, but Gaul stopped her. He grabbed her wrists with his hands and pulled her arms down.

"Not here," he said, almost hissing. "Anyone could be watching. Did you get what I asked for?"

"Right here," she said. Rather than hold it up, she surreptitiously held his hand down by his side. In the process, she palmed over the thumbnail-sized SD card she had pocketed earlier. Without acknowledging it, he curled his hand around the card. He slid his hand into his pocket.

"Say, I need to make a pit stop," he said. "Let's drop by the restroom first."

Inside the restroom, he went into the toilet stall closest to the far wall. After closing the door, he went through the motions of dropping his pants and sitting on the seat. He scoured the walls and ceilings for signs of cameras, though he had never noticed one in the restroom before. Based on previous experience, he decided the cameras would be in plain sight if they were there at all, and he saw nothing.

Gaul made a fast motion with his left hand to retrieve the SD card from his pocket. He turned over his belt to reveal a tiny zippered money pouch. A moment later, the card was in the pouch, zippered up, and Gaul was at the sink, washing his hands. Humming "Jumping Jack Flash," he looked in the mirror, self-satisfied. After quickly straightening his tie and combing his hair, he turned away from the mirror, then everything went black.

27

MISSED MEETING

Later the same day, Sam Chin arrived at Area 53. His visit was a little different from Gaul's: the senator, an old hand, was already up to date on the base's activities. For the new cyber colonel, the visit was a real eye-opener.

Instead of a big auditorium presentation, which had been a show for the senator's benefit, Fuchs escorted Chin to a small private conference room to make a personal presentation. After helping themselves to coffee and pastries, Chin decided to get down to business.

"You know, General, I thought I had seen pretty much all of the surprises the Army had in store, but I was wrong," Chin said. "This bunker is impressive."

"Well, we don't call it a *bunker*."

"Maybe not," Chin said, "but there's a reason why it's buried deep inside a remote mountain."

"True," Fuchs said in agreement. "Here at SubCyberCom, we've developed the ability to intercept and intervene in the signal communications of any military force in the world. We can read their traffic, send out false traffic in their native language, and even shut them down entirely. But no one can get to us."

"What guarantee do we have that the Chinese, and by extension the Persians, have not developed the same capability?" Chin asked.

"No guarantees," Fuchs said in a terse chop. Chin noticed her shoulders hunch up a little. Fuchs' entire upper body suddenly oozed tension. "We know they're working on it. We have an entire regiment devoted to countermeasures. Right now, we think we're safe, but that's why we have Operation Intangible."

"Operation Intangible?"

Fuchs nodded.

"I thought maybe General Forbus had already told you about it."

Chin shook his head slowly, showing no reaction.

Fuchs paused for a long moment before beginning.

"As you are probably aware, a section of the Patriot Act gives the President the right to take control of all communication in CONUS in the event of national emergency."

Chin nodded.

"By CONUS you mean not only the continental United States, but the outlying states and territories as well? Hasn't that been around in various forms since Eisenhower's time?"

"Not exactly. We didn't have the Internet in Eisenhower's time."

"You mean –?"

"I mean, if the President orders it, we are to implement Operation Intangible. Intangible is designed to make sure that no foreign power or enemy destroys or takes control of the national economy via the Internet."

"Well, the only way to do that is to shut it down!"

Fuchs nodded.

"Or at least take it over. Shut it down or take it over."

"And *that's* Operation Intangible? *That's* what SubCyberCom is for?"

"It's our mission, yes, but only part of our mission."

"And is Operation Intangible part of Project May Day?"

"Not part of it, not exactly. Intangible is operational. Like the football or the bombers or the subs, it's always there, awaiting activation, hopefully never being used. We train like we will use it tomorrow, but unless something extraordinary happens, we don't expect it to be used."

"I don't mean to sound indelicate, General, but isn't an attitude like that a setup for complacency and mistakes?"

Fuchs pressed her lips together and turned them up slightly in a grotesque grimace that barely resembled a smile. For the first time,

Chin noticed that she had made slight concessions to femininity. Her lips, though cracked, sported a pale rose lipstick. Her cheeks showed signs of powder, too, but he noticed that she wore no eye makeup at all. He imagined that if she wore bright red lipstick, she would look a lot like one of the crones he used to see populating the slots on weeknights at a casino for Las Vegas locals.

"Exactly what I tell my officers every chance I get, Colonel," she said. "But you come here representing General Forbus. I want to be completely honest."

"Got it," Chin said. "So you're saying that a run-through of Intangible is not part of the May Day exercise?"

"Exactly what I'm saying, Colonel," she said. Chin looked at her body language and had strong doubts about what he heard.

"I understand I'm not your only visitor today," Chin said. He wanted to change the subject so she would not suspect he had any real interest in Intangible.

"Yes, Senator Gaul was here this morning, but he's already left. I understand he is meeting with constituents in town."

"Already gone?" Chin found it difficult not to show an undue interest, but he was bitterly disappointed. He had counted on getting evidence from Gaul that would reveal Stormy's secret plans for May Day.

Fuchs watched him carefully; she could see him try to hide his disappointment without success. She was more successful at holding back her desire to smile.

"Yes, back to Vegas. It's tempting to say something rude about that, but it's actually my hometown, too, you know. She leaned forward slightly.

Chin nodded.

"So I've heard, but with all due respect, I have trouble picturing you in that city, General."

Fuchs smiled and laughed, a rare thing for her, but when she did, she laughed without restraint.

"Thank you for that, Colonel. Keep it up and you'll be on the fast track for your star."

Chin laughed with her.

"Good to know."

Fuchs seemed pleasant enough on the surface, but he had a feeling he would never have a future working for her.

"Colonel, it's been a pleasure showing you around, but I have a number of matters to attend to. I'll have an airman in a moment who can drive you back to your jet. Meanwhile, why don't you wait in the break room with a cup of coffee?"

"Thanks, General, I'll do that. Don't worry about me."

Chin stood up straight and saluted; she saluted back and waited for him to leave first. The colonel got the message and headed out, making sure he was pointed toward the break room. On the way, he started to pass a men's restroom, so he decided to make room for the coffee he was about to drink.

Chin used a private stall, as he preferred to do. He was never comfortable turning his back to a door, which is what you do when you use a standing urinal. Using a stall allowed him to stay aware of his environment, a habit that was about to save his life.

At a critical moment, the door to the small restroom opened. Chin heard someone step in. The sound must have registered at some deep level of perception, because he knew instantly that something was wrong. Whoever entered was not there for a call of nature. Beneath the stall partition he could see heavy field boots. Before he could process another thought the stall door slammed open, kicked by a heavy boot heel.

Chin was not caught completely by surprise, but his survival required excellent reflexes and split-second timing. He felt more than saw the truncheon swinging down toward his head. Chin slid inside the swing so that he could advance into the attack. He had nowhere to run, and running wasn't his style anyway. All of his martial arts training was for the attack, to end it quickly.

His only real impediment was the door to the stall, which opened inward. With his attacker filling the doorway, he had no room to maneuver. With advance warning, he might have slid under the partition, but there was no time.

Chin slammed into the door, smashing the closing edge against his attacker's arm. As the elbow shattered, the hand's grip on the heavy stick loosened. Sam recovered it in a single smooth move. He gripped the club as his arm continued in the same smooth circle, ending when the leading edge of the truncheon struck the attacker's temple with an audible crunch. The soldier dropped in a dead weight. Chin rolled the man over with his boot, literally a dead weight: staring blankly through open eyes, Colonel Trent Oliver.

28

TEMPTATIONS

As Fran Gaul slowly regained consciousness, a spiking headache became the complete center of his universe. He ran his fingers through his hair unconsciously, a habit borne of a narcissistic fear that it was thinning further.

Holy Mother of God. What did I do to deserve this hangover? I don't even remember taking a drink.

The senator struggled to open his eyes but failed. They felt like they were sealed with glue. For a time that seemed an eternity, he lay in bed. The headache consumed all of his energy and attention. No thought to move or to think could penetrate the power of its onslaught. Lying there, limp, was all he could do to cope. Accept it and wait for it to pass. He had awareness but no will. If a young child appeared and attacked him, he would be helpless to defend himself.

Time passed. Eventually, slowly, the headache began to subside. Tentatively, he struggled to open his eyes, with only the slightest success: he could see more light, but not enough to resolve any objects. Like the opening of a delicate flower, the pain waned slowly, but it eventually became more distant. As a result, it was quite some time before Gaul realized he could think again, if only in small efforts. He feared that a stronger effort would return the assault that stabbed at his temples.

As rational thought seeped into his consciousness, his mind turned to his predicament. He had no memory of anything that happened after he arrived at Area 53. He was sure he had not drunk himself into a stupor, since he did not do that anymore, and this was a top-secret military base. The mere knowledge of its existence was classified, Area 51 mania notwithstanding. What could he have done to bring this on? He was stumped.

Gaul turned his attention to his accommodations. Considering the hellholes he survived during his military career, these digs were not bad. The room had no windows, just a door. The bedroom appeared to be an unusual mix of both the masculine and the feminine – elements of each, but not a room either a man or a woman would likely decorate for themselves. Why did it seem so damned familiar? He sure didn't recognize it. There was a bed but no dresser, just a small dressing table and chair in front of a mirror. He looked at the mirror and knew instantly it was two-way. He was being watched, so he tried to act nonchalant. He counted on his adversaries, whoever they were, to fall for his Bruce Wayne playboy persona.

Looking around, he saw a small bathroom off in one corner; in another, a well-provided minibar. On top of the minibar sat a variety of premium liquor bottles, all unopened, and a large glass display jar with a metal top, the kind you might see in a doctor's office to hold cotton swabs. Inside the jar was, by all appearances, some extremely fine sensemilla bud. Rich green with finely woven golden and red threads. Marijuana. He opened the jar and smelled of the buds as an oenophile might a fine wine. Slowly, with a sad shake of his head, he returned the metal top to close the jar. Next to the jar, he found a few small bottles marked for a variety of painkillers, including OxyContin. He ignored them.

Gaul smiled to himself. He dwelled on grim thoughts he normally would ignore. Without knowing how he got here, he knew *why* he was here. His hosts, whoever they were, thought they knew his weaknesses. They thought they could get him drunk and stoned and knocked on his ass all the time. Well *screw* that.

But where *was* he? Why was he here? It would help if he could remember something, anything, about what had happened at Area 53, but he was drawing a blank.

The door opened.

29

MISSING SENATOR

"Does General Forbus know you're here?" the Vice President asked. They sat in her office in the White House. As much as she enjoyed the solitude of her Naval Observatory office, the need to keep an eye on the Oval Office had changed her work habits.

"Of course he does, Madame Vice President. Otherwise it would be a breach of the chain of command."

"It looks like you had a mighty eventful trip," she observed.

"That I did. There's gonna be a shitstorm really soon, once this becomes public knowledge."

"Does it have to be public knowledge?"

Chin gave her a disapproving sidewise glance.

"You can't have a death in the top staff of a four-star general with a theater command and not expect the news to get out. Especially after what happened to the Chairman."

"The death, sure. But the circumstances? Can't that be sanitized for the public?"

Chin looked at her again.

"Why would we do that? I must say, I didn't know your first instinct was to cover things up."

"It's *not, Sam*," she said, aggravated. "But we're juggling several balls in the air right now. Until we get Charley squared away, and now Stormy, too, I don't want to go showing our hand."

"Fair enough," Chin said.

Queenan's countenance changed for a moment: she giggled nervously.

"Daddy taught me how to play poker, you know. It used to embarrass the hell out of Albert, back in college, when I beat his buddies and took all their money. So I know when to hold 'em, and when to fold 'em. I can tell you right now, we won't be doing any foldin'."

"I bet," Chin said, smiling.

Then Queenan got serious again. "But you didn't get anything from Fran Gaul?"

"Hell, I never saw the senator. We had a straightforward plan to be there at the same time so he could do a handoff. But when I got there, he had already left. General Fuchs said he had left to meet with constituents and contributors, but his office denies any knowledge of his whereabouts. It's pretty unusual for a United States senator to have constituent meetings without someone on his staff knowing something."

"What are you saying, Sam?"

"I'm saying, Joanie, that we have a United States senator who has gone *missing*. Shouldn't the FBI be involved in this? Or the Secret Service?"

Queenan pursed her lips – a characteristic tell that she was giving serious thought to her subject.

"What does General Forbus think?"

"General Forbus, like any smart general who wants to keep his job, has no opinion at all about political matters, including the whereabouts of a potentially missing senator. He's not even particularly concerned about Stormy's man, the late Trent Oliver. Maybe because all's well that ends well. But he didn't mind me dropping it on your doorstep."

"So kind of him," Queenan said, smirking. "But he's smart, and right. We can let Gaul's office worry about him. With any luck at all, we'll dig him out of the woodwork before anyone notices he's gone. And we can leave Stormy to his own explanations. We need to him on the defensive while we figure out what he's up to."

"And they say Washington's no place for optimists," Chin said, muttering under his breath.

"What was that?" Queenan asked, a sharp tone cutting into her words.

"Nothing. It's just that in war, they teach us that hope is no substitute for a good plan. Right now, I don't see a good plan."

30

THE LAST TEMPTATION

"**W**hy, sugah, you're awake!" the girl squealed.

Fran Gaul examined the young woman in front of him with an experienced eye. She looked old enough to be legal in any state in the union, but not much beyond that. Minimal clothing and maximal makeup made her choice of professions clear: Nevada's second oldest talent pool, after the miners. He immediately knew where he was – if not *where* he was, at least what kind of where.

"Where *am* I?" he asked her.

"Why, sugah, you're with me!" The girl was slightly short, maybe five-two, with curves, slightly plump breasts that looked natural, and long strawberry-blond hair that set well against her pale skin. She scooted over to him and sat down, putting one arm around his waist and letting her opposite hand rest on his upper thigh.

"And I'm mighty grateful for it, too," he said, going into instant politician mode. "But I have to confess, I'm feeling a might fuzzy."

"I know," she said, cooing. "When they brought you in, they said you'd been on a bender."

Gaul started to object but thought better of it. No doubt she was completely unaware of any details except instructions to take good care of him. Under most any other circumstances, he would be quite happy for her take care of him. If nothing else, his captors had skillfully selected a girl of his favorite type: *female*. But he was committed to his cause. Charley Davidson was his *friend* as well as President of the United States. Gaul had a personal code of honor, though not as well defined as it might be. The priority of friendship versus patriotism was not always obvious to him, but when put together, they were compelling. At his core, Gaul was a patriot first and a party boy second.

"Not so much," Gaul said. He needed time to figure a way out, but time had almost run out. May Day was no more than two days away, maybe a little longer, depending on the time, but so far, he had no idea what day or time it was.

"But I *am* feeling a might under the weather. Can you help with that?"

"I know I can," she assured him.

31

MAFIA CONNECTION

"**L**et me have a Bud," Chin said to the bartender.

"Sure, if that's what you really want," the bartender said.

"What's that supposed to mean?"

"Just lots of talk that the Bud gets watered down."

"Yeah, yeah, old news. They did it so long ago, I can't tell the difference. Anyway, I'm not looking to get drunk. Gimme a Bud."

"You're the boss."

A moment later, sipping the beer from a frosted mug, Chin scanned the bar for patrons, friendly or otherwise. Happy hour was a half hour away, which meant it was less than half full, but the chatter was animated. Soon it would be packed – a working man's bar where people minded their own business. Nothing would make him happier than to do his business and get out before he was spotted by someone unexpected in the crowd. Before he even finished scanning the whole room, he found the target of his attention.

Chin sat down in the booth inhabited by a single man. He was a man whose dark, dangerous looks discouraged attention; a man nothing like he ever wanted to be, but everything like his uncle and grandfather, save the differences between Chinese and Sicilian heritage.

"I appreciate your coming here on such short notice," Chin said to him. "But I have to admit that I'm surprised you were close enough to make it possible."

Paul Palmio waved a hand in dismissal.

"Like the military," he said, "I work in more than one theater of action. Today I'm working the District. What can I do for you?"

"Senator Fran Gaul has gone missing in Nevada," Chin said. "He could be stashed away on a military base somewhere, but I doubt it. It's too dangerous."

"So you think *I* can find him?" Palmio asked. He smiled as if amused by the request of a young child.

"I have no idea what you can do," Chin said. "But you said you wanted to help. Someone killed Gus Caesare. It wasn't an accident. I'm certain of that. I can't prove it, but that someone might have been Colonel Trent Oliver, who I killed yesterday." Chin was not typically boastful. He rarely saw value in giving away how dangerous he could be, but he knew Palmio would respect the strength revealed. "I think that right before he attacked me, he may have made Fran Gaul disappear. Gaul may be alive or he may be dead, but I'm going to find him. He's the key to General Caesare's death. And he may be the key to saving Charley Davidson's presidency."

"Charley's the Man," Palmio said, making a thumbs up with his right hand. "What can I do?"

"Like I said, I don't know what businesses you're in. I don't want to know. But do you have any friends in the state? Friends who could make inquiries?"

"I can do that," Palmio said. He paused and looked down for a moment. He seemed to be making a decision. After a brief pause, he looked up, more relaxed, as if he had made a tough decision. He got up from the booth as if to leave. He fidgeted for a moment, thought better of it, and sat down again.

"You know, I was going to go and ask around, but I can do that right here. Let me make a couple of calls real quick." As he spoke, he thumbed a message into his phone. He looked up at Chin. They waited.

● ● ●

"Oh my Lord," Gaul said. He groaned unselfconsciously. "I think my recovery time is shot to hell."

"And you have *so much* to recover from," the girl said, still cooing – one of the things she was good at. She had identified herself as Shirley.

Shirley sat up in bed and leaned back against the wall. Gaul's head rested in her unclad lap while she stroked his hair.

"Sweetheart, you'll be the end of me yet, if I let you," Gaul said.

"And who says *you* get to decide?" she asked in challenge. Before he could answer, her lips opened without speaking a word.

Though Gaul had managed to avoid the drugs and alcohol offered, he had far less success holding back against the insistent sexuality. He started with a clear head but soon fell into a daze of sex and sleeping. He lost track of time. As long as Shirley kept him occupied, he worried about little else. He knew he had to get out, but he had glimpsed the security. An easy exit was not in the cards.

The Silver Does Ranch brothel sat in central Nevada, in an area so remote that even the prostitutes served it only on a rotating basis. Gaul had visited the ranch on two occasions, but he had no reason to recognize Shirley or the room, recently remodeled. He had no way to know where he was.

Paul Palmio found out with two phone calls, although he did have to wait several hours for a call back. When he got the news he was waiting for, he made a few more calls. With his last call, he arranged flight on a private jet to McCarran International Airport in Las Vegas, where he was met by colleagues whose "firm" occasionally partnered with his.

From McCarran he was taken to a medium-sized off-strip casino, where he picked up a waiting crew, which filled three black Lincoln Navigators.

When he saw the Navigators, Palmio scowled.

"Are you kiddin' me?" he shouted at the nearest driver.

"These just *scream* mob," he said. "Let's get something a little less flashy."

The result would have been laughable anywhere else but Sin City. Instead of three Navigators, they now had two stretch limos. The difference was, the limos were white with gold trim. They looked exactly like the limos that regularly chauffeured satisfied clients between Las Vegas and the out-of-county brothels. The limos were a marketing tool for the brothels, which were at least an hour's drive away. Contrary to popular mythology, prostitution was legal in only twelve of Nevada's counties; Las Vegas was not in one of them.

The shrewdness of the switch became obvious when they arrived at the brothel, where the vehicles got no second glances. Had Gaul's captors been paying attention, they would have been startled to see a dozen thirty-something men in dark tailored suits, all apparently in top physical shape, approach as if a single unit.

Had brothel security been watching, they would have seen four of the men peel off and circle around to the sides and back, but almost anyone could be excused for missing the quiet, fluid movements.

As it turned out, security was minimal beyond one-inch deadbolts on the doors and windows. Palmio's men battered through the front door with a two-man ram. A large guard, forty-something but built like a weightlifter on steroids, came around the corner, his gun in a belt holster. When he saw three Glocks and a Sig Sauer trained on the spot between his eyes, he raised his hands with care. His lone partner was less cautious and paid the price: watching from the kitchen in back, he raised his own weapon to initiate fire but hesitated. His indecision caught him between the desire to resist and the realization, coming too late, that resistance was pointless. He went down with a double-tap from Palmio's gun.

Fran Gaul should have been trying harder to escape, but at the moment he was working hard on something else: Shirley, who was bouncing up and down on him with great enthusiasm when the door burst open. Palmio and two of his men surged into the room.

"Playtime's over, Senator," he said. "You've got work to do."

Shirley bounced right off the bed and ran to a corner, where she crouched down as if to make herself invisible.

"Who are *you*?" Gaul asked.

"I'm the guy's taking you to see the President," Palmio said.

32

RESCUE

"**G**reat news," Chin said, talking on the phone. "I won't say much on the phone, but that which was missing is no longer."

"Does he have some good news for us?" Queenan asked.

"Don't know," Chin said. "I got a short text message, nothing else. I'll let you know the instant I can talk to him."

• • •

Gaul covered himself in bed sheets and ran into the bathroom. Shirley did not bother with cover; she ran out of the room with a squeak. None of Palmio's men were inclined to stop her, but they watched with great interest.

"I wouldn't mind a piece of that," the youngest one commented, a man not much older than the girl

"Keep your peter parked, Peter," his older partner said, placing a hand on the young man's shoulder as if to hold him back.

Palmio nodded at Peter, a wide man-boy of medium height, who picked up Gaul's clothing. He searched it thoroughly, every pocket, even the boxers, socks, and shoes. When he was done, he looked at Palmio and shook his head. Palmio sighed.

"According to my source, one of the soldiers on the base passed a flash drive to Gaul. It must have had something good on it."

"Either he never got it, or your information was wrong," Peter said.

"Too bad," Palmio said. "But just the same, the U.S. Army now owes me one. And that ain't shabby."

33

DIAGNOSIS REVEALED

General Strom Thornton's rages were legendary, hence his nickname. This time he stormed around his office, ranting, raving, muttering to himself. Trent Oliver's replacement in name only, Colonel Terry Cantwell, stood at stiff attention, quivering, as he watched the dark venting of one of the world's most powerful generals. His level of concern spiked when the worst happened: Stormy pulled out one of his cigars and actually *lit* it, right there in his Pentagon office! Shock fed fear for Cantwell, who struggled not to react.

Eventually the general's tirade decreased in amplitude. While Cantwell found it impossible to relax, his level of concern dropped enough to process what was going on. He was privy to Project May Day's higher goals, as was all of Stormy's staff, but conflicted about their purpose. The comparisons of Thornton to MacArthur were neither new nor discredited. Cantwell had taken a wait-and-see stance. Meanwhile, he had to help Stormy or kiss his career goodbye.

Eventually the general's tirade stopped altogether. Cantwell watched as he relaxed and began pacing. The cigar seemed to have a calming effect, which surprised Cantwell, who came from a family almost religious in its opposition to tobacco. He watched his new boss with the same alarm as a Baptist preacher at a whiskey-drinking poker tournament in a dance hall.

Cantwell fought the urge to look at his watch. His time in Stormy's office seemed interminable. Finally the general turned and looked at him.

"It's time for the press to learn what's going on," he said.

• • •

"Are you watching this?" Charley Davidson asked.

Tammany Dreidel shrugged his shoulders. In spite of his lack of hair, his suit was covered with flakes of dandruff.

"Sure. More press drivel. Things of which they know nothing."

Davidson stared at him.

"You and that English degree. How did you ever end up in politics?"

"Mister President, I could tell you, but then—"

"But then you'd have to *kill* me?" Davidson asked, scoffing. He stood up, tall and big like someone half his age, emphasizing his lack of susceptibility to such threats.

"No, but you might kill me," Dreidel said.

"Stop joking," Davidson said. "This is serious. Do you hear what they're saying?" He waved his hand toward the television screen. The picture was frozen on a photo of General Thornton.

"Yes, I heard. They're saying Thornton has electronic proof that Persia is getting tech support from China. They're suggesting that China may be the real player behind Persia's nuclear program."

"So tell me," Davidson said. "Tell me why, if Stormy has this proof, tell me why we're hearing this on television and not from him personally."

An hour later, the President made the same demand of his Cyber Commander. General George Forbus stood stock still, at full attention, as he got his first dressing down ever from a Commander in Chief. He had ample opportunity to think about his career and wonder whether it was time to retire, but Davidson cut his reverie short.

"General, do you hear what I'm asking? *Why* does the Army Chief of Staff have electronic intelligence that you do not have? Why have you not notified me of this connection between Persia and China?"

"Mister President, I'm going to do something for you that is no doubt extremely rare."

"Oh?"

"I'm going to tell you the plain, unvarnished truth."

"And that is?"

"And that is, this is the first *I've* heard of any connection between China and the Persian nuclear program. I admit it stands to reason, but neither I nor anyone on my staff has heard of this. For that reason, I consider it highly suspect until I can get confirmation."

The president gave him a grim look.

"It's all over the news, General. Just because it didn't come from you doesn't mean it isn't true."

"*Mister* President. You've been in politics what, ten years?"

"Thirteen," Davidson said through tight lips.

"So you, of all people, have to know you can't believe everything you hear on the news."

"Be-*lieve* it? It sure as hell better *not* be true!" Davidson's words escalated to a bellow.

"Mister President! Just give me a little time to get to the bottom of this. We were both blindsided. Give me a little time."

"Time, time, time," Davidson said, muttering. "What?"

Forbus gave him a funny look. "Mister President?"

"General, what are you doing here?" Davidson's eyes had a wild look of fear from disorientation.

"Mister President –" he said, but the President cut him off.

"Thank you, General, that's all," Davidson said, saluting.

● ● ●

When Forbus returned to his office at Fort Meade, Sam Chin was waiting for him, grinning, with another familiar face – Senator Fran Gaul. Forbus, not known for his charismatic ways, broke into a grin of his own when he saw the Nevadan.

"Senator, you don't know what a relief it is to see you," he said, reaching to shake Gaul's hand.

Gaul smiled wanly as they shook.

"Not too much the worse for wear," Chin said. "But you look like you could use some rest. What did they have you doing while you were held captive?" He gave Gaul a dry smile of innocence, having gotten a report firsthand from Paul Palmio. So far, though, Forbus had been spared the details.

"I, er, uh—" Gaul said, stammering.

"Never mind, Senator," Chin said. He slapped the senator on the shoulder like a politician. "How about the electronic surveillance data I asked for?"

"Oh, yeah, right here," Gaul said. He held out the tiny SD disk. Chin reached out and took it.

"How did you sneak it out, Senator?" Chin asked. "Surely they searched you for it."

"They were searching for a flash drive," Gaul said. "So I was kinda lucky. This was small enough to keep in my money belt's hidden pouch. A flash drive would never have fit, so they didn't even check it."

"What's on it?" Forbus asked.

"Don't know," Gaul said. "I'm not even the messenger. I'm just the lowly courier."

"Colonel?" Forbus said, looking at Chin.

"Right away, General," Chin said.

"Senator, if you don't mind, I'd like to ask you to stick around while Colonel Chin has that disk analyzed."

"I have a feeling we're going to have a lot to talk about," Gaul said. "Just give me a good wing chair. I can connect to my office on my iPad while we wait. They took it away from me at the brothel, but luckily we found it in the owner's office."

"Just don't tell them where you are or what you're doing," Forbus said. "Something major is afoot. We've had leaks that we can't pin down. Until we do, we have to be ultracautious."

"In that case, maybe I shouldn't work at all," Gaul quipped. "A little nap would hit the spot."

"Senator. Senator." Gaul woke with a start. One of Forbus' aides, a slender Hispanic captain with a toothbrush mustache, was shaking his shoulder gently.

"What? What?" Gaul's mind felt scrambled for a moment; he could make no sense of his environment. He had never slept or woken in this office before.

"Senator, you're at General Forbus' office," the captain said. Gaul, ever the politician, noticed a name tag that said *Ruiz*. "The general and Colonel Chin have asked for you. They have some news for you."

Gaul shook his head and blinked his eyes rapidly, trying to clear them. He stood and shook himself suddenly.

"Br-r-r-r-r-r!"

Captain Ruiz looked startled but said nothing.

"There! Now I'm awake." Gaul said. "Lead the way, Captain."

The aide led him into Forbus' private conference room, where he and Chin stood with grim looks. The room was decked out in techno-chrome and tech of all kinds – video, audio, even personal workstations. Chin, noticing a CRT, judged some of it a bit dated.

"Senator, how well do you know the President?" Forbus asked. He paced back and forth at the front of the room. Gaul noticed his restlessness but did not feel defensive about the question. He gave Forbus a probing look before answering.

"Depends on what you mean by 'well,'" Gaul said. He clasped his hands and leaned forward slightly, curious what was coming next.

"Don't dodge the question, Senator. How often do you speak to him? See him in person? Do you really know him personally, or is it just surface level?"

"What are you asking me, General? What's this all about?"

"I'm asking you if you've noticed a change in his behavior in the last year or so."

"Well, sure. You all know his wife Beth died last year. Everyone knows that. It was a big blow to him. Maybe he hasn't been the same sprightly guy I've known for the last dozen years. I know he still works out in his gym, but he *has* seemed distracted. Not himself."

"I'm afraid it's a little bit more than that, Senator," Forbus said. "Colonel?" He nodded to Chin.

Chin pulled out a remote unit. He pushed a couple of buttons on the unit and brought up a series of memos on the wall-sized display.

"Senator, we found a tremendous amount of material, so I'll spare you a lot of the details. I've highlighted some key spots."

They all looked at the display.

While modern medicine does not have a definitive diagnostic test for this disease, our testing suggests a ninety-percent probability that the subject is in the latter portion of early-stage Alzheimer's. By all indications, which are anecdotal at best, the President's symptomology was minimal at the beginning of his term. After the death of his wife, he took a noticeable turn for the worse. Fugue state episodes, though brief, are increasing in number and duration. Serious, permanent downturns and memory lapses after stressful life events are a hallmark of Alzheimer's.

"What the hell...?" Gaul said, jumping out of his chair.

"Just the beginning," Forbus said. "Colonel?"

Chin pushed another button.

Generals, we have a unique opportunity in the history of our great nation. We have an opportunity to avoid the mistake of the pacifist, panty-waisted civilians who would keep us from protecting ourselves against the nuclear pretensions of Persia and its secret attempts to create a new Islamic caliphate. With the President sidelined and unable to perform as Commander in Chief, we can take the necessary steps to ensure the security of our homeland.

"Holy fuck," Gaul said. "Stormy Thornton wants to take over the country. He's talking about a military coup. He figures Charley Davidson can't stop him."

"Effectively," Chin said. "And there's more."

FINAL PREPARATIONS

Back in his own office, Stormy Thornton was busy overseeing the final details of Project May Day. In his suite at the Pentagon, he held a videoconference with his commanders in the Persian Gulf theater.

"Gentleman," he said, beginning, but stopped short, remembering himself. "And lady," he said nodding to the one female officer in the group, a two-star admiral. She nodded back to thank him for his acknowledgement.

"We are in the final stages of preparation for Project May Day," he said. "In less than forty hours, we will activate all units. They will be activated on high alert. We will be at DEFCON 2."

Those words caused a considerable stir among the participants. General Windfire spoke up.

"Does that mean you anticipate this turning into a live-fire exercise?"

"Be prepared, gentlemen. I will be speaking to the President again soon. Be prepared to transition from Project May Day to Operation May Showers at a moment's notice."

THE MISSING PRESIDENT

"Tonight on the Roxy Report, we will be asking the question, *'Where is President Charley Davidson?'* He hasn't been seen in public for more than three weeks now, although the White House does manage to issue a steady stream of press releases of little or no value. In a moment, we will have a conversation with some of the people who know him best. Meanwhile, Washington is in chaos, what with the mysterious death of Chairman of the Joint Chiefs of Staff, General Gustavo Caesare. More than one wag is suggesting that the debonair general, long considered one of the most eligible bachelors in Washington, was actually gay. Some say he was secretly killed in the midst of a sordid orgy of sodomy and Satan only knows what else. I don't believe it for a minute, but I'm keeping an open mind until I get more information. And now one of our most secret sources has it that President Davidson's longtime friend and confidante, Democratic Senator and boozehound Fran Gaul, has gone missing as well. Roxy Report has confirmed that Senator Gaul has been missing for two days and no one in his office, in Washington or Las Vegas, can produce him. Stay tuned for our first conversation, with the President's Chief of Staff, Tammany Dreidel.*

Vice President Joan Queenan used her remote to mute the sound on the video screen. Sitting at the head of the table, she could easily view the screen at the far end. The others – Chin, Forbus, and Gaul – were at a disadvantage as they shifted their attention back and forth from the screen to the Vice President. None of them felt comfortable turning their backs to her, so they would sneak quick glances at the screen, then turn back.

"Doesn't know the half of it, does he?" she said to them.

"No, and it's a good thing," Chin said. "But the way this town leaks, he'll know soon enough. I recommend that we – that is, *you* – get ahead of this story."

"That's exactly what I intend, Colonel," she said. "Which is why I've asked one more person to join us." She turned to a speakerphone on her desk and pushed a button.

"Has he arrived?" she asked.

"Just walked in the door, Madame Vice President. Shall I send him on in?"

"Do it." Queenan turned back to her audience.

"I guess I need to hold a press conference or something," Gaul said. "Can't have my constituents getting all excited."

"Or something," Queenan said in a flat voice. She and Gaul had never had an affinity for each other's politics.

The door opened.

"Gentlemen," Queenan said, standing. "I think you all know Secretary of State Cameron Romulet."

Romulet's straight-backed appearance impressed even the military men. Gaul slouched back, intimidated, as the secretary strode forward. Romulet pretended not to notice as he greeted each with a personal remark. He turned to Queenan last.

"Madame Vice President, " he said. As he shook her hand, he gave her the slightest of bows with his head. He turned to address the group as a whole.

"I've reviewed the materials you had couriered to me. I appreciate the sensitivity of the materials and the need to keep them confidential. As you know, our situation is delicate. Although we are not there yet, we are threatened with a constitutional crisis. We must do everything we can to avoid that."

"As I see it, we have two problems," Queenan said. "We've got to stop Stormy. And we've got to stop Project May Day."

"Those are really the same problem," Romulet said. "All respect, I mean. It really comes back to a bigger, more fundamental problem."

"Which is?"

"Which is, Charley Davidson is probably no longer fit to be President. We must convene the Cabinet at the earliest possible moment to have you appointed, under the Twenty-Fifth Amendment to the Constitution, as Acting President. And if possible, we need to get him to resign."

PART III

36

SHOWDOWN BEGINS

"What is it, General? I thought you were busy with preparations for Project May Day. I'm looking forward to our little trip to Nevada tomorrow." Charley Davidson stood behind his desk with his arms crossed. Strom Thornton stood in front of him almost defiantly, not as a subordinate.

"May Day is occupying all my attention, Mister President. Even more than I expected."

"Which means?"

"Which means, Mister President, that I thank God we are proceeding with May Day. We are this far from having to turn this exercise into a real fight." He said this while holding his right thumb and index finger only a fraction of an inch apart. Thornton noticed that the President's hair and suit looked uncharacteristically mussed up.

"What? *Why?* You know my policy concerning Persia. We have every opportunity to keep peace with that country, General Thornton. I insist on it. I only agreed to this exercise because you swore our national security could be in danger unless we did something to keep them on their toes. I went along with that much, but that's all. So tell me now why this is necessary."

"Mister President, we are on the verge of a national emergency. We are picking up heavy signal traffic between China and Persia that proves *definitively* that China is behind the Persian nuclear initiative. Furthermore, we have evidence that they plan to use Project May Day as an excuse to launch a theater-wide strike against U.S. forces."

Davidson was now sitting, arms slack by his side. He looked at Thornton dully. His eyes reflected little of the light that had delighted so many fans and supporters over the years.

"May Day?" he said, echoing Thornton.

"Yes, Mister President. The schedule has been moved up by one day. We have to get you to our secure location immediately."

Tam Dreidel, Davidson's chief of staff, stood by. Nearby spots in the ceiling highlighted the sweaty sheen of his hairless dome.

"It's not that simple, is it? You can see he's in no position to stop us. Why not just leave him here?"

"If we do that, it's too easy for others to intervene. The success of this operation, to a point, depends on discretion. The fewer people who can get to him, the easier this will be. If we take him to Area 53, no one will be able to interfere."

"In that case, I'll stand by with the President to make sure he is secure until you are ready."

"You do that," the general said with a curt nod. He looked back at the President. Davidson just sat there, impassive, inexpressive, like an aging G.I. Joe doll. Thornton took a long, last look at him. Charley Davidson was once a man he enjoyed on the screen, then admired as Governor of California, then respected as his Commander in Chief. Now he felt nothing but pity for the old man. He shook his head sadly and headed out the door.

• • •

Not long after Thornton left the Oval Office, the interoffice phone buzzed on the President's desk. Davidson had been sitting at his desk passively. He did not seem to notice the buzzing at first, but after the third attempt, he pressed the button to answer. Before he could say anything, two Secret Service agents burst in, guns drawn. They scanned the room, swinging their Sig Sauers around like radar. Failing to find a problem, they relaxed and holstered their weapons.

Davidson looked at them, his face a blank.

"What's going on, gentlemen?" he asked.

"Nothing, Mister President," the senior agent said. "Except we were worried when you didn't respond to your phone."

"I was busy," Davidson said. "Is there something wrong with that? Can't the President of Calley-fornya get a little peace and quiet when he wants it?"

The two agents exchanged a look that said *here we go again.*

"Uh, sure, Mister President," the senior said. "But you have a visitor."

"Mister President, we need to talk." Cameron Romulet stood in the doorway with a grave look.

37

CABINET MEETING

In the Cabinet Room, department secretaries gathered for the historic meeting. The conclave was impromptu, so seating arrangements were first-come, first-served. As a result, secretaries who normally got little attention managed to find superior positions. The Secretary of Transportation, Theo Bantu, chose the seat to the right of the President's seat at the head of the table. Bantu was short, barely an inch over five feet tall; he tried to compensate with a heavy beard, which only served to make him look bug-eyed when he got excited. Secretary of Labor Danny Hedron sat at the left. The Secretary of Veteran's Affairs was a retired brigadier general; he sat next to Hedron. Most of the other department heads quickly followed.

"Say, Theo, you know what this meeting's all about?" The Secretary of Commerce, who had once held Bantu's position, walked up with an extended hand. He looked concerned.

"I doubt if I know any more than you, Jack," Bantu said, shaking Secretary Mack's hand. "I was in my limo en route to Capitol Hill when my secretary buzzed me to get over here pronto. Said an emergency Cabinet meeting had been called. I haven't even *talked* to the President in a couple of weeks, so I have no idea what's on his mind."

Moments later, most of the chairs at the main table were filled; aides sat in chairs lining the walls around the table.

"Where's Rick?" Hedron asked. In the President's absence, the large man dominated the room. He looked at the empty chair where the Attorney General normally sat, at an angle by the President's left elbow.

"Right here," Attorney General Richard Telepsen said, standing in the doorway. He stood there and scanned the room, as if counting heads. "We're just waiting on a few more folks." Telepsen was orange-haired and pink-skinned with freckles, so sensitive to ginger jokes that his enemies often used it to get under his skin.

"Like the President," the Secretary of Commerce said. Everyone laughed, which helped to reduce the tension evident around the room. No one knew why the unplanned meeting had been called. No one assumed it was for good news.

The Cabinet members waited. Some stood, but most sat. All knew each other to varying degrees. They had plenty to talk about, but no one wanted to start a conversation. The dark energy of the surprise meeting hung over the room like a heavy storm cloud not quite able to burst. Only Telepsen had interacted much with Davidson in recent weeks, so he felt the strongest sense of foreboding. Standing there, waiting, he felt like a heavy weight was pulling him straight down, into the ground. The feeling rooted him there, making him feel immovable. Having undergone hypnotherapy once to help him quit smoking, he recognized the feeling as similar, but with greater physical power. When he saw the approaching Secret Service agents, his stomach knotted up as well.

First into the room was Vice President Queenan, who moved to her seat at the distant end of the table. Next was President Davidson, who took his usual seat at the head of the table. He sat there expectantly, saying nothing. Tension in the room escalated as the Cabinet members looked at each other. Some studied the President and Vice President. Neither spoke. Finally, one more person entered the room.

Secretary of State Cameron Romulet stood in the entrance with his trademark stature. The silver-gray hair at the temples, relatively slight for a man in his early sixties, gave him a George Hamilton look of sophistication matched by few politicians.

"Mister President," he said, nodding to Davidson. Davidson turned and looked at him but said nothing. Romulet looked to the group, who now looked at him as one.

"I've called this meeting today to discuss appointment of the Vice President as Acting President as outlined in the Twenty-Sixth Amendment to the Constitution of the United States of America."

38

TWENTY-FIFTH AMENDMENT

The room burst into chaos as everyone stood, shouting and talking to no one and everyone.

Within moments, Attorney General Telepsen regained control of the room.

"Gentlemen! Ladies! If you please! Please sit down while we work through this." Looking at Romulet with a scowl, he said, "I take it you mean the Twenty-*Fifth* Amendment? I recall the Twenty-Sixth gives eighteen-year-olds the right to vote."

"Yes, yes, sorry," Romulet said, red-faced. He looked around the room. "We have an extraordinarily unique and difficult dilemma," he said to the group. "To help understand what has happened, what *is* happening, we have prepared small packets for each of you." As he spoke, he passed out nine-by-twelve manila envelopes, none of them thick enough to hold more than a dozen pages or so. Everyone opened their envelopes and made cursory glances at the material as Romulet spoke.

"If you will look at the top pages, you will see that the President has been diagnosed as approaching mid-stage Alzheimer's. Although he often functions normally, as if there is nothing wrong, more and more, those of us who see him regularly can see it in his performance. More and more, we worry that a crisis will occur with a vacant President at the helm."

"This is remarkable," spoke out one man. Doctor Martin Kriton stood at his full height of six feet and eight inches, but even so, no one noticed anything but the massive wart on his nose. "I can't believe you didn't consult me on this. I'm Secretary of Health and Human Services and an MD, for God's sake."

"Sorry, Doctor Kriton," Romulet said. "This whole situation has developed quickly, and not under my control. I called this meeting the moment it was brought to my attention."

"And the President...?" Kriton said, looking in Davidson's direction.

The president smiled and nodded at Kriton.

"Hello," he said. "Thank you for coming."

"Mister President –?" Kriton began.

"Yes, Doctor Kriton. Thank you for coming. Have you been briefed, or do I need to review it for you?" Davidson smiled, but the look on his face was empty, as if he was staring at nothing. To Kriton, he sounded almost robotic, not the Charley Davidson he had known for years.

"Yes, I mean, no, Mister President ..." Kriton began. His eyes shifted back and forth between the documents in his hand and Davidson, unsure where to stop. Although a medical doctor by profession, Kriton was an old-school Republican, not much younger than the President, who believed in loyalty before ideology. "Mister Secretary, how do you propose to proceed?"

"Let's do this formally," Romulet said. "Mister Attorney General, do you certify that we have a quorum?"

Telepsen responded without counting or looking around the room. He stood.

"Mister Secretary, the Cabinet does not operate under formal rules that specify or require a quorum present. However, in order to act under the Twenty-Fifth Amendment, we must either act with the President's acquiescence, or with a majority of the department heads, regardless of how many are present. A majority of the total members, not a majority of those present. So the question of a quorum is moot. In any event, all members except the Secretary of Homeland Security are present and accounted for."

"Thank you, General. Mister President, do you understand the matters before you today? I have here a letter authorizing the Vice President to become Acting President. Are you willing to sign this?"

Davidson smiled. His eyes continued to look glazed.

"Thank you all for coming today," he said. He clasped his hands together on the desk in front of him. The former champion bodybuilder and silver-screen heartthrob sat there as if waiting for a cue.

"Mis-tah Secretary. Mis-tah *Secretary*!" Brigadier General Abraham Ribstein, retired, stood up in protest. As Secretary of Veterans Affairs with a decorated military background of his own, he had closer ties to the military than anyone in the Cabinet, including Secretary of Defense Fleming D'Enfant. In moments of stress, he tended to let his guard down; his South Carolina-accented words slid out like honey on a hot stick.

"Mis-tah Secretary," he repeated again. "While I concede that un-dah the Twenty-Fifth Amendment this august body, with the support of the Vice President, may assume control of the Presidency, I refer to the words of the great Thomas Jefferson, as he wrote them in the Declaration of Independence: *Prudence, indeed, will dictate that Governments long established should not be changed for light and transient Causes.*

"Heed these words, my friends. What, truly, do we know that dictates an immediate need for usurpation of the presidency? Two or three pieces of paper that anyone could make up and hand out? Do we have independent confirmation? Second opinions? Can we be certain there is no hidden political agenda to seize power from the duly elected President of the United States? With all due respect, Mis-tah Secretary, we need more information. There is no compelling reason to act at this time."

"I'm inclined to agree, Mister Secretary," Kriton said in support. "An accurate diagnosis of Alzheimer's is notoriously elusive in anyone. The president may or may not have a problem, but if so, we are at the beginning of the investigation, not the end."

Interior Secretary Elizabeth Hornblossom spoke up for the first time. White-haired and short, but fit like the outdoorswoman she was, Hornblossom looked down to the far end of the table.

"Madame Vice President, where do you fit into all this? Are you in agreement with Secretary Romulet?" All eyes turned toward the woman who would be President.

39

CYBERWAR

The fundamental design flaw in highly secured locations like the White House, the Pentagon, or the Cyber Command office building at Fort Meade was simple: they were secured against invaders from without, trying to get in. Once inside, most security was assumed, but that assumption would today be tested.

On days when General Forbus was out of the office, the front desk to his office suite was handled by a young male civilian employee who did admin work not requiring a security clearance. When Forbus was in, Captain Ted Hambor held down the spot unless he was sent out on a task.

Hambor was thirty-two, a man with medium-brown hair and plain features unscarred by his time in Afghanistan. Ted had seen enough action for two quick promotions from second lieutenant but saved his own life by doing a favor for the right colonel at the right time. After finding himself with a promotion to captain and an easy assignment working for a four-star, he had had few worries other than how to get out from under the desk job and his career back in gear.

Now he was about to discover that war follows you everywhere.

He heard them before he saw them, four set of boots marching as one, with a cadence so precise that a civilian would swear it was one person with a heavy gait, but Hambor knew the difference. He stood up and looked around the door to see four soldiers marching directly toward him, in unison.

Normally there would be nothing unusual about soldiers marching around a base, but Hambor immediately knew something was wrong.

CyberCom soldiers had recently adopted a new uniform dictated by General Forbus. Forbus had decided to create a greater sense of identity among soldiers under his command, so he had created a pastel solid-blue fatigue. The result was made of the same material as army fatigues but matched the color of Air Force blue dress shirts.

These soldiers wore Army brown digital camo. They wore ball-cap hats that covered the tops of their heads, decorated in the same pattern. Their faces looked blurry and plain. The captain blinked his eyes several times, trying to resolve his vision well enough to see their faces, but without success. Then he noticed they all had sidearms – old Army Colt .45s, long abandoned as a military standard. As if on an invisible cue, the four simultaneously reached to their holstered guns and snapped off the leather safety straps.

Eyes wide, Hambor ran inside and slammed shut the outer door to the suite, but he knew he could not secure it in time; that would require stooping down and laboriously turning two locks, and the key was in a desk across the room. He ran back to warn Forbus after sliding a desk in front of double wooden doors.

"We're under attack!"

Forbus heard the shout when he stuck his head inside the general's doors. Hambor bolted for a nearby arms closet. Eyes wide, Forbus reached in his desk for his own favorite, a Heckler & Koch semiauto that was a good fit for his slightly smallish hand. After grabbing three extra magazines, he was ready to go.

Hambor caught the attackers by surprise. Their Kevlar was strong enough to resist the semiauto weapons' fire they expected to face. Kevlar was the reason Hambor's favorite weapon was a Mossberg semiauto shotgun – a street sweeper. A favorite in urban assault. The first two attackers went down under his fire, but he got too confident. In the time it took for him to draw first blood, the survivors ducked behind furniture and returned fire. Ted was caught up in the tunnel vision so common among those in firefights; he had no time to refocus his awareness. His inattention cost him his life but probably saved his boss.

As Hambor went down, Forbus burst out of his office, gun blazing. His face showed extraordinary calm, as if his body responded like an automatic pilot. He killed one of the two remaining soldiers with a well-targeted shot to the left femoral artery in the upper thigh. The second went down with two rounds to his chest, center mass, where he was best protected. A heavily muscled man, he flipped on the ground and shot back, hitting Forbus in his left shoulder. The general had time to notice the man's lower face was covered by a flesh-colored bandage, wrapped around from side to side. Forbus shot back one more time, this time causing a messy explosion of red brain matter when the hollow-point bullet exited the back of his attacker's head. Then the general passed out on the floor.

40

HOMELAND SECURITY

"**I**'d like to answer that, if you don't mind."

All heads turned back to the doorway.

"Sorry I'm late," said the Secretary of Homeland Security, Eleanor Roundy. Roundy wore a woman's suit with epaulets that tried to give her a military look, without much success; her grandmotherly hairstyle, a bun of artificial blond trying desperately not to look gray, made sure of that.

"I'd say you're just in time," Queenan said. Three people laughed uneasily.

"Understood, Madame Vice President."

Roundy turned her gaze from Queenan to scan the rest of the room.

"I'm sure you can all appreciate that the Vice President is in an awkward position," she began. "She just received news that, if correct and valid, strongly points to the need to disallow the President's authority – *at least temporarily*. But as Vice President, she can be seen as benefitting from the result, if being President can truly be considered a benefit."

"Thank you, Madame Secretary," Queenan said, interrupting her. "I may be in a tight spot, but it's my job to do it. My friends, there is more to this situation than simply the President's medical condition. We are at the cusp of a dangerous military confrontation that could result in a war with Persia, or worse."

The Secretary of Defense groaned.

"Not May Day again!" he mocked. "How many times do we have to tell you?"

"Once was quite enough, Mister Secretary," Queenan said. There was ice in her voice, and steel as well. The Cabinet members slowly turned their attention, and respect, to her. She looked down the table. Everyone, including Davidson, looked at her for the next move. He smiled and nodded to her, as if giving permission.

"It is no secret that Project May Day is a military exercise scheduled to take place tomorrow. There are events related to it that I am not at liberty to disclose. Suffice it to say that what it now threatens is to turn into a regional war, or worse, *if* we are not careful."

"Which means there must be no doubt as to who has command authority," Roundy said.

"And absolutely no doubt about the integrity of that authority," Romulet said. He sighed as if bearing the weight of a thousand worlds. "This is not an irrevocable decision. But at least for now, I must move that we vote to make Acting President the Vice President of the United States, Joan Queenan."

"Second the motion," Roundy said quickly.

"Mister Attorney General, would you please review the details of the Twenty-Fifth Amendment, so we can all be on the same page?" Romulet asked. When he looked at Telepsen, everyone in the room followed his gaze.

"Certainly," Telepsen said. He picked up an iPad and opened a document he had previously prepared.

"Presidential authority may be ceded, temporarily, to the Vice President as Acting President."

"Under what circumstances?" Kriton asked.

"The president may voluntarily cede authority, as George H.W. Bush once did for minor surgery. So did Bill Clinton, if I recall. Those were short-term circumstances that simply allowed for the fact that the President would be unconscious due to surgical anesthesia, and to give the Vice President the authority to act in the event of an emergency. Our situation today does not appear to fit that mold.

"The other way is by action of the Cabinet. A majority of the Cabinet may vote to make the Vice President *Acting President.*

"In either case, the President may intervene to end the acting presidency, by delivering a message to Congress. At that point, the Cabinet may appeal, but only directly to Congress. And at that point, it would take a two-thirds vote of Congress, of each house individually, to override the President's prerogative of office."

41

THE REAL BRAINS

Lieutenant General Claudia Fuchs sat in her private secure computing room in Area 53. Here she could communicate with almost any online computer system in the world and hack virtually all of them. She could communicate directly with the command and control systems of every ship in the U.S. Navy, of every plane in every branch of the military, of every tank, of every individual soldier wired into a personal network. At the same time, her room was physically and electronically secure against signal leak or tapping of any kind. She and her team had taken Operation Intangible far, far beyond anything envisioned by Charley Davidson, George Forbus, or Stormy Thornton. With these tools, she knew, she could take complete control of the U.S. military. But to what purpose? Fuchs was a patriot. At the moment she was unclear whether her patriotism was best offered to Stormy or the President. She was prepared for either possibility, but soon she would have to make a decision. Meanwhile, the next step was hers. Tapping away, she sent spurious transmissions to each of Stormy's theater commanders. The final message went to the base commander at Fort Meade.

• • •

"Mister Secretary, before we proceed, I would like to ask once more, for the record, for the President to take this step voluntarily." As Ribstein spoke, everyone's eyes turned to Romulet and Davidson, who stood immediately next to the President. Romulet turned to look directly at Davidson, who looked at him as well.

"Mister President, do you understand why we are gathered here today?"

"I understand you want to take my job away from me," Davidson said. A few people laughed uncomfortably, while most shifted silently in their seats. "But I'm still not clear on the details. I'm not surprised you inside-the-Beltway types want my job, but I never thought you would do this to me, Joanie!" he choked out, looking at Queenan. He looked stressed and distressed; those nearest him could see teardrops squeezing out the sides of his eyes.

Queenan looked dismayed.

"I, I'm not doing anything, Mister President. There are events far beyond my control or yours. The important thing is to protect America. The Cabinet is doing what it must to make sure that nothing goes wrong in the next few days. After this May Day crisis is past us, we can take stock of things again."

"Reichstag fire!"

The room went quiet. Two seats down from Queenan sat the Secretary of Agriculture, Hank Thompson, who had said nothing up to this point.

"Excuse me?" Queenan said. She turned her body toward the linen-suited Thompson and scooted her chair back, to have a better look at him.

"Reichstag fire!" he repeated. "This is just a ploy. It's an excuse to seize power. You have no real evidence. You've provided no real evidence of an imminent foreign threat. It's all hearsay. Once you've taken over, who's to stop you?"

"*We* will," Romulet said. "The Cabinet."

"Well ex-cuuuuse me, Mister Secretary," Thompson said. "But if you'll read that amendment a little more closely, you'll see that the *only* person who can take away the power of the Acting President is the President himself. The Cabinet has no removal authority at all, not for the President, not for the Vice President, and certainly not for the Acting President."

"Not a problem," Romulet said. "She did not initiate this. *I* did. And now, if there's no further discussion, I think it's time we take a vote. All those in favor, signify by raising your right hand."

Romulet raised his hand, as did Roundy, Telepsen, and quite a few others.

"Okay, all those opposed?" He watched hands rise from Kriton, Thompson, D'Enfant, and three others. Everyone in the room was a vote counter; they all knew the result, but Romulet announced it for the record.

"By a vote of ten to six, Vice President Joan Queenan is now *Acting* President. Under the circumstances, I'm not sure congratulations are in order. Madame President?"

"Please don't call me that, Mister Secretary," she said, "or any of you," she said as she scanned the room. "I'm not the President. It's an important distinction to be made. And I don't think Madame Acting President really has the right ring to it, do you? So Madame Vice President is still the best. I've always liked being an MVP," she quipped. Everyone laughed, happy to break the tension.

Suddenly two Secret Service agents burst into the room.

"We have a security emergency! Everyone downstairs *now!*"

Within moments, the entire Cabinet, the President included, were hustling down a small corridor. Two agents led the way and two took the rear, while teams of four surrounded Queenan and Davidson. One of the lead agents pointed a remote device toward a utility room, which emitted an audible click. The door drifted open a few inches. The second leader flung it open so hard that it bounced off a rubber stopper and back into her face. She grimaced and opened it again, this time with more finesse. She turned to the group, waved, and shouted, "Follow me!" while her partner held it open.

Everyone in the crowd heard the echoing sounds of her shoe leather against the metal stairs as she raced downward. Those closest saw her draw a handgun with her right hand. In her left, she held a flashlight that lit the way.

"Make way for the President!" one of the Secret Service agents shouted. Queenan and Davidson looked at each other. The Vice

President was used to deferring but was unsure what to do, so the President decided for her.

"After you, Madame Vice President," he said, bowing at the waist with a sweep of the arm.

Queenan stopped and looked at him, his countenance as placid as ever.

"Thank you, Mister President."

Queenan ran down the stairs. Three agents followed. After them came Davidson and three more agents. The Cabinet members followed closely behind.

Ten minutes later, all were gathered in the Situation Room. With more than two dozen people present, it was a tight squeeze. As everyone shuffled around awaiting word from the Secret Service agents, Queenan spoke up.

"Before we go any farther, there's a little detail we have to attend to. Technically speaking, I'm not Acting President until the Cabinet conveys a notice of presidential incapacity to the Speaker of the House and the President pro tempore of the Senate. So if you don't have a letter already drawn up, we need to get one, pronto. The last thing we need is a lawyers' contest over who was in charge at what time. I assume Secretary Romulet has the letter?" She looked around the room, as did everyone else. Soon everyone was shrugging their shoulders.

"Where is Cameron Romulet?" she asked.

42

STORMING THE WHITE HOUSE

Having finished her preparations, Claudia Fuchs reached the general on a secure line. She crossed her arms and stood tall in a position of dominance that she favored.

"Communications initiated, sir. We should be hearing from the theater commanders shortly, as well as NSA. The White House is under imminent military threat. What troops will you call in for support?"

"We will follow protocol, General. However, General Forbus has been compromised. Continue to route all communications directly to me."

"Yes, sir." She disconnected. The plan was turning out different from what they had envisioned, which was to be expected, but the result was even better than hoped for. The Magic Glass dashboard in front of her allowed for both graphic and textual displays, all updated in real time. Peering, she stood and scanned the Persian Gulf region for updates of American, Persian, and Chinese ships. The objects were a little fuzzy. Cursing to herself, she pulled out a pair of reading glasses, a crutch she hated because they were so necessary. Now she could see that both sides had planes in the air – not only fighters, but AWACs communications and flying refueling depots. The few Russian vessels lent a small presence, staying at the periphery of the theater. Signals intelligence indicated they were providing some communications support to the Persian navy, but Fuchs could take control of their data streams at any time. She turned her attention to a CNN webcam facing the White House from Pennsylvania Avenue. From the east end, she could see tanks turning onto the street in front.

"Ho-lee shit," she swore softly to herself. "It's really happening. Now let's see if Stormy can pull this off." She relaxed, sat back in her chair, and sipped a glass of Chardonnay as she considered Bayesian probabilities and Markov chains describing the many permutations of possible events to come.

• • •

"Where is Cameron Romulet?"

Kriton started to stand as if to answer, but he felt someone tugging on his suit jacket. He turned to see Defense Secretary Fleming D'Enfant motioning to him. He put an index finger across his lips to signal silence. When Kriton sat down, D'Enfant leaned over and upward to whisper into his fellow secretary's ear.

"Bide your time," he said. His voice reminded Kriton of the softness and fragility of a cobweb, which is what he thought of when he looked at the SecDef's combover. "Stormy's about to make his move."

"This will never work," Kriton said. "The President and Vice President were supposed to be *secured*."

"They're right here, aren't they?" D'Enfant said. "We're secure. *They're* secure. There's been a change in plans. Watch for what comes next."

Out in the corridor, large young Marines with automatic weapons scrambled right and left looking for the Secretary of State. They approached their work in pairs. At each door, one stood off at an angle, gun pointed at the door, as his partner slowly reached for the doorknob, standing at the side, turning the knob, carefully opening the door. Behind each, they knew, could lurk sudden death.

Like all the other rooms, the door to the men's restroom opened inward. When the two Marines approached it, they moved with methodical caution. The restroom was at the end of a narrow corridor, which made it impossible to fan out to the sides. They were at the mercy of any enemy who was armed and waiting for them to enter.

The men edged their way up. When the lead was ready, he nodded to his partner, who nodded back. They burst into the restroom, rifles ready but unneeded. They saw no one in the room. The leader looked around, swinging his gun point like a radar beacon.

"Mister Secretary!" he shouted. "Secretary Romulet! Cameron Romulet!" he shouted, each time with a slight change of intonation.

"Right here."

He turned and looked toward the corner stall.

The soldier walked carefully, the way you might when afraid of waking an infant. He held his rifle to his shoulder, monitoring through his scope, ready to shoot at any moment. Cameron Romulet sat there in the stall, helpless as the soldier pointed the muzzle directly between his eyes. Romulet was certain the man was about to shoot, but he refused to close his eyes. Instead he stared directly at the young man, who hesitated. That hesitation saved the Secretary of State's life.

"Hey!" the soldier's partner yelled, when he saw the lead drawing down on Romulet. The first man hesitated and jerked his arm in indecision; that was all it took. His partner double-tapped him with two quick shots, sending him flying into the back wall. Kevlar protected him from the first shot, but the second one went high and entered at the throat. The shot was not an instantaneous kill, but it was messy. The soldier thrashed around on the floor as he bled out. Romulet had turned away at just the right moment, which kept blood off his face but not his suit jacket. He jumped up and ran out the door while the man who saved his life examined his former buddy, now a twitching corpse.

• • •

"Mister Secretary, do you have the paper we discussed?" Queenan asked. She brushed her hair out of her face, a movement that had become increasingly common throughout the day as events challenged her normally perfect countenance. She retained her composure, but the stress showed in the deterioration of her hairdo. As Romulet emerged, she stared.

Everyone in the room gaped at his blood-spattered suit. For a man they had never seen with a wrinkled shirt or a scuffed shoe, the spectacle in front of them was unprecedented.

"Right here, Madame Vice President. Fortunately for history, they survived without bloodstains. At any rate, my office took the liberty of writing up these draft letters. They are sufficiently terse to satisfy everyone, I think. Given the gravity of the circumstances, I request that everyone here sign the letters, which we will send immediately to the Congressional leadership."

"Do you expect me to sign it, even though I voted against it?" D'Enfant asked, indignance choking his voice.

"How about me?" Kriton asked.

"I knew the vote would not be unanimous," Romulet said. "And yet, I think it is important that we convey our support *as a Cabinet* for the Acting President. So I have drafted a letter with room for two groups of signatories – those with the affirmative, and those with the negative. You can formally consent to the process and sign the letter of conveyance, without supporting the vote. Does that meet with your approval?"

Romulet held out the draft to D'Enfant. Kriton read over his shoulder. Both read for a moment. As they finished, each looked at the other, serious and unhappy, but they nodded, first to each other, and at last to Romulet. The Secretary of State smiled.

"Excellent," he said. The room burst into applause. President Charley Davidson stood in a back corner quietly, unnoticed. He watched but said nothing, wondering if it was time for his workout yet.

"Now we've got to get these documents to the Speaker and President pro tempore as quickly as possible. The Vice President is not Acting President until they are delivered."

"Just a technicality," said someone in back.

"More than a technicality," Romulet said, looking toward the end of the table. "We expect the need for immediate action on a foreign front. If she gives orders and her authority can be disputed, then we have a true constitutional crisis."

"I thought that's what we just had," Kriton said.

"Not even close, Mister Secretary," Romulet said. "We just worked through the correct functioning of the Constitution. That amendment is used rarely, true, but that does not mean a crisis when it *is* used. The crisis would come from *not* following the Constitution."

"I stand corrected," Kriton said, looking unhappy.

"Do we have to deliver that letter by hand?" Queenan asked. "Can we deliver it electronically?"

"We could scan it and e-mail it as an attachment," Romulet said. "Then confirm via videoconference."

"I can take care of that," Attorney General Telepsen said, holding out his hand for the letter.

"Take at least two Marines with you," Romulet said, handing it over. "And make copies for everyone here."

A few minutes later, Telepsen returned with a look of dismay. In his hand, he held two dozen copies of the letter, along with the original.

"Get it all done?" Romulet asked. Looking more closely, he asked, "What's the matter?"

"I got it scanned and copied," Telepsen said. "But all communications with the outside world are shut down."

"Huh? What're you talking about?"

"Just what I said. There's nothing going in or out of the comm room. They said they're being jammed or something."

"Or something?"

"With the emphasis on *something*. I know the Situation Room is supposed to be a lead cage, but isn't the whole idea of a comm room to *communicate*? Otherwise, what's the point?"

"True," Romulet said. "Did you make inquiries?"

At that moment, they heard the rumble of Army boots in the corridor outside. He looked outside the door to see a squad of Marines running toward him. The leader waved at the others to stop. He walked briskly up to Romulet.

"Colonel Thomas Hawke. Sir, the White House is under attack. I am under orders to protect you and all others in the room against any attempt to take it by force. The Secret Service will take personal charge of the President and Vice President. We will rely upon your leadership to keep the Cabinet orderly."

"Under *attack*?"

"No time. Use the media center to monitor events. Now, in the room, close the door, and lock it."

Inside the Situation Room, Romulet closed the door and stood squarely in front of it. He stood close enough that blood smeared off his jacket onto the door.

"What's up?" Ribstein asked.

"You'll know soon enough," Romulet said. "The Situation Room toilet is so small, it makes an airplane toilet look like a suite at the Ritz Carlton. Why do you think I made a pit stop?"

• • •

Fuchs continued to monitor the march of military forces, including APCs and tanks, up Pennsylvania Avenue. At times like these, she wished she was in a room with large wall monitors; she was so big that sitting at a desk console was no fun at all.

Watching the screen, she saw the entire block filled with vehicles. Two tanks joined together and turned front and center, as if preparing to knock on the front door – which, by all appearances, is exactly what was about to happen. Their cannons pointed directly toward the north face, the face that tourists on Pennsylvania Avenue saw every day of the year. Troops were spread out behind the tanks, but some were starting to creep forward toward the cover of the trees and hedges. Fuchs watched the drama with silent intensity as it unfolded. At first she nodded to herself, approving of orders well written and executed as planned. Then she looked closer and frowned.

"Stormy, dammit," she said, muttering to herself. "Can't you, just this once, stick to a plan?"

43

MESSAGE BOY

"**M**adame Vice President, if I may?"

Fleming D'Enfant turned to face the Cabinet and attending Marines and Secret Service.

"Army Chief of Staff Strom Thornton has acted to assure the orderly execution of government," he said. "We have uncovered strong evidence, which he will be transmitting on television any moment now, that points to a Persian conspiracy to attack the White House and hold the Cabinet hostage."

"Oh, you mean the way *he's* attacking the White House and holding us hostage?" Telepsen asked. "We need to turn on the media center right now."

Queenan turned to D'Enfant.

"Is this part of Operation Intangible?" she asked.

D'Enfant stared at her.

"Where did you hear about *that*?" he asked in a tone more suitable for an underling.

"Never mind where I heard about it," Queenan said. "Answer the question. Is this or is it not part of Operation Intangible?"

D'Enfant squeezed his lips together in irritation. He scowled.

"No, we rolled Intangible up into Operation Integrity. It's much wider in scope now."

"*Wider?*" she asked. "How *much* wider? Wider *how?*" Her face was twisted in anger, a horrific face, a face no one in the room had seen before.

"Just look out the front door," D'Enfant said. He looked and sounded lame, as if he wished he could drop straight down through the floor and never be seen again. Just then, Queenan heard a voice from the other side of the room.

"Madame Vice President," Roundy said. "You've got to see this."

• • •

Fuchs continued to monitor her dashboards to make sure everything was going as planned. Most importantly, she had segmented operations so that units normally in communication with each other were left on their own. Internal networks were maintained, but internetwork links and external links to the outside world were severed, without exception. She waited to see who would prevail, the President or the General. Due to the shutdown of White House communications, she had no idea that Joan Queenan was now Acting President.

• • •

Queenan stared at the screens sitting side by side. The images were disparate but connected in a way that few others than she could appreciate. On the left, she saw a CNN screen displaying documents about Persian plans to attack the White House and Capitol Hill. On the right, she saw images of the White House surrounded by U.S. Army troops, including tanks with their cannons aimed squarely at the center of the White House.

Colonel Sam Chin, who had been nearby but silent during the entire escapade, finally walked forward and spoke up.

"Madame Vice President, I think it's time for me to do my job. Let me deliver that document to Congress for you. Personally."

Queenan turned to look at him more closely than usual: He thought of her look as sardonic.

"And how do you propose to do *that?*" she asked. "Have you looked out there? It's not just tanks in front. Look at the troops on the south lawn."

"That's my job, Madame Vice President. And in case you're wondering, your Secret Service man in charge is one of my all-time best friends, Dennis Camacho. We've already got a plan figured out."

"Then go to it, Colonel." She didn't smile, but her look conveyed confidence. She handed him the envelope and saluted him. He almost smiled but caught himself and saluted back. Then he was gone.

Inside the Situation Room, the Cabinet huddled and waited. Everyone watched the TV monitors that lined the walls. Most of them focused on CNN or the C-SPAN webcams, while others watched the White House security cameras providing three-hundred-sixty-degree coverage of the grounds. Army troops on the east, west, and south sides had all established positions. Having done sizable damage to the lawn, they were now dug in. So far, no one was moving in to take direct control of the White House.

• • •

Sam Chin never acted on impulse. When he offered to deliver the document to Capitol Hill, he already had a plan. Now that he had permission, his plan seemed like a far less certain proposition.

In a narrow corridor of the White House basement, Dennis Camacho waited for Chin. The longtime Secret Service special agent was average in height and build. His salt-and-pepper hair and horn-rimmed glasses marked him to the outside world as unexceptional – exactly as his job required. He was stone-faced except when he spoke; then he erupted with a passionate voice.

As Chin approached, he saw the look on his old friend's face – a look of urgency, the look of a man with a mission. Camacho waved and said, "Follow me." He headed off at a trot. Chin raced to catch up.

"I'm not going to explain this route to you," Camacho said. "Just take my word that Stormy doesn't know. Neither does anyone else in his command." What followed for Chin was a jumble of corkscrew turns in utility tunnels. Without a map, he was directionally challenged. Eventually he followed his friend up a small stairwell that led to a utility door. With a push of the handle, they were outside. When they emerged,

Chin saw they were in Lafayette Park – not an optimal location for the trek to Capitol Hill, but it would do.

With Chin in uniform, they had no trouble walking out to Pennsylvania Avenue. Army vehicles and troops continued to rush from all directions toward the White House, ignoring them.

"Looks like you've got Capitol Hill to yourself, Sam," Camacho said. "Now I have to get back inside."

"Thanks, Dennis," Chin said, slapping him on the shoulder in affection. "I'll see you again when this is all over."

"Wait! I almost forgot!"

Chin stopped.

"What is it?"

"We've taken the Speaker and Senate president pro tempore to a safe location for the duration of this emergency. Even I don't know where they are."

Chin swore. He stood for a moment, looking off to the side, as if trying to recall a long-lost memory.

"I've got an idea. Leave this to me. You get back to the Presidents."

Camacho flashed him an informal salute with his fingers, grinned, and turned on his heel. He ran back into the stairwell as Chin raced toward the Capitol.

Once there, he entered through the front. He looked around in surprise. Except for a bit more foot traffic than usual and a louder buzz of chatter, you would never know that only a couple of miles away, the Army was threatening to attack the White House. Chin pulled out his satellite phone and verified that he had a signal again – not so much a gamble that paid off as his only play. He punched in a number for his forensics unit.

"I need to know *now* where the Secret Service has the House Speaker. Can you tap their networks and get back to me pronto?" Chin listened for a minute and nodded. "Christ, that was *fast!* Sometime soon, you're going to have to show me how you do that. Later." He hung up and headed for a little-known sub-basement break room normally used by the lowliest of House employees. His memory of the building layout was rusty, but good enough to get him there. He was in such a hurry that he rushed right into a duo of Secret Service agents protecting the room, guns already drawn. When they saw him, they all aimed directly at him.

Chin threw his arms out for protection, waving at the agents.

"Colonel Samuel Chin, Cyber Command," he shouted. "I have an urgent message from the President for the Speaker of the House and the Senate President pro tempore."

The agents hesitated for a moment.

"I've got to get confirmation for this," the senior man said. He started to speak into a microphone attached at his shoulder. When he did, the younger one looked at him for a moment; that was all Chin needed. He leaped for the less experienced man and put his handgun to the man's throat.

"We don't have time!" Chin shouted. "There's a national emergency, and we can fix things if I can just deliver this letter - *right now!*" The senior agent hesitated; he stood in place with his gun arm outstretched in Chin's direction but had no clear shot. As he stood there, motionless, Chin edged his way through the door with his hostage serving as protection.

He entered the room only to see a roomful of Congressional leaders cowering against the back wall. He continued to hold his gun to the Secret Service agent's throat as he shouted.

"Colonel Samuel Chin, United States Army, Cyber Command. I'm here under the direct order of the Cabinet and the Acting President of the United States, Joan Queenan."

A collective gasp arose from the room.

44

FACING THE TROOPS

After a wait that seemed like forever, a courier showed up to deliver a message to Queenan. She listened and nodded. Looking at the cCabinet, she stood and addressed them directly.

"Our message has been delivered directly to the Speaker and President pro tempore of the Senate. Now we have to find a way to announce it to the world," she said. "Without any external telecomm, we have no way to get the word out."

"I think I can help."

All eyes turned to look at the confident visage of Charles Russell Davidson, President of the United States.

• • •

Davidson led the group out of the Situation Room, up a series of stairwells he seemed to know perfectly. The route took them around and out the front, north face of the White House. As he, Queenan, and the Cabinet approached the massive doorway, they looked out in amazement at the assemblage of U.S. Army trucks, tanks, and soldiers facing them. Several military helicopters, with machine guns cocked and ready, hovered nearby. All guns seemed to point directly at them.

Davidson started to walk out by himself, but Queenan hurried forward.

"With all respect, Mister President," she said, "it would be better if you let me handle this."

They stopped and looked directly at each other. Davidson had his hand up over his eyes to shield them from the sun, but Queenan was facing away from it.

"It's not about you, sir. If I'm going to have their respect, I have to earn it. You can't earn it for me."

Davidson looked at her. This time she did not see an empty shell. She saw the man who had selected her for Vice President.

"I know you can do it," he said. "I wish I could."

"I know," she said. Then she turned toward the tanks and walked into history.

45

TAKING CONTROL

"First they killed the Chairman, and now they've killed General Forbus," Stormy Thornton said. He was videoconferencing with Claudia Fuchs, who remained in her secure room in Area 53.

"I haven't seen any ELINT on it," Fuchs said, puzzlement showing on her face. "Do you have direct confirmation?" Watching him pace in and out of view as he talked, she picked up a bottle of water and took a long swig while awaiting his reply.

"From a captain on the scene, yes," he said, turning to face her. "We also have confirmed data that the White House has been targeted for an external attack."

"It's a good thing you anticipated that with your troops," she said, carefully walking a thin line between honesty and flattery. "But isn't this a day early? May Day is tomorrow."

"Granted," Thornton said. "But events accelerated the timetable for us. We have good reason to believe the President and Vice President have both been targeted."

"In that case, shouldn't they be physically separated, sir? Aren't they both at the White House right now?"

"Yes, yes ... how did you know that?"

"At Cyber Command, we make it our business to know. Sir. Why else would you recruit me?"

Thornton stared at the phone as if it were a hand grenade, letting that sink in for a moment. He had this sudden feeling that in a heartbeat, Claudia Fuchs could go from being his number one asset to his number one nightmare. In the digital domain, she could do things that no one else could approach. No one he could trust, at any rate. Removing her from the scene would not be a simple matter, or even a certain one.

"General, I have been given orders by the President to activate Operation Integrity. We must protect the President and Vice President at all costs. Furthermore, we must protect our assets in the Persian Gulf that are under imminent threat. We must engage in preemptive action against our preidentified target array in Persia."

"Sir, we do not own our own comm at this time. If we send orders to our ships through standard comm, the Chinese will intercept it and use it against us."

"That's why I'm counting on you, General. Forget about the comm. Implement Operation Integrity and take direct control of the ships. *You* control the horizontal. *You* control the vertical. *You* pull the trigger. *You* lead us into battle."

"Yes, sir!" Fuchs saluted into thin air and disconnected.

● ● ●

Joan Queenan walked across the White House lawn and straight up to the closest tank. Television cameras from CNN, NBC, CBS, ABC, FOX, BBC, Al Jazeera, and a half-dozen other overseas news networks followed her steps. They broadcast her movements in real time to more than one-third of the world, none of whom knew that she was now Acting President. To all watching, it appeared that the tank's cannon lowered imperceptibly, as if targeting her.

As she approached, a general officer emerged from behind the tank, armed only with a sidearm in a belt holster. He approached warily until he recognized her. Then he saluted.

"Madame Vice President!" He curled his spine backward in a parody of spinal rectitude. Queenan saluted back.

"At ease, General. General, you are hereby notified that pursuant to a vote of the President's Cabinet and the Twenty-Fifth Amendment to the Constitution, I have been appointed Acting President due to presidential incapacity."

"Presidential incapacity? With all due respect, ma'am, I see the President standing right over there. Doesn't look incapacitated to me."

"He doesn't look it, General, but the first time you get a chance to chat with him, you'll get the idea. *If* he recognizes you. His memory is going. The president has been diagnosed with Alzheimer's."

The brigadier general stood there, stunned. His mouth hung open for a moment.

"But I can't expect you to take me at my word, General," Queenan said. She held out an iPad that had been delivered with the courier from the Capitol. She tapped the screen twice, activating a video.

In the video stood a group of Democratic and Republican Congressional leaders, each recognizable. The woman standing in front spoke first.

"I, Angela Percussi, Speaker of the United States House of Representatives, hereby certify that I, as well as the President pro tempore of the Senate, Joe Jalisco, have received a letter from the President's Cabinet, signed by all members, testifying that they have voted to make the Vice President, Joan Queenan, Acting President due to presidential incapacity. The details will be forthcoming, but I understand the President has an illness that cannot be cured. Our prayers are with the President for a speedy recovery, and with Acting President Joan Queenan. We must all offer her our support and guidance in the coming days and weeks."

The general looked at Queenan with new respect. She gave him a serious look with flat-lined lips, neither a smile nor a frown.

"I'm satisfied, Madame *Acting* President. If I may, I'd like my tech to transmit this to all the troops. Clearly we're not needed here."

"Perhaps not, General. Stand down. Have *everyone* stand down. But until we get this sorted out, stick around. Turn the troops around, facing outward. Before this is all over with, I may yet need your help."

46

VIDEOCONFERENCE

"**D**amn! Now she's just rubbing it in!"

Fran Gaul's Senate colleague and would-be presidential contender Jon Thum watched MSNBC's video of Queenan in front of the troops facing the White House. They stood in Gaul's Senate office, watching with drinks in hand. Gaul, who knew more about the situation than his buddy would ever suspect, just chuckled.

"No, but she *is* taking advantage," Gaul said as they watched the screen. The only audio came from a clueless pundit making lame observations. Everyone watched as, by all appearances, Queenan dismissed Brigadier General Richard Thornbridge after showing him a video on an iPad. As he walked away, apparently giving orders to his officers, Queenan walked up to the nearby tank as casually as if she was inspecting a flower garden. A young soldier with an automatic weapon stood near an open hatch.

They watched as Queenan appeared to identify herself. When the soldier scrambled to salute, she saluted back and waved him down. The soldier approached her timidly, gun pointed toward the ground. She waved him over. Clearly surprised, he handed the weapon to her. She cocked and examined it, pointed it to the sky and peered up the scope, popped the magazine and slammed it back in, and finally handed it back to the soldier, nodding her approval. His instant grin would adorn more than five dozen magazine and news websites in the coming week.

"Shee-it, pardner, I hope it's not too late for you to run for re-election," Gaul said to Thum. "Coz you ain't got *nothin'* on her."

• • •

Army Chief of Staff Strom Thornton stood in front of his media center wall. His conference room rarely held more than three people, because it was designed specifically for multiuser videoconferencing. Upon his wall he saw, in real time, all his theater commanders. Half of them had a direct hand in the preparations for Project May Day, while the others stood by for unexpected events.

"Commanders, thank you all for getting with me as we count down to H-hour and D-day."

The generals and admirals, who had video setups similar to Stormy's, exchanged glances across the screens as if they were in the same room together.

"General Thornton, sir, a lot has changed in the last twenty-four hours. Is Project May Day still a go?"

"Not only is May Day a go, General Windfire, but we have initiated protocols to convert our bearings from May Day to May Showers."

"May Showers?"

"Operation May Showers. Generals, we have intercepted traffic between the Persian and Chinese fleets indicating plans to attack our forces at the tail end of the May Day exercise, when our forces normally would be the least prepared."

Windfire looked at him with skepticism.

"General, we have that traffic. We cannot confirm. In any event, forewarned is forearmed. We are ready for anything they could hope to throw at us, sir." Windfire stared hard at Thornton, as if challenging him.

"Just because we are ready does not mean they *know* we are ready, General."

"All due respect, General, we have not used stealth in our preparations. We've made *sure* that anyone paying attention *knows* that we are ready to give fire at a moment's notice."

"Still..."

"Listen to him, General."

Everyone turned to the new voice. In a new window of the videoconference app, the face of an angry General George Forbus popped up.

"Everyone but me, General!" Forbus said, challenging Stormy with a glare as well as his words.

"Huh?" Thornton said, clearly flabbergasted.

"You invited all the theater commanders, even SpaceCom, but somehow I got left out. A man doesn't earn four stars by committing common oversights."

"No, he earns four stars by learning who will step up to the plate when the ball needs to be hit out of the park," Stormy said, huffing. "You haven't got what it takes, General."

"Haven't got what it *takes?*" Forbus demanded. "Haven't got what it *takes?* You see where I am right now?"

As he spoke, his angry voice rose in tone. The camera pulled back to show Forbus sitting upright in a hospital bed, a large bandage across his left shoulder and chest.

"I was *attacked* in my *own office* this afternoon! By soldiers all missing in action, presumed dead, in Afghanistan! How do you explain *that*, General?"

"Well...well..." Thornton said, stumbling, flabbergasted. Playing defense was not a role he was used to. "Have you questioned them?"

"No, they're all dead. We thought one might live, but when I shoot, I don't aim for the foot. I may be a desk jockey now, but I've maintained my proficiency with firearms. Anyway, close-up work with a Mossberg doesn't require skill, just intention.

"Generals, I am here right now for several reasons. The main reason is that I should have been invited but I wasn't. I wasn't invited because General Thornton thought I was dead. He thought I was dead because he arranged for it, just as he arranged for the death of General Caesare."

The theater commanders, who had been watching Forbus closely as he spoke, abruptly changed their attention to Thornton, who looked down.

"What else?" Windfire demanded.

"I'm also here because the general plans to use fake intelligence to make it look like we are about to be attacked. He's even trying to make it look like we have been infiltrated from within."

"Why would he do that?"

"Because he disagrees with the President's Persian policy, General. As many of us do. But the difference is, we are loyal to the nation and to the Constitution, so we suck it in. Instead, General Thornton discovered, before anyone else, a huge secret: the President has Alzheimer's."

The generals looked back and forth at each other. Too many surprises in too short a period of time.

"Then it's true?" General Gerard Behrsberg asked. Behrsberg was commander in chief of the Space Command, having been appointed by Davidson only a few months before.

"It's true," Forbus said, shaking his head. "I've seen the paperwork – the *real* paperwork. Plus I've seen the private physician's notes. The president is near the end of the early stage. For a normal person, that means stay home, have a part-time caregiver, and give up the car keys. If he's a hunter, he gives up his guns. For the man with his finger on the nuclear trigger..."

"That's all well and good, but you're accusing a top commander of engineering a coup d'état. He's the Army Chief of Staff, for God's sake!" Behrsberg said. "We need more evidence than just your word."

"Will *my* word be good enough, General?" A new window popped open. This time, the face of a civilian appeared – Acting President Joan Queenan.

47

GENERAL SHOWDOWN

dmiral Tanner McDonough stood at the helm of the *U.S.S. Ronald Reagan*. He looked out and saw stars everywhere, a sign of clear skies in all directions, in spite of a persistent weather bulletin that promised rain showers. He despised weathermen as he did all incompetents.

McDonough's rough complexion reflected the harshness of life at sea. He was not quite as fit as many of the top commanders, and recently hip problems forced him to use a cane, at least until he could find time for a hip replacement. At this point in his career, that could mean retirement, and he wasn't ready.

His carrier group took the lead position in the Project May Day exercises. Elements of his task force had new orders, received in the last hour from Stormy Thornton on a hardware-encrypted device known to only one of his sailors, a former Navy SEAL sidelined by injuries. His personal loyalty was beyond question. Having sustained his injuries on a covert mission the previous year in the Country Formerly Known as Iran, he was completely on board with Operation May Showers.

McDonough called in the ship's commander, Rear Admiral Nelson Briggs. Briggs wore thick-lensed spectacles that would have been impossibly heavy in the days of glass lenses.

"Admiral, prepare for new orders," he said to Briggs. "Due to new intelligence received, we are officially transitioning from Project May Day to Operation May Showers. Do you understand what that means?"

"Aye, aye, *sir!*" Briggs said in answer, saluting. He waved over his executive officer, who waited nearby.

"You heard the man!" he said in a bellow. "DEFCON 1! We're going to war! You prepare the ship, while I relay operational orders to the other vessels. We need our birds in the air and our sharks underwater. Tell them to arm the darts."

• • •

"Generals, at three thirty-eight this afternoon, the Speaker of the House of Representatives and the President pro tempore of the senate received notification of the President's incapacity from the Cabinet. The vote was ten to six. Effective the moment they received the notification, I became Acting President."

"Did you take the oath of office?" Behrsberg asked.

"There is no oath of office for Acting President," Queenan said. "Not in the Constitution anyway, and Congress never passed legislation to that effect. Just the oath of office I took on Inauguration Day, which is almost identical in form and substance."

"Still, it wouldn't hurt," Behrsberg said.

"General, we're on treacherous ground here. Without question some people will accuse me of engineering a takeover of the presidency. As you will discover, I did not initiate these proceedings. They were initiated by the Secretary of State, Cameron Romulet. So if I took an oath of office that wasn't needed, it might be seen as my trying to completely take over the presidency. Which I'm not. I encourage all of you to reread the Twenty-Fifth Amendment, so you can be certain of the mechanism. The president has the power to reassert his authority at any time."

"Kind of tough making decisions under those circumstances," Behrsberg said, relenting. "I don't think any of us envy you your position." Several of the generals agreed by shaking their heads vigorously. "What are your orders?"

"Project May Day, Operation May Showers, and all related operations and activities are hereby canceled until further notice. Stand down. Prepare to return your forces to their prior positions of two weeks ago, pending our review. These are direct orders."

Thornton jumped to his feet and shouted, "Madame Acting President, I must protest!" He began pacing in a fury. "We have incontrovertible evidence that the Persian Navy plans to launch nuclear missiles at our carrier group, preceded by a Chinese cyber attack. We cannot back down at this time."

"We can and will," Queenan said. She scowled; she had never liked the man and no longer felt the need to pretend. "I've seen the data. There is no reason to believe Persia can deliver its two nuclear bombs as airborne warheads. General, you are relieved of your command. You are to remain in your office, which is now under guard until we can determine whether a court-martial is in order."

Open-mouthed, Thornton ran to his door, where two large MPs, one with non-comm stripes and the other a major, turned and glowered at him without saluting. He walked back to the video monitor and poked a button on his keyboard.

"You're going to thank me for the video you're about to see." Looking back at his captors, who remained at the door, he picked up a remote unit and clicked. A live feed of Tammany Dreidel, the President's chief of staff, came on.

"General, I have the letter right here," he said with an oily smile. In his hand, he held a letter of two sentences, clearly printed on White House stationary. He held the letter up so that all could clearly see the words: "I hereby declare my incapacity ended. I resume all rights and responsibilities of President of the United States." It was signed by Charley Davidson, whose signature was familiar to all.

48

OUT OF CONTROL

Back on the helm of the *Ronald Reagan*, Nelson Briggs had barely gotten orders out to the fleet before the new orders came in: stand down. Swearing, he phoned Admiral McDonough, who had briefly left the deck. McDonough reappeared in moments.

"Admiral, we have new orders directly from Admiral Bana."

"Bana? Why him? He's Acting Chairman of the Joint Chiefs. He doesn't order us. General Thornton is commander for the duration of the exercise."

"Sir, General Thornton has been fired. We are ordered to end the exercise immediately. We are back to DEFCON 3. Apparently the general was not authorized to make that call, and he got canned. Queenan is Acting President. She ordered Acting Chairman Bana to take control of the situation. He has ordered us to recall all vessels."

McDonough stood there with his mouth hanging open.

Goddamn. I can't believe I let Stormy rope me into this conspiracy of his. It's every man for himself. I stayed out of those damn videoconferences of Stormy's, so maybe there's no record. Stormy may have the brains and balls of an ox, but he's no rat. As long as I play it straight, I have a chance.

"Sir?"

He snapped his mouth shut.

"What happened to Charley Davidson?"

Briggs tilted the left side of his head down while presenting a half-smile on his right. It was a subconscious tick of his that told McDonough that he was not unhappy about some turn of events.

"They say he has Alzheimer's. He's still President, technically, but the VP's Acting President now."

"I'll be double-damned. Have you given the stand-down orders yet?"

"No, sir, just about to."

"Get to it, man! The last thing we need is an accidental war."

Briggs scrambled to pick up the nearest phone and started shouting out orders. Before he finished the first call, McDonough was back on deck, furiously figuring out how to keep his head down.

• • •

During Queenan's exchange with the other commanders, Forbus was distracted by messages he received on the iPad – it had so many custom mods required by the military that he called an mPad – sitting on the food tray by his hospital bed. He pulled up a real-time map showing ocean and air activity of U.S. armed forces in the Persian Gulf region. He watched in horror as he saw some U.S. forces still preparing to attack. If he could realize it so easily, he knew the Chinese were way ahead of him. How far would they go?

While Queenan talked with the other generals, he sent her a text message. His large fingers had trouble keeping pace: the tiny virtual keyboard, he thought, was made for children, not men. Queenan had never given him her private mobile number, but his position gave him better access than any one person on the planet, or at least, so he hoped. *Persian Gulf on the brink*, he texted. *Communications to the region compromised and jammed.*

"Generals, we have breaking news in the Gulf, so we have to cut this short. The president's letter does not take effect until it is delivered to the Congressional leadership, which is under lockdown in an undisclosed location. Given his condition, it will have to be backed up by a personal appearance. Until such time as we have confirmation of that delivery, I am retaining authority as Acting President.

"Generals, we are on the brink of a war that no one asked for or needs. Our satellites show elements of the *Ronald Reagan* carrier group still preparing to attack. *Stand down.* Anyone not willing to implement my orders can feel free to resign his command right now."

• • •

Back on the *Ronald Reagan*, Tanner McDonough watched the radar screen in horror.

"Admiral!" he shouted. Nelson Briggs, on the other end of the command deck, turned around abruptly.

"Sir?"

"We have orders to stand down!"

"Sir, I have given the orders to all the vessels in our fleet and verified."

"Our new destroyers are not obeying orders, Admiral," McDonough said. "The *Zumwalt* is headed upstream. According to our projections, she will be within target range of Tehran within three hours. The *Michael Monsoor* and the *Lyndon Johnson* are headed downstream, toward the Chinese fleet."

Briggs punched buttons on a communications console while he spoke. McDonough noticed sweat beading between the short-short bristles on the top of his head and unconsciously wiped his brow; he never liked his men to see him sweat, even on the battlefield.

"Sir, no response from the *Zumwalt*. Or the *Michael Monsoor*. Or the *Lyndon B. Johnson*."

• • •

Queenan stared at the generals and admiral. They looked back at her, unflinching. Finally Windfire, his aging face prickly with a day's growth, spoke up.

"The problem, Madame Acting President, is that our communications are spotty. We're communicating with our forces in the Gulf, but we're not the only ones. All electronic means have been compromised. It appears that Stormy, I mean, General Thornton, has control over the Cyber Command."

Queenan look at Forbus.

"General, how could that be? Who's taken control of your command?"

Forbus just stared.

Queenan looked at the Secretary of the Navy, a political appointee she had never had dealings with before

"Mister Secretary? Let's get the admirals on the line to explain this situation."

The secretary, a former yacht manufacturer, nodded at one of the non-comm specialists in the corner of the room. Within seconds, Admiral Bana was on the screen, but his back was turned as he spoke into his own communications console, to persons unknown. Suddenly a voice blared at him through a speaker, and he turned around abruptly. When he saw Queenan on the screen, he flushed but snapped to attention and saluted.

"Madame President!" he snapped.

Queenan sighed.

"Just to be clear, Admiral, I'm Acting President. But until Charley Davidson says otherwise, I'm your Commander in Chief."

"Ma'am!"

"Admiral, I've ordered a complete stand-down of all forces, and yet our three most modern destroyers have gone rogue. What's going on? Tell me about these ships."

"Ma'am, the *Zumwalt* class are ships with multiple missions, but they are best suited for land attack. You can see them up here on the display."

"They look like the old ironclads."

"That's what everyone says. They are replacing battleships, so they are also suited for surface attack and support as well. The main thing is, they have a completely integrated cybernetic system for fire and navigation control."

"You mean remote control, like drones?"

"In theory, yes, ma'am. Though it's never been tested."

"Was that test part of Project May Day?"

"Well, uh…"

"Well? Was it or wasn't it?"

"Ma'am. I honestly don't know. I'm not privy to all of General Thornton's plans."

Windfire cleared his throat judiciously.

"We need to get this matter settled, pronto. And we need to make sure Stormy is secured, without outside communications, so that if Dreidel does make it to Capitol Hill, he still can't do anything to reactivate Project May Day, or May Showers, or whatever the hell it's called now."

• • •

After leaving Capitol Hill, Sam Chin had rushed to Forbus' hospital room, where he watched the entire conference from a corner with no video coverage. As soon as it disconnected, he spoke to the general, whose face showed evidence of far more pain than he had allowed the other commanders to see.

"Sir, I'd lay hundred-to-one odds that the keys to the treasure room, so to speak, are out in Nevada, at Area 53. General Fuchs' operation out there looked pretty complete to me. It's isolated and secured. I think it will even take a nuclear blast, as long as it's not a dead-on hit. When's the last time you communicated with her?" He watched the African-American general as he carefully tried to get comfortable on his hospital bed.

"Well, I was busy, you know. But my understanding is that communications with Area 53 went silent at exactly the same time as the White House and Capitol Hill – which are still off-net, you know. Their local nets remain functional, but they have no Internet and no external e-mail. Phones are down, too. So the troops that Stormy sent in are now being used to protect them, just in case."

"Yes, sir. Sir, I volunteer to go to Area 53, right now, to personally shut down the operation. We don't know whether General Fuchs was part of Stormy's operation, or if she's just following orders, but either way, she's about to get us into a shooting war."

"Go, son, and take some troops with you." He stopped for a moment, failing in his effort to suppress a groan. "But we sure as hell don't have any time to waste. Let's get you some very special wheels."

• • •

Moments later on a helipad outside the building, Forbus gave Chin some final instructions. He sat in a wheelchair, the bandaged leg sticking out into the air, as the colonel prepared to step into the waiting Marine helicopter.

"Hand this letter directly to General Fuchs," he said, passing over an unmarked envelope. From the thickness Chin could tell it contained a single sheet of paper.

"This letter gives you complete command authority over Area 53. It orders General Fuchs to come to Fort Meade immediately for a review of the last two weeks' events."

"Won't I have a problem with any other general staff on the base?"

Forbus shook his head, the tension evident. Chin watched him manage the pain but said nothing.

"Area 53 is run by a three-star because of the seriousness of the subject matter, not because it's top-heavy with generals. You'll be in charge until we get things sorted out. It will be your job to determine all the plans, who is behind them, and who is culpable."

"Culpable?"

"Yes. Most soldiers just follow orders and do their jobs. In our business, need to know is very restricted. They may be puzzled or surprised by their orders, but they just follow them. Most will put a happy face on it and assume that there's a bigger picture out there that makes everything right."

"Hasn't it always been that way in military affairs? I don't mean just here and now, but throughout history."

Forbus grunted. As he spoke, his Mississippi accent seemed thicker than ever.

"We're warriors, not historians. History is for the survivors. For now, let's focus on surviving. Speaking of surviving, we have a very special plane for you to travel in. It's a souped-up version of the old Oxcart series the Agency created out at Area 51 in the fifties and sixties. It'll do Mach 4.1 on a good day."

"Jesus, Mach 4! Will I pass out?"

"Be sure to let me know."

• • •

Chin's enthusiasm for his mission waned when he saw the plane that was supposed to take him to the airfield at Area 51. Its long neck and minimal body looked more like a snake with fins than a bird with wings. He craned his own neck in an attempt to get a good look at the cockpit, but it was no use; wherever the seats were, they were buried in the neck. He imagined it would be as comfortable as Harry Potter's bedroom under the staircase, without the family ambience. Beyond the plane, the late-afternoon sky was roiling with storm clouds anxious to break loose, providing a dramatic backdrop for this strange plane. While he stood in the hangar that housed the carbon-composite miracle of engineering, he felt a hard slap on his shoulder, from behind.

"You old dog!"

Even before turning, he recognized the booming voice of Fran Gaul.

"You're not goin' somewhere fun without me?"

Chin turned and looked at the senator.

"This ain't exactly a fun-vee," he said with a broad smile. "Are you the reason I got a bird with an extra jump seat?"

"Exactamundo. Well, not exactly. It's a fringe benefit of getting the fastest plane on the planet, which the generals and politicians decided to make functional as well as fast. So sometimes it ferries VIPs halfway around the world on a moment's notice."

"Must be kind of expensive to use as a taxi," Chin said.

"Sssht. Guys like me know how to spend money, but guys like your boss know how to *use* money. Today it's my job to escort you and actually get you inside Area 53. This is one of those times when being an old-timer comes in handy. I was part of the Armed Services crew that actually helped build the place."

"Area 51?"

"No, Area 53. It was carved out of that there Nevada Test Range back in the nineties, after they ended the nuclear testing. Way back when, in the fifties, I guess, they divided the range into fifty-two numbered areas – and you know which one is most famous. Area 51. But later we added one more. It's never been anything but a center for cyber command activities, even before there was a Cyber Command."

49

SECRET BACK DOORS

The officer and his men approached the front door of Area 53 – at least, what they were told was the front door – with a healthy dose of skepticism, since the idea of attacking a nuclear-hardened structure with a light-weapon platoon seemed just plain silly. Still, orders were orders.

Two doors were jammed into the side of the mountain. One was a structure of heavy corrugated metal, a half-moon lying on its flat side, large enough to accept huge trucks. Only the wavy structure of the metal kept it from looking like a gigantic guillotine. The approach to the door was a winding road built into the natural floor of the mountain structure. The towering sides of nearby mountains, along with the winding passes, provided substantial protection against an attack by air.

To the left the soldiers approached a second smaller door just large enough to accept them walking in single file. Made of the same heavy metal as its larger counterpart, it had no doorknob, latch, handle, or any other obvious means of opening. Not even a lock was visible. Above the door was an array of three swivel-mounted cameras protected by a box made of bulletproof polycarbonate. The thickness suggested it could protect at least against nine-millimeter ammunition, which was more than they were packing.

Major Arnold Rodriguez walked up to the door alone. His lieutenant watched while the sergeants tried without success to discern a pattern to the camera movements. An operator, perhaps more than one, was controlling the cameras.

Not knowing what else to do, Rodriguez walked up to the door and rapped on it with his gloved knuckles.

"Hello! Anyone home?"

He felt silly shouting to a metal door, but he was sure a microphone was hidden somewhere. He was certain they were seen and heard. More striking was the stillness of the barren Nevada desert around him. The surroundings felt eerie, reminding him of a movie moment where a character suddenly seems frozen in time and steps outside of his own body, noticing the complete stillness of everything around him. The ground and rocks were a uniform tan, except for the oily green creosote bushes dotting the landscape. The perfectly still little leaves on the bushes betrayed not a hint of a breeze. Not a bird or insect was to be seen or heard in the sky; snakes were surely hiding in the rocks nearby, but they were not apparent. Though still only late spring, the solar onslaught was relentless though not yet deadly. Still, only the shade of the mountainside kept the heat in check.

• • •

On another side of the mountain, Sam Chin and Fran Gaul crawled up the traces of a wash formed from an old rain gutter. Rain was not common in the desert, but when it came, it often struck with a fury that cut deep alleys into the sandy earth, which tended to be half filled with detritus: large sharp rocks carried by sudden flooding. When the desert showers ended, the flooding ended like a spigot turned off, and the rocks dropped in place.

Gaul provided a running commentary for Chin. The senator's physical condition had deteriorated since his military days. Since he had to lead the way, the going was slower than Chin liked.

"Back when they first started marking out the Nevada Test Range into areas, they discovered there were quite a few old, played-out mines. Silver mostly, but some gold as well. Probably some uranium, too, if they looked for it, but no one's looking anymore. They found quite a few old prospectors. They managed to run them off with various forms of encouragement."

"I'll bet," Chin said, with no attempt to hide his sarcasm. He was in better physical shape for this kind of fieldwork. Gaul was out of shape, but by moving slowly and having dressed for safari, he had yet to break a sweat. He was helped by Chin carrying the heavier pack.

"We're looking for an old mine entrance that was never really covered over properly. It's not much more than a cave that was useful because it's a natural tunnel into the mountain."

"So you cut a secret entrance into the mine shaft?"

"Something like that," Gaul said.

"How can you be sure no one knows about it anymore? For that matter, how can you be sure it even works? When was the last time you used it?"

"I can't be sure," Gaul said. "And it's been years. We're winging it, my friend. But now you know why I told you to bring some C-4, just in case."

"Is that the entrance?" Chin asked. He pointed at a dark indentation in the side that seemed roughly man-sized. He thought of his childhood distaste for dark, enclosed spaces; it had never been tested in all his years as a soldier. Now it would be. He had a bad taste in his mouth, so he swallowed and ignored it. He focused his thoughts entirely on getting inside the mountain.

"Let me lead, Sam," Gaul said. "I've been here before. If I need your help..."

"You know where to find me."

Gaul nodded, already walking into the mountain.

• • •

Rodriguez hammered the door with the side of his closed fist. He was a big man; his hands were massive even without the gloves, but the effort was futile. The doors were solid, not hollow. They were so well anchored that his pounding barely made a sound, even in the midst of the desert silence, but still he pounded. The major had no thought of actually breaking through the door, but he did harbor hopes of getting someone interested enough to open the door at least for a moment.

Eventually the pounding paid off. He heard an electronic crackle come from a heretofore unrevealed speaker. Then a voice spoke.

"You have no authorization to enter this facility," the voice said with authority. "You are ordered to leave immediately and return to base."

"Our orders are to enter *this* base," Rodriguez replied.

"This base is sealed by orders of Lieutenant General Claudia Fuchs, operating under direct orders from the President of the United States. We have orders to protect and defend. If you do not leave immediately, we are under orders to remove you by all available means."

• • •

The cave they entered was little more than a crevice, but Chin saw signs of previous use. The sides of the cave were worn smooth; the path was unnaturally clear; and here and there he saw a corner brace, which made him wonder about the reliability of those weak spots. The key, he knew, was to keep moving.

"No lights?" Chin said, joking.

"Just something else to lose, break, or steal," Gaul said. "That's why I tried to make sure our packs came with a little bit of everything in them." Chin looked at him skeptically with those words. Gaul's pack looked like it weighed less than twenty pounds, but Chin knew his own was almost three times that. While he watched, Gaul took off his pack, opened a side pocket, and pulled out two LED flashlights. He handed one to Chin and switched on the other. As it did, he heard the beady rattling sound that made his stomach clench.

"Watch it!" Chin hissed, pulling back. In spite of the light, Gaul had almost stepped on an angry rattlesnake. Chin threw a rock on the deadly creature – hurting it enough to scare it off, but not enough to kill it. It slid off between the rocks without another sound. Gaul just looked at it.

"This way," he said. He waved for Chin to follow him. After no more than ten slow minutes of maneuvering on the sharp rocks, they found themselves at the end of the corridor, facing a sheer wall that went straight up, beyond the reach of their lights. Into the stone wall was set a steel ladder that climbed up into the darkness. A few feet away, they saw a thin drip of water, steady enough to result in moss and algae along the drip line. Chin looked at Gaul.

"*This* is a mining shaft?" he asked.

"No, we just came through the shaft," Gaul said. "Or, rather, what's left of it. Now we're in the part the Air Force built. Didn't I tell you this would be fun?" he said, grinning.

"I was glad when they outfitted me with boots," Chin grumbled. "But now I see that the soles are smooth. With the moisture on the ladder, they're going to be slick as hell."

"Gripe, gripe, gripe," Gaul said. "I thought Army officers were *tough*. Now in flight survival school..."

"Yeah, yeah, yeah," Chin said, climbing behind Gaul. "Just tell me what's going to happen when we get to the top."

• • •

At the words from the hidden speaker, Rodriguez' men tensed up. All weapons were unlocked, cocked, and ready but had no targets except rocks. Then they heard the metallic movement of a device rising up from the rocks above – then another, then another. Three automated chain guns with advanced optic devices, controlled remotely from inside the mountain, raised into the air on heavy metal poles. As they locked into their positions, the barrels of the guns wound downward to point at the soldiers from above. The enlisted men and non-comms tensed, but the major responded calmly to the threat.

"We are here under the order of General George Forbus, commander in chief of Cyber Command and commanding officer of this facility. I hold a letter in my hands – I'm holding it up so you can focus on it – assigning command of this base to Colonel Samuel Chin."

"Are you Colonel Chin?" the voice asked.

"No, I am Major Arnold Rodriguez, operating under orders from Colonel Chin."

"When you can produce Colonel Chin, we can let you in."

Meanwhile, the guns remained pointed at the troops.

• • •

Although the ladder seemed endless, it did not take Gaul and Chin long to approach the top. As they did, Chin's left foot hit a wet spot on a rung and slipped. His right foot groped for purchase, desperately. The minute the burden of the weight went to his hands and upper arms, he knew he could not hold on long without at least one foot on a rung. His heart pounded with fear as he stabilized first his right foot, then found his way back with the left. The slick soles were slippery on the wet, mossy rung, so he took extra care. After a moment he was safe and catching his breath; the whole thing was over before Gaul even realized what was going on.

The ladder rose ten feet higher than the stepping-off level, which was a much larger space than the trail through the crevasses from which they had just emerged. As their glow sticks began fading, they walked around a corner and stopped. In front of them, they saw a seven-foot metal door so secure the mountain appeared to have been built around it. Gaul walked directly up to the security keypad and punched in a number. He was rewarded with a loud electronic click.

"Follow me," he said to Chin. Together they walked through the back door of Area 53.

• • •

As the soldiers watched the elevated automatic weapons, several of them experienced a simultaneous revelation.

"Say, Major –" the lieutenant began.

"Doesn't look like any kind of gun I ever saw," one of the sergeants said for him.

"It's got a long barrel with a hole at the end, and it's pointed at us," another sergeant said. "That's good enough for me."

"But what's that over there?" the first one asked, pointing to a fourth platform that held a device looking more like a flat TV satellite dish than a gun.

"Whatever it is, it's pointed at us, too," the first non-comm said.

"Say, I think that's –" the major started to say, but he froze. Suddenly, without warning or any prior awareness of his next action, he and all his men found themselves running away from the entrances as fast as they could move. The heat ray seemed to follow them as they ran. After a quarter of a mile, they slowed down and stopped.

"What the hell just happened?"

"That, gentlemen, was an active denial system," Major Rodriguez said. "Funny thing is, I just had a briefing on it last week."

"Nothing funny about it," one of the Ranger NCOs said. "It was like a cross between a TASER and a welding torch. My skin felt like it was burning off. I can fight a man, but I can't fight a ray gun."

"That's a ninety-five-gigahertz beam," Rodriguez said. "It only heats up a tiny fraction of the skin, less than a half-millimeter. Regular microwave ovens are 2.45 gigahertz, which is enough to penetrate seventeen millimeters. We can consider ourselves lucky, I guess."

Rodriguez looked at the battle-hardened watch on the inside of his left wrist. Its nonelectronic quartz action allowed it to keep ticking even after taking an electromagnetic licking. If it was one of those new i-watches, he found himself thinking, it would be junk now.

"I hope we bought the colonel enough time," he said. "Because I think we're out of tricks. Anyone feel like ringing the doorbell again?"

● ● ●

As Chin and Gaul entered the corridor, they saw soldiers scurrying around them. A couple of them glanced at Gaul, the only man or woman in sight not in a military uniform, but they kept going. A loudspeaker filled in most of the blanks for them.

"*General quarters—man your defensive assignments. Our front entrance is under assault per the Operation May Showers battle plan contingency ninety-one Q. Prepare to engage the enemy.*"

The voice was digitally crisp and loud to the point of being unnerving. At those words, two corporals rushing past Chin and Gaul stopped to pay closer attention to the visitors.

"Say, who are you two?" one of them demanded, looking at Gaul while the other started pawing his backpack.

"I'm Colonel Samuel Chin," Chin said with a growl. "Since when does a corporal go making demands of a colonel?"

"Since that colonel was a filthy infiltrator," the corporal said and nodded. Behind them, two more soldiers smashed them in the back of their heads with rifle butts.

50

ENTERING THE DRAGON

Chin and Gaul awoke almost simultaneously, as they had been struck carefully and were not out long. Each was lying on a wide wooden plank hanging from the side of a mountain. The planks were attached to the wall with large steel chains attached to iron rings driven into the mountain, with walls of stone on two sides. The fourth wall was formed of metal bars.

"Where are we?" Gaul said, groaning. He opened his eyes slowly and looked around. "Looks like a dungeon cell on Han's island in *Enter the Dragon*," he said, groaning again. "I hope you're Bruce Lee," he said.

"Only if you're Roper," Chin said. He tried to laugh but it was a thin laugh; he was feeling feeble. "But right now, I'd even settle for Williams."

"Wasn't he the one who died?"

"He died so that Bruce Lee and John Saxon could live," Chin said. "Now it's our turn."

"That's for me to decide," a new voice said.

Chin and Gaul looked up.

"Over here," the female voice said. Then they saw the speaker, too high above them to reach. Presumably there was a camera as well, but they could not see one.

"Shades of *Enter the Dragon*," Chin said. "Are you Han?"

"No, I'm General Claudia Fuchs, commander of this base. Hasn't been *that* long! You should recognize my voice, Colonel Chin."

"If you know who I am, you should have a pretty good idea of why I'm here. With no good reason to hold us like this."

"Yes and no. Yes, we've been monitoring electronic transmissions worldwide, at least as they pertain to Project May Day or Operation May Showers. No, I don't know your assigned role in the operation."

"I'm here under direct orders of General Forbus, who is acting under the direct orders of the Commander in Chief of the United States. If you will focus your camera on the document I am holding up, you will see that General Forbus has given command of this base to me, and you are directed to proceed to Fort Meade immediately for debriefing."

"You're very convincing, Colonel. Even though I know the full range of plans for Operation May Showers, including the anticipated cyberwarfare, social engineering, and plain old duplicity, I'm torn. Is your job here really a trick to fool me into giving up control of the base under spurious circumstances? Or are you really here as the general's representative?"

"Of course I'm here as the general's representative," Chin said. "This is no exercise. Think about it. You're in total electronic lockdown here. Even though you know what's going on practically everywhere in the rest of the world, you still don't know what's going on in the White House. General Thornton has attempted a coup this afternoon. Surely you've seen it. Surely you saw the Vice President, I mean, Acting President Queenan, when she stood those troops down. Do you really think that was part of some CIA-inspired battle plan?"

"We don't have time to sort this out, but using Ockham's razor as my guide, I have a pretty strong suspicion. You two come with me."

With that, the door to the cell opened electronically. Two soldiers entered and quickly unlocked their shackles. As Gaul and Chin emerged from the cell, a bit dazed but no worse off than before, Fuchs marched up with a retinue of four APs – the Air Force version of MPs. She slowed only long enough to return Chin's salute and continued down the hall without a word. The colonel and the senator fell in behind the general.

The seven strode quickly through a narrow, winding hallway. Chin wondered about that: The functional utility of narrow halls was suspect, because it was so hard to get large furniture and equipment in and out. He gathered they were based on the internal topography of the mountain, an interesting subject he never expected to get a chance to pursue. Soon they arrived at an electronic cage room just like Fuchs', but large enough to accommodate a half-dozen workers. At the moment, there were only two.

While the Cyber Command's base in Area 53 was littered with mid-level officers, as in most of the military, the real work was still done by the non-commissioned officers. These two would not be chiefs for a couple more years, but they already had a lot of responsibility. Fuchs had tasked one of them to monitor the events outside the White House; the other, the activities in the Persian Gulf.

The two sat at workstations no different from Fuchs', except they had to share the space. They were used to it: Teresa McNeil, 30, was Caucasian but slightly dark-skinned; her red hair was dark, and her five-ten height made her as tall and as gawky as a newly elevated thirteen-year-old. Her partner and occasional sex mate was the same age, shorter, but bulky and self-confident from pumping iron in his free time.

"Look, look!" McNeil said, pointing to her screen.

"Now what, Terry?" Thad Jackson asked. He craned his neck over in a manner designed to be obviously, playfully, intrusive. She swatted him away.

"No, look! See these intercepts that Stormy leaked to the networks? They're not *real!*"

Jackson hissed lightly.

"Show me," a commanding voice said, behind them. The two sergeants whirled around to see General Fuchs. "How can you possibly know that?"

"Because *we created them as part of the original exercise for Project May Day!*" McNeil shouted. "It's dummy data, like in a video game," she said. "Only for real."

"Things are hoppin' today," Jackson observed. "I thought the action was all going to be tomorrow for May Day. Did you see the video in front of the White House, General?"

"No, I was busy making inspections. What's been happening?"

"You really haven't heard?"

"I just told you –"

"We have a new Commander in Chief, at least for now. Acting President Joan Queenan. Look." They all turned to the monitor of CNN news, which replayed the video of Queenan and the tanks over and over again. Fuchs watched in rapt attention. She turned to her visitors.

"You said you were acting under the orders of the Commander in Chief," she said to Chin. An accusation resounded in her voice and flashed from her eyes.

"Yes, I did," he said. He could not hide the sly grin creeping onto his face. "And we are. Vice President Joan Queenan is now Acting President Joan Queenan. And just in case you're wondering, I've seen enough to believe she will be POTUS before the term is over."

"Sweet Jesus," Gaul said, without a trace of reverence. "If she's President, Speaker Percussi will be next in line. She hates my guts because I beat her handpicked feminist girlfriend when I won my first Democratic nomination ten years ago. We've got to protect Queenan at all costs."

"Nothing like well-motivated civic virtue," Chin said with a wry smile.

"Son, you don't want to know what passes for civic virtue in the District."

"Or on the Strip."

"Touché," Gaul said. He laughed without hesitation. "Now let's go save the country."

"The country?" Chin said. "The *world*."

"The *world*," Gaul said, snorting. "Saving America *is* saving the world."

● ● ●

"We don't have a moment to waste," Fuchs said. "Just before your men showed up at the front door, I was monitoring activities in the Persian Gulf. Stormy gave the order for Operation May Showers. I was implementing the battle plan. Now you're saying it's all over?"

"Stand down, right now," Chin said. "Those are the President's direct orders. I was present when she gave those orders to Wild Bill Windfire and all the other theater commanders. She fired Stormy on the spot. You need to do whatever it takes, right now, to turn our ships around."

Fuchs pressed her lips together, clearly tense. Her mind raced with the possibilities. Was he on the level? Or was this an extremely sophisticated ploy to test her readiness? Tests like these were known to destroy previously certain promotions.

"I'm almost convinced," she said in a halting voice. "Bringing a United States senator is a nice touch, I must admit."

"Honey, I helped build this place when you were playing games on your daddy's Commodore 64. I *had* to come. I'm the only one who knows about the back door. Course, we have to have a war, this ain't too bad a place to sit it out."

Fuchs glared at Gaul but said nothing.

"I need assurances. What else you got?"

"Fair enough, but this better do it," Chin said. "We don't have a moment to waste. Go ahead and open a comm channel to the White House. If you get Secret Service, get me Dennis Camacho. He's in charge of the White House detail and we go way back. Otherwise, ask for the Acting President. Her code name is Blondie."

"Blondie. Marvelous."

Within a few moments, Joan Queenan's face filled the screen. Fuchs stood ramrod-straight and snapped out her best salute but had time to notice that Queenan's hair and makeup were as perfect as ever; little did she know how disheveled Queenan had been earlier in the day. She tended to think of such things as narcissistic and had always discounted the Vice President because of it, but suddenly Fuchs wondered if it was really Queenan's personal form of extreme self-discipline. She could respect that.

"Madam Acting President!" she said. "What are your orders?"

"Stand down, General. Shut down Project May Day, Operation May Showers, Operation Integrity, and everything else Stormy had his hand in. I've appointed General Forbus as acting Chief of Staff of the Army, which means I need you to step up and run the Cyber Command. We both know that on a technology level, you've been in charge for a while now. Now you need to take your game to the next level for a full command. Are you up to it?"

"Yes, *ma'am*!" Fuchs said.

"We can talk about the details later. For now, I want you to get to work to turn our ships and planes around. Have we armed any nukes?"

"Uh, uh..."

"Disarm them. Immediately."

"I'm on it now," Fuchs said. Even before this conference, her probability assessments had already calculated the likely winner of this competition. Within moments, she issued orders she had drafted hours before. Almost immediately, the satellites and telemetry began showing signs that American ships were turning back to their prior assignments.

51

ACTING PRESIDENT

I need to stay on top of what's happening here and now. I also need to think ahead. I never formed a comprehensive strategy for governing the way Charley had to. I was always treated like an afterthought that could turn into an aftershock. Now I'm in his shoes. I get it. For now, I go with Charley's way. But by next year, when I run on my own, I have to have my own approach. I have to figure out who I can trust.

"We need to get over to Capitol Hill," Queenan said. She and the entire Cabinet, along with Davidson and their security escorts, had returned to the Cabinet Room to watch events unfold. The cloudy spring afternoon had turned to early evening; dusk almost completely to night. "They may know I'm Acting President, but I doubt that it's sunk in. I need to get over there and seal the deal in person. I need to give reassurances to Congress and the country that the government will continue. I need to reassure anyone who is worried about the generals taking over."

"If I may say, Madame President," Camacho said, "let's take the underground route. We've got enough trams for everyone. We can go through the new tunnels we've set up. The streets outside right now are pretty chaotic. We've got the U.S. Army and an army of protesters and rubberneckers out there like it's a reality TV show. And then we've got another element out there, I suspect, anxious to stir things up. Maybe worse. Plus it would mean a convoy of limousines almost as long as the drive itself."

"It's your call, Special Agent Camacho," Queenan said. "Let's do it."

Camacho nodded.

"Let's go."

With that, they fell into line. Camacho led them to a stairwell under a larger staircase. To Queenan, it seemed like the entrance to a dungeon; Davidson's mind wandered to a movie he had once starred in, where his character was being led away to torture. In his mind he tensed up, waiting for a chance to break free and save everyone.

Eventually Camacho led them through a door. The door opened to a track that looked like something from a game center with go-karts lined up, one behind another. The difference was, these were electric golf carts customized for a special use. The seats were nicer, but perhaps more importantly, the engines were almost twice as fast as traditional golf carts. The drain on the batteries was tremendous, but the underground route was not far.

"How far do we have to go?" Martin Kriton directed his question at Hank Thompson.

"I don't know, a mile or so," Thompson said.

"Several miles," Bantu interrupted. "Even a straight line is more than a mile. Between the utilities and the sewers, this little tunnel does a lot of zigging and zagging."

"You oughta know," Thompson said to the Secretary of Transportation. "Just as long as we don't have to walk it."

"I don't mind," Kriton said, smiling. As he spoke, he looked down at Thompson, almost a full foot shorter than his eighty-inch height.

"Hey, go for it," Thompson said, but Kriton didn't budge.

Not much time was required for everyone to find a cart. Most of the Secret Service agents were walking or jogging. A few rode in the front and back carts, with the Presidents. Conversation among the department heads assumed a tone of normality as they reverted to typical banter about taxi drivers, bodyguards, schedulers, and admins.

Then, all at once, the carts stopped.

"What the –?"

Camacho was startled but caught his words. Just as he began to speak into his collar mic, he saw the heavily armed soldiers, heads covered with balaclavas, approaching around a bend at a rapid pace.

"We've got visitors," he heard in his earpiece.

Then he heard gunfire.

52

UNDERGROUND ASSAULT

Queenan and Davidson were separated by three carts, each with their own squads of Secret Service bodyguards. At the first sound of gunfire, Queenan jerked around toward the direction of the gunfire in back. Davidson was back there, too, she knew. Before she could do or say anything, her protectors grabbed her and quickly moved her off the cart.

"Go – go – go!" one of them shouted. Instead of trying to protect her in place, where they were trapped and the strength of the assault was unknown, they opted to get her into a narrow worker's stairwell that led up to the street. Half of the group followed. A few hundred feet away, a Marine found a second stairwell for Davidson and the remaining Cabinet members. While they scrambled, Camacho barked instructions into his body mic for limousines to meet them on the street.

• • •

The presidents' group emerged moments later into a cement cylinder that opened to the street above ground. With most of the group clustered at the top near the door, Queenan's lead bodyguard spoke up.

"We're waiting for limos," he said to the group. He noticed that few of the Cabinet had not made it; he was concerned, but his only mission was to protect Queenan. "We don't want to be loose on the street without them."

He spoke into his body mic, then listened.

"Several Cabinet members have been shot," he said. "Three Tangos down, two Tangos loose. Let's stay alert."

The wait seemed like an eternity, but it was less than five minutes. To the civilians, it felt like a fire drill that wasn't a drill after all.

"Okay, let's go!"

The lead agent, who held a Hechler & Koch MP5 machine gun, opened the door and led the group out. Every Secret Service agent was visibly armed with MP5s or Glock handguns.

Outside the door was a swirling chaos of street people, rubberneckers, protestors, street organizers, food vendors, police, and soldiers without any orders other than stay in position. Their lieutenant had strung them in a line along the block where Queenan's group emerged. When he and his men saw armed civilians running from the utility door, they immediately converged on the group, guns leveled at the bodyguards.

"Halt!" the lieutenant cried out. "Hands up! Drop the weapons!"

"Secret Service!" the agent yelled back. "And the President of the United States!"

The lieutenant and his nearest sergeant looked at each other.

"What happened to Charley Davidson?" he asked.

Halfway down the block a similar scene took place as Davidson's group emerged from a second tunnel. At the same moment, a squad of eight limousines and five motorcycle cops slid up and parked in a line at the curb, like waiting taxis.

A second sergeant came running up to the lieutenant.

"We got President Davidson!" he said.

"Wait a minute!" the lieutenant protested to Queenan's bodyguard. "We can't have two presidents –"

"Can it," Dennis Camacho said, running up to the group. "Watch it on TV when you get home. Meanwhile, we've got to get Acting President Queenan and President Davidson into these cars pronto."

The lieutenant looked back and forth between Queenan and Davidson, and the dozen Cabinet members. The department heads looked familiar, but he could not place them. Finally he gave the only order that would cause him fewer problems than it would create, at least for now.

"You heard the man!" he shouted to the two sergeants. "Let's get 'em outta here!" He used hand signals to deploy his men, who completely surrounded the convoy, guns pointed out toward the crowd.

The Secret Service agents started to shuffle their flock randomly into the limousines, but Camacho stopped them.

"Wait!" he shouted. He waved over three supervisors and gave them their orders. The all nodded in assent and sped to their assignments. Soon they were directing the Cabinet members, four to a car, into their limousines. Queenan and Davidson went in separate cars along with their bodyguards.

A pair of motorcycle cops rode in front, two rode alongside the rear vehicle, and the fifth officer rode alongside the fourth. Sirens blaring, the convoy pulled away as fast as soldiers could clear onlookers from the path ahead.

Inside the limousines, only Davidson was relaxed. Having performed in so many actions films, where the work was physically grueling and the environment more deadly than some actual battlefields, his hold on reality was in doubt, but not his courage. He was determined to show them the stuff of a true leader.

Camacho had stationed himself in Queenan's limousine; it was clear to him who would be President when the smoke cleared. He continued shouting orders into his suit mic, clearing the way ahead. Suddenly he heard something that made him sit straight up and look out the rear window, where he saw a squad of a half-dozen motorcycles speeding to join them.

• • •

At first glance, the motorcycles appeared to be more police. The shape and coloring seemed the same, but he knew differently. His rear guards began pulling their weapons, but not before two of the new arrivals pulled theirs and shot them down, sending the police and their motorcycles spinning off into a crowd on the sidewalk. One of the pair slapped a magnetized device outside the gas tank of the rear vehicle. The other four attackers separated and sped up, each targeting another limousine.

As they did, the bomb detonated with a *whump*, immediately followed by the explosion of the rear limousine's gas tank – an enormous explosion that sent pieces of the car flying everywhere. The nearest onlookers screamed and ran for safety, but several were struck down by shrapnel.

The attackers easily took out the only motorcycle officer on the side. They both fired at him; one shot struck the biker's back while the other went wild and blew out the front tire, which sent him careening. Clear of motorcycle police except for the front pair, who continued to lead, they let up their guard to focus on finding and killing Queenan. Each pulled a bomb out of a bag and pulled up to a limousine, prepared to bomb them as well.

Neither lived to make another mistake. When the rear decoy car exploded, soldiers up and down the street came running. Two lines of ten soldiers each, led by a lieutenant, knelt and opened fire on the two attackers. Both went down within two seconds, but one still managed to slap his bomb on the side of the fourth limousine in the line. In moments it exploded like the first one, with more spectators and several soldiers going down under flying metal.

The rear pair, seeing the ambush, did quick 180s and tried to flee but were surrounded by a ring of soldiers before they could accelerate away – a ring of automatic rifles. They barely surrendered in time avoid the same fate as their comrades.

The front limousines sped away, untouched and now unthreatened, while the rear contingent – Cabinet members – remained trapped behind the flaming hulk of the fourth vehicle. From the third limo, Queenan looked out the one-way glass of the rear window.

"The secretaries made it!" she said to Camacho. "It looks like they're going to get around the burning limo and follow us." Camacho, who maintained continuous communications with the other cars and more security ahead of them, nodded.

A few moments later, they pulled into the Capitol driveway.

53

CAPITOL HILL

The scene outside Capitol Hill was not much less chaotic, but once the limousines entered the secured driveway, everyone relaxed noticeably, like overfilled balloons slightly deflated. Troops had been moved from the White House and lined the driveway, assuring their safety.

Queenan emerged first. She did not lead the entourage; they simply followed her as she strode into the building with forceful confidence. Moments later, as she waited at the door to the emergency joint session that had convened in the last hour, she heard the words, "the Acting President of the United States, Joan Queenan."

As she walked into the room and up the center aisle, the Republicans clapped and cheered loudly, while most Democrats clapped with a limp enthusiasm that made it clear they would rather be elsewhere, perhaps a dentist's office. As she walked, she stopped to shake hands and talk to members. She was particularly enthusiastic with the House veterans she had known during her tenure there. Queenan walked up to the podium left vacant by the House Speaker, who sat with the Senate Majority Leader in slightly elevated seats behind the podium.

• • •

Queenan quickly dispensed with formalities and got down to business.

"My friends," she began, "it's been a hell of a day."

The room erupted. Rather than slam the Speaker's gavel down for silence, she waited for it to come down on its own. Not the first time this would happen, she figured.

"Today our country has faced not one, not two, but three major crises," she said. The room was suddenly reduced to an unnatural quiet.

"And we met each one successfully." The room seemed to breathe as one person, a person exhaling mightily in relief.

"As far as I know, you have only heard of one of these crises. Let me talk about how and why I got here, and then we can talk about our other problems – which, I'm astounded to discover, have not leaked to any print or electronic media anywhere. We *know* that will change.

"First, let's talk about why I'm here. A few months back, General Strom Thornton, now the former Army Chief of Staff, discovered that President Davidson has Alzheimer's Disease. He suspected it. He had a physician secretly assess the President for the condition. I have learned that Alzheimer's is almost impossible to diagnose with certainty, but someone in close contact with the patient can often assess the situation accurately.

"What happened next threatened the very foundation of this country. General Thornton, who disagreed with President Davidson's decision not attack Persia with military force, decided to *take control of the government*. His original plan was to take the President hostage in a secret base in the Nevada desert, have me killed while I visited the Vatican, and to use a military exercise as cover to launch an invasion of Persia. There are details about this that can never be revealed for reasons of national security, but the bottom line is, the general almost got us into a shooting war with Persia *and* China. With Russian ships on hand, too, who knows what they might have done?

"Thornton's coup d'état was based on the assumption of a President unable to do his job. By making me Acting President, the cabinet has foiled his plan and shut down the coup. I have fired General Thornton. The military exercise was canceled before it got off the ground, though you might say it was already taxiing for takeoff. We stopped the general in the nick of time. The Persians and Chinese, and the Russians, too, all understand that we have no hostile intentions. I am following President Davidson's policies to a capital tee until his status can be resolved."

"Madame Speaker! Madame *Speaker*!" An urban Democratic congressman from Queenan's hometown of Houston stood in protest.

"Madame Speaker, I have unimpeachable evidence that President Davidson has declared his incapacity ended. Under the Twenty-Fifth Amendment, that is sufficient to return him to his duties."

Percussi rose and spoke at the microphone in the center aisle.

"If there is a letter from the President declaring his incapacity ended, then you are correct. His authority reverts immediately. But for that to happen, that letter must be presented to me as Speaker, and to the Senate President pro tempore. Neither of us has seen such a letter."

At that, the Congressman stepped forward.

"Madame Speaker, I have that letter, signed by the President, delivered to me by his chief of staff, Tammany Dreidel. I submit it now for your consideration."

At this, both chambers exploded with noise and energy. The Democrats had marginal control over both houses, but the party leadership had no notion of whether their greatest advantage would come from supporting Davidson or Queenan.

The entire room was suddenly silenced by the next turn of events. President Charley Davidson walked up the center aisle slowly, with deliberation, up the same path Queenan had walked only moments before. But instead of shaking the proferred hands, instead of trading inside jokes with the senators and representatives, he just walked. His cadence seemed robotic, almost programmed. There was no spontaneity or life to his movement.

Davidson walked up the stairs and around to the podium where Queenan stood.

"Madame Acting President, if I may have a word, I think I can clear things up."

Queenan looked at him, puzzled, unsure what to do. Davidson held up his palm at chest height.

"Trust me," he said. "I'll be right back."

Then Charles Russell Davidson, President for two years, three months, and nine days, turned to his audience and made a startling announcement.

"I hereby resign as President of the United States, effective right now."

Again, pandemonium. He waited. His acting career had made him a master of timing, a learned skill that would be one of the last to die with his dementia. When he felt he had waited just long enough, he held up his hand for silence.

"Just like you, I just found out about my illness. I was shocked. But not surprised. We know these things about ourselves, if we only pay attention.

"On a good day, I'm great. No one can stop me. On a bad day, I'm rediscovering the joys of fried chicken, which is not good for me. Today has been so-so. They tell me the stress of my job makes it worse. I can believe it. So today, I am trusting my own judgment. Ten years ago, I chose Congresswoman Joan Queenan to be my Vice President."

At that, Queenan touched his shoulder, then leaned over and whispered in his ear. He grinned.

"Excuse me, *three* years ago. Now you see why I must resign. I did not pick her for window dressing. I picked her because I knew, from learning about her as a *person*, that she could do the job. Now she *must* do the job. I hope you will give her your support. I do. Thank you."

Republican and Democrat alike, every member present stood and applauded the outgoing president with enthusiastic respect. Queenan stood back and let Davidson have the limelight for this one last time. Davidson smiled and waved to the crowd as if he had just received an Academy Award. Eventually the commotion died down. As all the members sat down again, Davidson quietly stepped back and disappeared from the light. Speaker Percussi stepped forward.

"Thank you, Mister President, for an unbelievably gracious decision. Now I have to ask, is there a judge in the house?"

Everyone laughed and looked around at each other. After a moment, a rustling revealed the emergence of three Supreme Court justices, watching events unfold from a remote corner.

"Mister Justices, could you help us out for a moment?" Again the entire room, including the justices, laughed as one.

Moments later, the three appeared on the dais next to Queenan, accompanied by Percussi. All three were appointed by a Democratic president, but Queenan looked at the most senior of them, the only white male.

"Mister Justice Annandale, would you do the honors?"

Annandale smiled and said nothing but held up a Bible in his left hand.

"Perfect," Queenan said. The oath of office did not take long.

"Repeat after me," Annandale said after she placed her hand on the Bible he had provided.

"I, Joan Katherine Queenan," he said.

"I, Joan Katherine Queenan," she repeated.

"Do solemnly swear."

"Do solemnly swear."

"That I will faithfully execute."

"That I will faithfully execute."

"The Office of President of the United States."

"The Office of President of the United States."

"And will to the best of my ability."

"And will to the best of my ability."

"Preserve, protect, and defend the Constitution of the United States."

"Preserve, protect, and defend the Constitution of the United States."

With that, the room erupted in cheers and applause as Annandale shook her hand in congratulations.

54

ROGUE TRAFFIC

Half a continent away, Sergeant Thad Jackson continued to monitor Persian Gulf naval traffic. His job was much easier than before: Now all he had to do was make sure the Americans were getting the hell out. So far, so good.

Until now.

The movements of the American fleets were easy to track because they all moved away from the Persian Gulf. As they went south out the Gulf of Oman, some peeled off with the *Reagan* convoy, east toward the Gulf of Aden. This route kept them skirting the coast of the Arabian peninsula, with a fast track to the Red Sea if needed. The *Washington* carrier group headed down into the Arabian Sea, with a southern bearing toward India that would take them between Malé and Sri Lanka – or so he thought the first time he looked. Now, after more than two hours of movement, the trend was clear: the three new destroyers from the *Reagan's* carrier fleet had struck out on their own. Two headed directly for the Chinese fleet, while the other went straight for the northern end of the Persian Gulf.

"That's the route to Kuwait City," Jackson said to Chin, who watched over his shoulder. General Fuchs had already headed back to Area 51, from which she would fly out for Andrews Air Force Base.

"Yes, if Kuwait City was your destination, son," Chin said to the young soldier. "But this is all about Persia. With that in mind, what is his likely target?"

"Not *Tehran?*"

"Bingo! If he goes all the way north, it's what, 460, 480 miles from the coast to the capital? And his missiles, half of them with twenty-five-kiloton Mark Fours, can easily fly more than twice that distance. Now, my question to you is, why are these ships not under our complete control? What has gone wrong?"

Jackson gulped. "Sheer speculation, sir, but I can think of two viable hypotheses."

Chin raised his eyebrows. "*Hypotheses*? Did a lowly Army grunt just use the word *hypotheses* in a complete sentence?"

Jackson smiled weakly. "Uh, yes, sir."

"God, make this man an officer! Better yet, make him my boss! Damn, too young ... anyway, go on, sergeant. Tell me your *hypotheses*."

"The first one is that someone has control of three of our ships. Presumably a Stormista, but there's no evidence one way or another."

"A what?"

"A Stormista. You know, one of Stormy's troops, his closest supporters. I doubt we've identified more than a handful."

"Which will change, as soon as we can organize an ID project. Meanwhile, what's number two? Number one sounds possible but remains unsupported."

"Number two has the virtue of simplicity, sir. Software bugs."

"What? *Software* bugs? In a war exercise?"

"Yes, sir. Isn't that the whole point of a war exercise? Unit testing, then system testing. We test all the parts, separately and in unit, to make sure we can execute the battle plans we've written."

"Er, I never would have thought of that. But it's a testable hypothesis, right? Can you find the bugs? Can you at least take command of the missiles? Keep 'em from arming?"

"Yes, sir, all those things are possible, but I'm only one man. Get me a team in here, and we have a shot at it."

"Do this, son, and you'll be in OCS by the end of the week. Now, go pick your team."

"Yes, sir!"

● ● ●

In the Situation Room, President Queenan monitored events in the Persian Gulf on a bank of video monitors, one of which displayed Colonel Chin.

"So if I understand this correctly, Colonel, you think we've lost remote control of our ships due to a *software* error? That you can't identify? Do we have to worry about them attacking their targets?"

"We can identify it, Madame President, but it's an unknown, so we can't say how long it will take. Until we identify it, we can't say how hard it will be to fix. Best guess, they are simply locked into their previous instruction set."

"Do we even know if the bug enhances the likelihood of them firing on their targets?"

"Again, unknown."

"What about communications with the ship's officers?"

"We're locked out of all electronic transmissions."

Queenan paused. Another idea occurred to her.

"What about traditional communications?"

"You mean flags? Semaphore?"

"If it can keep us out of a war, why not?"

"Hmmm. I don't know why not; I can't do that, but I can get it done."

"Keep that can-do attitude, Colonel."

"Yes, ma'am. Is that all, ma'am?"

"It is for now, but don't go out for coffee or pizza, know what I mean?"

"You kidding? I've got a whole battalion of pizza boys dying to serve their country. Or at least their colonel."

Queenan called the Secretary of State with her plan.

"The only problem I see, Madame President, is *they don't know you.*"

"True enough. And I don't know them. But we don't have time for diplomatic hand-holding right now, do we? Lives are at stake. Nations."

"We'll make the connection and get their ambassadors on the line."

"Any progress, Colonel?"

"Not yet, Madame President. We don't have any assets in the area that can get close enough for semaphore."

"You mean because all the assets under control have moved to the south?"

"Exactly. It could take hours, and we don't have hours. The northern destroyer, which I now see is the *U.S.S. Admiral Zumwalt*, is less than two hours from its optimal targeting point. If it's going to attack, it could attack any time after that."

"And before that? Could it attack earlier, from a *suboptimal* location?"

That thought stopped Chin flat; he grimaced. *She should have been a general*, he thought. *She thinks like one.*

"Yes, ma'am. I'm afraid it could."

"Well, I guess it's a good thing I'm not a drinking girl," she said.

"Ma'am?"

"Because if I was, I think I'd be slamming the bottle pretty hard right about now."

"Madame President, we've arranged the video hookups," Romulet said from the video console.

"Everyone?"

"Yes, ma'am. And without further ado, President Joan Queenan, let me introduce our guests. First, the Premier of the People's Republic of China, Xi Linghou."

"Premier Xi, *ni hao ma?*"

Xi's face lit up at her use of correctly intonated Mandarin. He responded in kind, but his voice was largely overshadowed by that of the English translator.

"Thank you, thank you. I see your use of the common language continues. Congratulations on your recent promotion."

"Thank you. Yes, I practice when I can, but I do not get much chance. Perhaps I can practice on you?"

Xi laughed at that. They both knew how common it was for his fellow countrymen to ask English speakers for a chance to practice. He needed no practice, but putting everything through translators gave him time to gauge reactions and think.

At just about the same time, he and Queenan noticed the looks of surprise and confusion on Romulet's face.

"Shall you tell them, or shall I?" Xi said to Queenan, smiling.

"Go ahead."

Xi looked at them all from his monitor.

"I met your honorable President many years ago, when she was married. Her husband was your ambassador, and I was a deputy foreign minister. Albert Queenan and I worked together many times. His wife and my wife were – *are* – friends. Now we meet again under much different circumstances." Xi's face took a grim turn.

"And, I'm afraid, dangerous circumstances. Your ships are threatening my ships. Your ship is threatening Persia, perhaps with nuclear weapons. That is a risk we cannot face. If you do not stop them, I will have no choice. I have been told you do not have control of these ships."

It was Queenan's turn to look startled. Where did he find out they were out of control?

"I don't know where you got your information about our ships, Premier Xi ..."

"Are you saying it is incorrect?"

"No, I must be honest. We discovered several hours ago that the problem is most likely a software bug. A programming error. We have a team of experts working on it right now."

"You have a team of six young programmers. Non-commissioned officers and corporals. That is hardly what I call a team of experts. Someone must take control of these ships, quickly, or we can take no chances. We will have to deal with it the old-fashioned way."

"Mister Premier, I respect your intentions. I hope you respect mine. If you don't mind, please keep Ambassador Wu online so that we can stay in touch the moment we find something out."

Xi laughed.

"I'm not going anywhere," his translator relayed.

• • •

"We finally got inside the opsys," Jackson said.

"Opsys? Pretend you're talking to a politician, son, or a young child."

"The operating system. It's the governing program that runs everything else. You know, like Windows on a PC, only for a destroyer."

"Got it. What else?"

"I'm not clear on whether a bug is involved, sir. We discovered some independent processes that we don't recognize."

"Independent processes? You mean like viruses?"

"Yes, sir."

"See, I'm catching on. I may be an old man of forty-two, but I can still learn."

Jackson laughed. "Yes, sir."

"The question is, are they bugs, or are they viruses? Are you saying someone could have planted them? Are you saying someone else is in control of our ships?"

"Uh, yes, sir, that is now a high-probability scenario."

"Do we know who?"

"No technical evidence, sir. But I suspect that when events play out, the answer will be obvious."

"Damn, you *are* going to Officers' Candidate School. We need more officers who can read between the lines. But I'd be happier if we were in control now. Can you retake control?"

"We're working on it."

● ● ●

Romulet returned to the ongoing videoconference. As soon as he appeared, Queenan pushed a button to mute the sound on all other stations.

"Madame President, I've got some of our Foreign Service and Agency boys working on this."

"No girls?"

"Hell, I don't know. Probably some. Maybe. All respect, Madame President, I'm speaking generically."

"Understood. Continue."

"Anyway, they've been breaking out the probabilities, and a few float to the top. You want the long story or the short story?"

"Pretend I'm a fan of *The Three Bears*. Give me the medium story."

"Okay. It comes down to this: Who has control, and what do they plan to do with it?

"As for control, it could be a rogue American unit, but we've pretty much ruled it out."

"Pretty much?"

"Enough to move forward to other possibilities. Not enough to rule it out altogether, but it goes to the bottom of the list."

"Okay."

"Next up, it has to be Chinese, Persian, or Russian, in that order. It comes down to resources and willpower. On resources alone, we could include the Israelis and the Ukrainians, and maybe even the Romanians, but they have no reason."

"Why are the Russians at the bottom?"

"Mainly because they've been off our radar lately. We haven't been locking horns. President Bukin's busy rearranging the Russian oil cartels. True, we're not bosom buddies, but we've been leaving each other alone. My read from their ambassador is, they want to leave it that way for now. They're happy to sell missiles to the Persians and let it go at that."

"Why not the Persians?"

"All our intelligence suggests they have been focused on their nuclear weapons for some time now. Their cyber capability is not world class at this point. That's why some mysterious interested party was able to infect their uranium-separation facilities with the Stuxnet virus some years back."

"And that leaves..."

"The Chinese, I'm afraid. Not a new story, as you are well aware. This is cyberwarfare. From a digital perspective, it's far worse than anything in the Cold War. Not many people understand that, but it may be the major challenge for your administration. President Davidson was quite interested until his wife died. Then he started losing touch."

"Understood." They were both quiet for a moment, reflecting on the events and on Davidson's life.

"Okay, suppose it's the Chinese. What will they do with it?"

"It comes down to whether they *want* us to know it's them. Are they unrealistic enough to think they can hide it from us? Look at it the other way: What if they decided to flaunt it? What if their goal is to make us lose face internationally?"

"An international 'you got served.'"

"If that means what I think it does, yes. But consider one more possibility: What if they intend to use our ships to attack Persia?"

55

ENTERTAINMENT EXPLOIT

"So let's say the Chinese have taken control of your opsys," Chin said.

"Not *my* opsys," Jackson said. "The ship's."

"Whatever," Chin said, echoing the phrase he had heard so often from his teenaged niece. "The point is, how do we get it back?"

"You mean electronically? Not physically? Because this is the military. Why can't we just send in some SEAL teams to retake the ships the good old-fashioned way?"

"Don't lecture me on tactics, son. We're getting down to the wire here. We don't have time for anything except cybermagic. Can you or can't you do it?"

Jackson sat there, wordless.

"*I* can do it."

• • •

"What if we can't get control of the ships?" Queenan asked.

"A better question might be, what if the Chinese *do* have control of them. What could they do with them? Anything obvious would be an act of war. Somehow, I don't think that's what they have in mind."

"Why not?"

"Because throughout the many centuries, no, make that *millennia*, of being the dominant civilization of the world, they never have been oriented toward aggressive action outside their sphere of influence. They're more passive-aggressive."

"Maybe they want to use them as a bargaining chip."

"Maybe, but again, that's an act of war. No, whatever they have planned, they don't want it to be public knowledge."

"So let's find out and keep it to ourselves."

"Easy to say, but not so easy to do. Any word from Colonel Chin?"

• • •

"*You* can do it?" Chin asked Teresa McNeil, who had been out of the loop lately while Thad Jackson ran the show.

"Oh, yeah. It's not *his* opsys because he didn't help build it," she said. "But *I* did. My team. The team I was on, I mean. We built in a back door, just for fun. A stupid, crazy back door that they would never expect."

"Go on."

"Just look at the three ships that went nomad on us."

"What about them?"

"You Army guys! Don't you ever read up on, like, ships and stuff?"

Chin pressed his lips together.

"Get to the point."

"The point is, these ships are all from our new *Zumwalt* class of destroyers. We're just now breaking them in. May Day was their first test."

"Go on. What's special about them?"

"Oh, they're special. I'll pull up some photos and specs while I lay it out for you."

McNeil went over to her terminal and sped through a fast series of keystrokes that Chin did not even try to follow. In moments, an early photo of the *U.S.S. Zumwalt* came up on the screen.

"Holy cow!" Chin said. "That's the *Zumwalt*? It looks like an iron-clad out of the Civil War."

McNeil laughed. "You aren't the first to say so, sir. It's a stealth destroyer, designed to reduce its radar profile. It has an integrated power system that can intelligently control power between the weapons and propulsions systems."

"By 'integrated,' do you mean computer controlled?"

"Exactly, sir. Automation is one of its main features. Fewer man-power requirements. In fact, we can control it from here. Or at least, we thought we could. That was the design. We expected to work out the kinks during the war games."

"And the other two?"

"The *U.S.S. Michael Monsoor* and the *U.S.S. Lyndon Johnson*. The *Zumwalt* is only slightly older. We intended to use the May Day exer-cises to test our ability to remotely control them and fight with them as a group."

"And the weapons systems?"

"Lots of them, sir, but the key is the ballistic missiles. They're all nuclear capable."

"So tell me about this back door of yours, Sergeant. You've set your-self up to be the big hero here, so I damn well hope you can deliver."

"It's the media center," she said, grinning like a kid. "We built a hack into the media center. It has an independent satellite uplink to the Boxstar Entertainment satellite. It runs no matter what's going on with the operating system, because Boxstar has its own governing software."

"You mean like the media center in the rec room?"

"The very same."

"But if it's not hooked up to the operating system, where does it get you?" Chin asked.

"That's the right question!" McNeil said, still grinning. "And the answer is, we modified the media servers to take control of the main opsys surreptitiously."

"You mean a secret switch? Are you serious?"

"I'm totally serious. There's only one problem."

Chin groaned. "Now what?"

"It's never been tested. We were going to do that –"

"I know, I know. In Project May Day."

● ● ●

"Madame President, it has indeed been a pleasure to renew our old acquaintance, but I'm afraid our matter at hand requires a decision."

"What decision would you like me to make, Mister Premier?" Queenan had to suppress a smile at her question, because she knew that whatever he told her, it would not be the true answer.

Xi had to suppress a smile, too, but for a different reason: He knew she would never agree to any decision he asked for outright.

"My experts tell me that they are receiving telemetry from your ship in the northern Persian Gulf. They are certain that it is preparing to launch missiles in the direction of Tehran. The two ships approaching our fleet are also acting like they will attack."

"How would you know that, Mister Premier? Our satellite photos are just as good as yours, and we see no sign of activity."

"We no longer rely on photography, Madame President. Our radio satellites can pick up the slightest electromagnetic signatures from the ship. We have some very smart men who can tell us what those signatures mean."

"What do you propose to do, Mister Premier?"

"I am told we have no more than one hour before the ships launch their missiles. So you have thirty minutes to stop those ships, or we will stop them for you. With the greatest of regret."

• • •

Chin threw commands at McNeil as he paced behind her in the cage.

"Okay, Sergeant McNeil, you want to be a star, now's your chance. Hack the entertainment satellite, hack the media centers on all three ships, hack the operating systems, and retake control of the ships. Use Sergeant Jackson and anyone else who can help you. You do this, and you can join him at OCS."

"On it already, sir," McNeil reported.

"I just got new information. We have thirty minutes, not one second longer, to get this done. Otherwise, the Chinese plan to blow those ships out the water – *if* they can. Justified or not, we will be in a shooting war."

• • •

"It is five minutes until we are forced to take action, Madame President. I fear where it will lead."

"My people are on it, Mister Premier. I expect word any moment."

Xi smiled a little smile to himself. The new President would be humbled today. The United States would start learning its new place in the world, with China back at the top. At the top where it had always been until the British colonial invasion of the early nineteenth century.

• • •

"Five minutes, Sergeant. Where are we?"

"I've coded a virus, sir. I'm executing the distribution mechanism right now."

"Which means?"

"We're uploading it to the satellite. It will take control of the satellite just enough to download to the ship's media centers. After only a few cycles, a few milliseconds, it should process and download. But how long before it takes over the operating system is anyone's guess."

"Can't you be more specific?"

"'Fraid not. Not this time, sir. We don't know the specifics of the bot they used to take our ships. I do know that no matter what, *my* bot will reboot the system and intercept foreign instructions before they can execute. The software will recognize what belongs. And what doesn't."

Together they watched a dashboard on glass, showing the progress of the bot as it uploaded to the satellite, downloaded to the rec rooms, and infiltrated the target ships. The graphics showed an image of the virus spreading through the command and control systems of each ship. *Reminds me of an old aspirin commercial on TV*, he thought. *The way it shows it spreading to the whole ship.*

The wait was interminable, but the clock said they still had a minute and a half left.

• • •

"We're in! We're in!" Chin shouted to Queenan on the phone.

"It's over?" Queenan asked, with hope in her voice.

"Yes, yes! Call the Chinese, fast!"

• • •

"Mister Premier, I have good news."

"We have one minute, Madame President. What is your news?"

"We're all clear. We have regained control of our ships. Your people should be able to verify that our ships are now reversing their courses. You have no reason to feel threatened."

"*I* never feel threatened, Madame President. But I *am* happy to know that the Persian people are safe, and that we do not have to worry about clouds of radiation in our backyard. Naturally, I need to ask my people to verify your, uh, your claims."

• • •

"Yes! Yes!" McNeil and Jackson danced around inside the electronic cage, hugging each other with glee. Chin watched in amusement; his glee sprang largely out of relief now that the May Day crisis was past – just as May Day was coming to the rest of the world. He looked up at the clock on the wall for the time – half an hour in. A close call, but the international day of protest had arrived without conflagration.

• • •

Queenan had debated with herself long and hard about how to handle this phone call. After her promising but problematic interaction with Premier Xi, she decided this should be a one-on-one. Like most of what she did now, she preferred a videoconference instead of a plain phone call. In cases where trust was at issue, it was much easier to assess her counterpart's sincerity when she could see a face. She counted on body language to help her interpret intentions.

"Madame President, he's here."

She looked up to her video monitor to see the Persian president, Fahrook Arkhami. Queenan did not completely trust first impressions, but she had learned to pay close attention to them. This time, she paid close attention to her visceral reaction. She was not disturbed by the result. She would give this man a chance.

"Mister President, I am pleased to meet you," she said through a translator.

"Madame President," he said with the slightest of nods.

"Mister President, I know the last few hours have been difficult."

"Indeed they have, Madame President. Your politicians have a tradition of casting aspersions on the sanity of Persians, especially when we called ourselves Iranians. Now we worry the same about you. Are you in control of your country?"

"Not the way you are, Mister President," Queenan said. "If you know anything about America, you know that no one is in control."

At that, Arkhami, along with unseen advisors in the background, laughed loudly with sounds almost like dogs barking.

"Excuse me if I laugh, Madame President. It is not often I find a leader who will make jokes about her own country. Especially when the jokes are so true. And at the same time, not true."

Queenan smiled wanly but said nothing.

"You are not saying much, Madame President, so I guess I will have to say it for both of us. As you know, I made much progress toward convincing your President Davidson that we of Persia are serious. We are sincere about our desire to re-enter the international arena, the world of serious nations. What can I do to make you take us seriously?"

Queenan looked at him long and hard before answering or even formulating an answer. So much rode on this assessment, she knew. She felt so inadequate. Assessing a total stranger when the fate of entire region could hang in the balance ... that would take some getting used to.

"It's not rocket science, Mister President," she said after a moment's hesitation. "You don't mess with us, and we won't mess with you."

-END-